Charlotte Mary Yonge

Modern Broods

Outlook

Charlotte Mary Yonge

Modern Broods

1. Auflage | ISBN: 978-3-73261-927-6

Erscheinungsort: Paderborn, Deutschland

Erscheinungsjahr: 2018

Outlook Verlag GmbH, Paderborn.

MODERN BROODS,
OR
DEVELOPMENTS UNLOOKED FOR

BY
CHARLOTTE MARY YONGE.

"*Youth and age are scholars yet but in the lower school.*"

—TENNYSON.

London
MACMILLAN AND CO., Limited
NEW YORK: THE MACMILLAN COMPANY
1900

RICHARD CLAY AND SONS, LIMITED,
LONDON AND BUNGAY.

First Edition, October, 1900.
Reprinted, November, 1900.

CHAPTER I—TORTOISES AND HARES

"Whate'er is good to wish, ask that of Heaven,
Though it be what thou canst not hope to see."

—Hartley Coleridge.

The scene was a drawing-room, with old-fashioned heavy sash windows opening on a narrow brick-walled town-garden sloping down to a river, and neatly kept. The same might be said of the room, where heavy old-fashioned furniture, handsome but not new, was concealed by various flimsy modernisms, knicknacks, fans, brackets, china photographs and water-colours, a canary singing loud in the window in the winter sunshine.

"Miss Prescott," announced the maid; but, finding no auditor save the canary, she retreated, and Miss Prescott looked round her with a half sigh of recognition of the surroundings. She was herself a quiet-looking, gentle lady, rather small, with a sweet mouth and eyes of hazel, in a rather worn face, dressed in a soft woollen and grey fur, with headgear to suit, and there was an air of glad expectation, a little flush, that did not look permanent, on her thin cheeks.

"Is it you, my dear Miss Prescott?" was the greeting of the older hostess as she entered, her grey hair rough and uncovered, and her dress of well-used black silk, her complexion of the red that shows wear and care. "Then it is true?" she asked, as the kiss and double shake of the hand was exchanged.

"May I ask? Is it true? May I congratulate you?"

"Oh, yes, it is true!" said Miss Prescott, breathlessly. "I suppose the girls are at the High School?"

"Yes, they will be at home at one. Or shall I send for them?"

"No, thank you, Mrs. Best. I shall like to have a little time with you first. I can stay till a quarter-past three."

"Then come and take off your things. I do not know when I have been so glad!"

"Do the girls know?" asked Miss Prescott, following upstairs to a comfortable bedroom, evidently serving also the purposes of a private room, for writing table and account books stood near the fire.

"They know something; Kate Bell heard a report from her cousins, and they have been watching anxiously for news from you."

"I would not write till I knew more. I hope they have not raised their expectations too high; for though it is enough to be an immense relief, it is not exactly affluence. I have been with Mr. Bell going into the matter and seeing the place," said Miss Prescott, sitting comfortably down in the arm-chair Mrs. Best placed for her, while she herself sat down in another, disposing themselves for a talk over the fire.

"Mr. Bell reckons it at about £600 a year."

"And an estate?"

"A very pretty cottage in a Devonshire valley, with the furniture and three acres of land."

"Oh! I believe the girls fancy that it is at least as large as LordColdhurst's."

"Yes, I was in hopes that they would have heard nothing about it."

"It came through some of their schoolfellows; one cannot help things getting into the air."

"And there getting inflated like bubbles," said Miss Prescott, smiling. "Well, their expectations will have a fall, poor dears!"

"And it does not come from their side of the family," said Mrs. Best. "Of course not! And it was wholly unexpected, was it not?"

"Yes, I had my name of Magdalen from my great aunt Tremlett; but she had never really forgiven my mother's marriage, though she consented to be my godmother. She offered to adopt me on my mother's death, and once when my father married again, and when we lost him, she wrote to propose my coming to live with her; but there would have been no payment, and so—"

"Yes, you dear good thing, you thought it your duty to go and work for your poor little stepmother and her children!"

"What else was my education good for, which has been a costly thing to poor father? And then the old lady was affronted for good, and never took any more notice of me, nor answered my letters. I did not even know she was dead, till I heard from Mr. Bell, who had learnt it from his lawyers!"

"It was quite right of her. Dear Magdalen, I am so glad," said Mrs. Best, crossing over to kiss her; for the first stiffness had worn off, and they were together again, as had been the solicitor's daughter and the chemist's daughter, who went to the same school till Magdalen had been sent away to be finished in Germany.

"Dear Sophy, I wish you had the good fortune, too!"

"Oh! my galleons are coming when George has prospered a little more in Queensland, and comes to fetch me. Sophia and he say they shall fight for me," said Mrs. Best, who had been bravely presiding over a high-school boarding-house ever since her husband, a railway engineer, had been killed by an accident, and left her with two children to bring up. "Dear children, they are very good to me."

"I am sure you have been goodness itself to us," said Magdalen, "in taking the care of these poor little ones when their mother died. I don't know how to be thankful enough to you and for all the blessings we have had! And that this should have come just now, especially when my life with Lady Milsom is coming to an end."

"Indeed!"

"Yes, the little boys are old enough for school, and the Colonel is going to take a house at Shrewsbury, where his mother will live with them, and want me no longer."

"You have been there seven years."

"Yes, and very happy. When Fanny married, Lady Milsom was left alone, and would not part with me, and then came the two little boys from India, so that she had an excuse for retaining me; but that is over now, or will be in a few weeks time. I had been trying for an engagement, and finding that beside your high-school diploma young ladies I am considered quitepassée—"

"My dear! With your art, and music, and all!"

"Too true! And while I was digesting a polite hint that my terms were too high, and therewith Agatha's earnest appeal to be sent to Girton, there comes this inheritance! Taking my burthen off my back, and making me ready to throw up my heels like a young colt."

"Ah! you will be taking another burthen, perhaps."

"No doubt, I suppose so, but let me find it out by degrees. I can only think as yet of having my dear girls to myself, *moi*, as the French would say, after having seen so little of them."

"It has been very unfortunate. Epidemics have been strangely inconvenient."

"Yes. First there was whooping cough here to destroy the summer holidays; then came the Milsoms' measles, and I could not go and carry infection. Oh! and then Freddy broke his leg, and his grandmother was too nervous to be left with him. And by and by some one told her the scarlatina was in the town."

"It really was, you know."

"Any way, it would have been sheer selfish inhumanity to leave her, and then she had a real illness, which frightened us all very much. Next came influenza to every one. And these last holidays! What should the newly-come little one from India do, but catch a fever in the Red Sea, and I had to keep guard over the brothers at Weymouth till she was reported safe, and I don't believe it was infectious after all! Still, I am tired of 'other people's stairs.'"

"It is nearly five years since you have been with them, except for that one peep you took at Weston."

"And that is a great deal at their age. Agatha was a vehement reader; she would hardly look at me, so absorbed was she in 'The York and Lancaster Rose' which I had brought her."

"She is rather like that now. I conclude that you will wish to take them away?"

"Not this time, at any rate till the house is fit to put over their heads. Besides, you have so mothered them, dear Sophy, that I could not bear to make a sudden parting."

"There will be pain, especially over little Thekla and Polly. But if George comes home this spring, and I go out to Queensland with him, perhaps I should have asked you to take this house off my hands. May be it would be prudent in you to do so even now, considering all things; only I believe that transplanting would be good for them all."

"I am glad you think so, for I have a perfect longing for that little house of my own."

"You will be able to give them a superior kind of society to what they have had access to here. There is a good deal that I should like to talk over with you before they come in."

"Agatha seems to be in despair at her failure."

"So is all the house, for we were very proud of her, and, of course, we all thought it a fad of the examiners, but perhaps our headmistress might not say the same. She is a good, hardworking girl though, and ambitious, and quite worth further training."

"I am glad of being able to secure it to her at least, and by the time her course is finished I shall be able to judge about the others."

"You thought of taking them in hand yourself?"

"Certainly; how nice it will be to teach my own kin, and not endless strangers, lovable as they have been!"

"It will be very good for them all to see something of life and manners superior to what I can give them here. You will take them into a fresh sphere, and—as things were—besides that, I could not—I did not know whether their lives would not lie among our people here."

"Dear Sophy, don't concern yourself. I am quite certain you would never let them fall in with anything hurtful."

"Why, no! I hope not; but if I had known what was coming, I don't think I should have asked you to consent to Vera and Thekla's spending their holidays at Mr. Waring's country house."

"Very worthy people, you said. I remember Tom Waring, a very nice boy; and Jessie Dale went to school with us—I liked her. Fancy them having a country house."

"Waring Grange they call it. He has got on wonderfully as upholsterer, decorator, and auctioneer. It is a very handsome one, with a garden that gets the prizes at the horticultural shows. They are thoroughly good people, but I was afraid afterwards that there had been a good deal of noisiness among the young folks at Christmas. Hubert Delrio was there, and I fancy there was some nonsense going on."

"Ah, the Delrios! Are they here?"

"Yes, poor Fred did not make his art succeed when he had a family to provide for, and he is the head of the Art School here. His son has a good deal of talent, and very prudently has got taken on by the firm of Eccles and Co., who do a great deal of architectural decoration. The boy is doing very well, but there have been giggles and whispers that make me rejoice that Vera should be out of the neighbourhood."

"Is she not very pretty?"

"You will be very much struck with her, I think; and Paulina is pretty too, and more thoughtful. She would not go with Thekla, because Waring Grange is far from church, and she would not disturb her Christmas and Epiphany. She is the most religious of them all, and puts me in mind of our old missionary castles in the air."

"Ah, what castles they were! And they seem further off than ever! Or perhaps you will fulfil them, and go and teach the Australian blacks!"

"A very unpromising field," said Mrs. Best, "though I hear there is a Sister Angela at the station who does wonders with them. I hear the quarter striking

—they will be back directly."

"Ah! before they come, we ought to talk over means! Something is owing for these last holidays. Oh! Sophy, I cannot find words to say how thankful I am to you for having helped me through this time, even to your own loss! It has made our life possible."

"Indeed, I was most thankful to do all I could for poor Agnes' children; and though I did not gain by them like my other boarders, I never *lost*, and they have been a great joy to me, yes, and a help, by giving my house a character."

"When I recollect how utterly crushed down I felt, seven years ago, when their mother died, and Aunt Magdalen refused help, and how despairingly I prayed, I feel all the more that there is an answer to even feeble almost worldly prayer."

"That it could not be when it was that you might be enabled to do the duty that was laid on you, my dear."

And with the exchange of a kiss, the two good women set themselves to practical pounds, shillings, and pence, which was just concluded when the patter of feet up the stone steps and voices in the hall announced the return of Mrs. Best's boarders.

Just as Magdalen was opening the door, there darted up, with the air of a privileged favourite, a little person of ten years old, with flying brown hair and round rosy cheeks, exclaiming breathlessly, "Is she come?"

The answer was to take her up with a motherly hug, and "My dear little Thekla!" There was not time for more than a hurried glance and embrace of the three on the steps of the stair, in their sailor hats and blue serge; but when in ten minutes more, the whole party, twenty in number, were seated round the dining table, observation was possible. Agatha, as senior scholar, sat at the foot of the table, fully occupied in dispensing Irish stew. She had a sensible face, to which projecting teeth gave a character, and a brow that would have shown itself finer but for the overhanging mass of hair. Vera and Paulina were so much alike and so nearly of the same age that they were often taken for twins, but on closer inspection Vera proved to be the prettiest, with a more delicately cut nose, clearer complexion, and bluer eyes; but Paulina, with paler cheeks, had softer eyes, and more pencilled brows, as well as a prettier lip and chin, though she would not strike the eye so much as her sister. Little Thekla was a round-faced, rosy little thing, childish for her nearly eleven years, smiling broadly and displaying enough white teeth to make Magdalen forebode that they would need much attention if they were not to be a desight like Agatha's.

She sat between Mrs. Best and Magdalen; and in the first pause, when the first course had just been distributed, she looked up with a great pair of grey eyes, and asked, in a shrill, clear little voice, "Sister, may I have a bicycle?"

"We will see about it, my dear," returned Magdalen, unwilling to pledge herself.

"But haven't you got a fortune?" undauntedly demanded Thekla.

"Something like it, Thekla. You shall hear about it after dinner." And Magdalen felt her colour flushing up under all those young eyes.

"Kitty Best said—"

But here Mrs. Best interposed. "We don't talk over such things at table, Thekla. Take care with the gravy. Did Mr. Jones give a lesson, this morning?"

"Yes, a very long one," said Vera.

"It was about the exact force of the words in the Revised Version," added Agatha, "compared with the Greek."

"That must have been very interesting!" said Magdalen.

Vera and her neighbour looked at one another and shrugged their shoulders; while some one else broke in with the news that another girl had not come back because she was down with influenza; and Magdalen, suspecting that "shop" was not talked at table, and also that the Scripture passage could not well be discussed there, saw that it was wise to let the conversation drift off, by Mrs. Best's leading, into anecdotes of the influenza.

All were glad when grace was chanted, and the five sisters could retreat into the drawing-room, which Mrs. Best let them have to themselves for the half hour before Magdalen's train, and the young ones' return to the High School. She was at once established with Thekla on her lap, and the others perched round on chairs and footstools. Of course the first question was, "And is it really true?"

"It is true, my dears, that my old great aunt has left me a house and some money; but you must not flatter yourselves that it is a great estate."

"Only mayn't I have a bicycle?" began Thekla again.

"Child, I believe you have bicycles on the brain," said Agatha. "But, sister, you do mean that we shall be better off, and I shall be able to go on with my education?"

"Yes, my dear, I think I can promise you so much," said Magdalen, caressing the serge shoulder.

"O thanks! Girton?" cried Agatha.

"There is much that I must inquire about before I decide—"

Again came, "Elsie Warner has a bicycle, and she is no older than me! Please, sister!"

"Hush now, my little Thekla," said the sister kindly; "I will talk to Mrs. Best, and see whether she thinks it will be good for you."

Thekla subsided with a pout, and Magdalen was able to explain her circumstances and plans a little more in detail; seeing however that the girls had no idea of the value of money, Paulina asked whether it meant being as well off as the Colonel and Lady Mary—

"Who keep a carriage and pair, and a butler," interposed Vera.

"Oh no, my dear. If I keep any kind of carriage it will be only a basket or governess cart, and a pony or donkey."

"That's all right," said Agatha. "I would not be rich and stupid for the world."

"Small fear of that!" said Magdalen, laughing. "Our home, the Goyle, is not more than a cottage, in a beautiful Devonshire valley—"

"What's the name of it?"

"The Goyle. I believe it is a diminutive of Gully, a narrow ravine. It is lovely even now, and will be delightful when you come to me in April—"

"Shall I leave school?" asked Vera. "I shall be seventeen in May."

"You will all leave school. Mrs. Best has made it easy to me by her wonderful goodness in keeping you on cheaper terms; but if Agatha goes to the University you must be content to work for a time with me."

"Oh!" cried Thekla. "Shall I have always holidays? My bicycle!"

Everybody burst out laughing at this—not a very trained cachinnation, but more of the giggle, even in Agatha; and Magdalen answered:

"You will have plenty of time for bicycling if the hills are not too steep, but I hope to make your lessons pleasant to you." She did not know whether to mention Mrs. Best's intention of soon giving up her house, which would have much increased her difficulties but for her legacy; and Agatha said, "You know, I think, that Vera and Polly both ought to make a real study of music. They both have talent, and cultivation would do a great deal for it."

Agatha spoke in a dogmatic way that amused Magdalen, and she said, "Well, I shall be able to judge when we are at the Goyle. Vera, I think you sing—"

Vera looked shy, and Agatha said, "She has a good voice, and Madame Lardner thinks it would answer to send her to some superior Conservatoire in process of time."

Vera did not commit herself as to her wishes, and Mrs. Best returned to say that if Miss Prescott wished to see the headmistress it was time to set out for the school; and accordingly the whole party walked up together to the school, Magdalen with Agatha, who was chiefly occupied in explaining how entirely it was owing to the one-sidedness of the examiners that she had not gained the scholarship. Magdalen had heard of such examiners before from the mothers of her pupils.

She had to wish her sisters good-bye for the next three months, not having gathered very much about them, except their personal appearance. She administered a sovereign to each of them as they parted. Agatha thanked her in a tone as if afraid to betray what a boon it was; Vera, with an eager kiss, asking if she could spend it as she liked; Paulina, with a certain grave propriety; and Thekla, of course, wanted to know whether it would buy a bicycle, or, if not, how many rides could be purchased from it.

When they were absorbed in the routine of the day, the interview with the head mistress disclosed, what Magdalen had expected, that Agatha, was an industrious, ambitious girl, with very good abilities quite worth cultivating, though not extraordinary; that Vera had a certain sort of cleverness, but no application and not much taste for anything but music; and that Paulina was a good, dutiful, plodding girl, who surpassed brighter powers by dint of diligence. The little one was a mere child, who had not yet come much under notice from the higher authorities.

On the whole, Magdalen went away with pleasant hopes, and the affectionate impulses of kindred blood rising within her, to complete her term with Lady Milsom, by whom she could not well be spared till towards Easter; while, in the meantime, her house was being repaired.

CHAPTER II—THE GOYLE

"A poor thing, but mine own."—Shakespeare.

"Thaay stwuns, thaay stwuns, thaay stwuns, thaay stwuns."

—T. Hughes, *Scouring of the White Horse.*

Magdalen Prescott stood on her own little terrace. Her house was, like many Devonian ones, built high on the slope of a steep hill, running down into a narrow valley, and her abode was almost at the narrowest part, where a little lively brawling stream descended from the moor amid rocks and brushwood. If the history of the place were told, it had been built for a shooting box, then inherited by a lawyer who had embellished and spent his holidays there, and afterwards, his youngest daughter, a lonely and retiring woman, had spent her latter years there.

The house was low, stone built, and roofed with rough slate, with a narrow verandah in front, and creepers in bud covering it. Then came a terrace just wide enough for a carriage to drive up; and below, flower-beds bordered with stones found what vantage ground they could between the steep slopes of grass that led almost precipitously down to the stream, where the ground rose equally rapidly on the other side. Moss, ivy, rhododendrons, primroses, anemones, and the promise of ferns were there, and the adjacent beds had their full share of hepaticas and all the early daffodil kinds. Behind and on the southern side, lay the kitchen garden, also a succession of steps, and beyond as the ravine widened were small meadows, each with a big stone in the midst. The gulley, (or goyle) narrowed as it rose, and there was a disused limestone quarry, all wreathed over with creeping plants, a birch tree growing up all white and silvery in the middle, and above the house and garden was wood, not of fine trees, and interspersed with rocks, but giving shade and shelter. The opposite side had likewise fields below, with one grey farm house peeping in sight, and red cattle feeding in one, and above the same rocky woodland, meeting the other at the quarry; and then after a little cascade had tumbled down from the steeper ground, giving place to the heathery peaty moor, which ended, more than two miles off in a torr like a small sphinx. This could not be seen from Magdalen's territory, but from the highest walk in her kitchen garden, she could see the square tower of Arnscombe, her parish church; and on a clear day, the glittering water of Rockstone bay.

To Magdalen it was a delightful view, and delightful too had been the arranging of her house, and preparing for her sisters. All the furniture and contents of the abode had been left to her. It was solid and handsome of its kind, belonging to the days of the retired Q.C., and some of it would have been displaced for what was more fresh and tasteful if Magdalen had not consulted economy. So she depended on basket-chairs, screens, brackets and drapery to enliven the ancient mahagony and rosewood, and she had accumulated a good many water colours, vases and knick-knacks. The old grand piano was found to be past its work, so that she went the length of purchasing a cottage one for the drawing-room, and another for the sitting-room that was to be the girls' own property, and on which she expended much care and contrivance. It opened into the drawing-room, and like it, had glass doors into the verandah, as well as another door into the little hall. The drawing-room had a bow window looking over the fields towards the South, and this way too looked the dining-room, in which Magdalen bestowed whatever was least interesting, such as the "Hume and Smollett" and "Gibbon" of her grandfather's library and her own school books, from which she hoped to teach Thekla.

Her upstairs arrangements had for the moment been rather disturbed by Mrs. Best's wishing to come with her pupils; but she decided that Agatha should at once take possession of her own pretty room, and the two next sisters of theirs, while she herself would sleep in the dressing room which she destined to Thekla, giving up her own chamber to Mrs. Best for these few days, and sending Thekla's little bed to Agatha's room.

And there she stood, on the little terrace, thinking how lovely the purple light on the moor was, and how all the newcomers would enjoy such a treat.

She had abstained from meeting them at the station, having respect to the capacities of the horse, even upon his native hills, and she had hired a farmer's cart to meet them and bring their luggage. Already she had a glimpse of the carriage, toiling up one hill, then disappearing between the hedges, and it was long before her gate, already open, was reached, and at her own *own* door, she received her little sister, followed by the others. And the first word she heard even before she had time to pay the driver was, "My dear Magdalen, what a road!"

Poor Mrs. Best! as the payment was put into the man's hand, Magdalen looked round and saw she looked quite worn out.

"Yes," said Paulina, "bumped to pieces and tired to death."

"I was afraid they had been mending the roads," said Magdalen.

"Mending! Strewing them with rocks, if you please," said Agatha.

"And such a distance!" added Paulina.

"Not quite three miles," replied Magdalen. "Here is some tea to repair you."

"My dear Magdalen"—in a chorus—"that really is quite impossible. It must be five, at least."

"Your nearest town ten miles off!" sighed Vera.

"Your nearest church," cried Paulina.

"Up in the wilds," said Agatha.

Magdalen felt as if these speeches were so many drops of water in her face and that of her beautiful Goyle, but she rose in its defence.

"It actually is less than three miles," she said. "I have walked it several times, and the cabs only charge three."

"That is testimony," said Mrs. Best, smiling; "but hills, perhaps, reckon for miles in one's feelings!"

"Particularly before you are rested," said Magdalen, setting her down in a comfortable wicker chair. "You will think little of it on your own feet, Vera, and the church is much nearer, Paulina, only on the other side of the hill."

"May I have a bicycle of my own?" burst in Thekla, again; while every one began laughing, and Agatha told her that Sister would think her brains were cycling.

> "With centric and concentric scribbledo'er
> Cycle and epicycle orb in orb."

"Epicycle?" cried Vera. "I saw it advertised in the *Queen*. A splendid one."

"Ah! Magdalen, you will think I have not taught them their Milton," said Mrs. Best, as both elders burst out laughing; and Agatha said, in an undertone, "Don't make yourself such a goose, Vera."

"I should think it rather rough sailing for bikes," said Paulina.

"I should have thought so, myself," returned Magdalen; "but the Clipstone girls do not seem to think so. I see them sailing merrily into Rockstone."

"You have neighbours, then?" said Vera.

"Certainly. Rockstone supplies a good deal. Here are various cards of people whose visits are yet to be returned. Clipstone is further off; but the daughters will be nice friends for you. I met one of them before, when she was staying at Lord Rotherwood's. But I am afraid your boxes are hardly come yet. Still, you will like to take off your things before dinner, even if you cannot unpack."

She led the way, and disposed of each girl in her new quarters, explaining to Agatha that her's and her little lodger were only temporary; but it struck upon her rather painfully that the only word of approbation or comfort came from Mrs. Best, and there were no notes at all of admiration of the scenery.

"Well," she said to herself, "much is not to be expected from people who have been tired and shaken up in a station cab over newly-mended roads! Were they as bad when I came? But then I could look out, and did not hear poor Sophy's groans all the way. I rather wish she had not come with them, though I am glad to see her again for this last time."

Meantime the four girls had congregated in the room appropriated to Vera and Paulina. "Here are the necessaries of life," said Agatha, handing out a brush and comb. "That slow wain may roll its course in utter darkness before it comes here."

"To the other end of nowhere," said Vera.

"And I am so tired," whined Thekla. "These tight boots do hurt me so! I want to go to bed."

Paulina was already on her knees, removing the boots and accommodating a pair of slippers to the little feet.

"We might as well be in a desert island," continued Vera, "shut up from everything with an old frump."

"Take care," said Agatha, in warning, signing towards Thekla.

"I am sure she looks jolly and good-natured," said Paulina.

"But did you hear what Elsie Lee always calls her, 'our maiden aunt'?"

All three laughed, and Vera added, "All the girls say she can't be less than fifty."

"Topsy! You know she is only sixteen years older than I am."

"Well, that's half a hundred!"

"Sixteen and nineteen, what do they make?"

"Oh, never mind your sums. She has got the face and look of half a hundred!"

"Now, I thought her face and her dress like a girl's," said Paulina.

"Yes," said Vera, "that's just the way with old maids. They dress themselves up youthfully and affect girlish airs, and are all the more horrid."

"That's your experience!" said Agatha. "But there's the waggon creeping up at a snail's pace. Let us run down and see after our things."

CHAPTER III—THE FIRST SUNDAY

"Speed on, speed on, the footpath way,
  And merrily hunt the stile-a;
A merry heart goes all the way,
  A sad tires in a mile-a."

—Shakespeare.

Sunday morning rose with new and bright hopes. The girls looked out at their window, and saw that it was a beautiful morning, and that the spring sunshine glowed upon the purple summits of the hills. Agatha supposed there would be a pleasant walk to church; Paulina said she had heard good accounts of the services in that part of the country; Vera hoped that they would see what their neighbours were like, and Thekla was delighted with the jolly garden and places to scramble in.

On this first Sunday they were let alone to explore the garden before the walk to church, which Magdalen foresaw would be a long affair with Mrs. Best. After their decorous stillness at breakfast, it was a contrast to hear the merry voices and laughter outside, but it subsided as soon as she approached, though she did not hear the murmured ripple, "Here comes maiden aunt! Behold—Quite a spicy hat!"

In truth, Magdalen's hat was a pretty new one, not by any means unsuitable to her age and appearance, and altogether her air was more stylish than the country town breeding was accustomed to; her dress perfectly plain, but well made.

Vera was perhaps the most sensible of the perfection of the turn-out; Agatha chiefly felt that her more decorated skirt and mantle had their inconveniences in walking through the red mud of the lanes, impeded by books and umbrella, which left no leisure to admire the primroses that studded the deep banks and which delighted Thekla in the freedom of short skirts.

Magdalen herself had enough to do in steering along such a substantial craft as poor Mrs. Best, used to church-going along a street, and shrouded under a squirrel mantle of many pounds weight.

Barely in time was the convoy when at last the exhausted lady was helped over the stone stile that led to the churchyard. Highly picturesque was the grey structure outside, but within modernism had not done much; the chancel was feebly fitted after the ideas of the "fifties," but the faded woodwork of the nave was intact, and Magdalen still had to sit in the grim pew of her predecessors.

The girls' looks at each other might have suited the entrance to a condemned cell, and the pulpit towered above them with a faded green cushion, that seemed in danger of tumbling down over their heads.

The service was a plain one, but reverent and careful; the music had a considerable element of harmonium mixed with schoolchild voices, and the sermon from an elderly man was a good one; but when the move to go out was made, and the young ones were beyond ear-shot of their elders, the exclamations were, "Well, I never thought to have gone back to Georgian era."

"Exactly the element of our maiden aunt."

"And nobody to be seen."

"Naggie, why do they shut one up in boxes?"

"Just to daunt Flapsy's roving eye, Tickle, my dear."

"Don't, Polly. There was nobody to be seen if we hadn't been in a box. Of course no one comes there but stately old farmers and their smart daughters. I saw one with a Gainsborough hat, and a bunch of cock's feathers, with a scarlet cactus cocking it up behind."

"Flapsy made use of her opportunities, you see. Being 'emparocked in a pew' cannot daunt her spirit of research."

"Now, Nag, I only meant to show you what impossible people they are."

"Natives who will repay the study perhaps," continued Agatha, reading as though from a book of travels. "We were able to observe a group of the aborigines at their devotions. Conspicuous was a not ungraceful young female, whose head, ornamented with a plume of feathers, towered above the enclosure in which she was secluded, while an aged fakir, hakem or medicine man pronounced from a loftier structure resembling a sentry box."

"Children, children, that's the wrong way," came Magdalen's voice from behind. "You must turn into that lane. Wait a moment."

They waited till Mrs. Best's lagging steps allowed Magdalen to come up with them, but dead silence fell on them when Mrs. Best observed, "You were very merry." They could not speak of the cause. Perhaps Magdalen divined something, for she said, "We hope to make some improvements, and so indeed does Mr. Earl, but he is very poor. Besides, newcomers must work slowly."

The doubt whether she had heard Agatha's speech made the girls conscious enough to keep from responding, as she meant them to do, by cheerful criticisms, and indeed the task of cheering and dragging on Mrs. Best was quite enough to occupy her. There was only three years difference in their ages, but this seemed to have made a great interval between one whose *métier* had been to be youthful and active, and her who had to be staid and dignified.

The early dinner passed in all demureness and formality, and the poor visitor was too much tired for any more services to be thought of for her. Magdalen explained that when the days would be longer, she thought of walking to Rockstone for evensong, but now the best way was to go to the chapel at Clipstone, which was nearer than either of the others.

"There is a lovely little chapel there, beautifully fitted up by Lord Rotherwood and Sir Jasper Merrifield, for the hamlet," she said.

"How far?" asked Mrs. Best.

"About a mile and a half across the fields; further by the road. You will find your bicycles available when you know the way."

"Don't we go to Rockstone?" asked Paulina. "I am sure there is a really satisfactory church there."

"St. Kenelm's, do you mean? That is not so near as St. Andrew's Church, but that is very satisfactory, and I go to one or other of them on week-days. It is too late to come back on these spring Sundays."

"I should not like to live among so many churches," said Mrs. Best, "and so far from them all!"

"You love your old parish church, like a faithful old churchwoman," said Magdalen. "Well, you see, I am faithful enough to go to my parish in the morning, but I think we may be discursive afterwards. There is a Sunday school in which I was waiting to offer help till our party was made up."

Magdalen had looked twice for a responding smile, first from Agatha, and then from Paulina, but none was awakened. The girls clustered together in the bedroom, and the word "Goody" passed between them.

"Tempered by respect for my Lord and Sir Jasper," added Agatha.

"And avoiding St. Kenelm's because it is the real correct church," said Paulina.

"Oh, yes!" cried Vera. "Mr. Hubert Delrio went to see it in case Eccles and Beamster should have an order. We must go there."

"Of course," said Paulina, with a sympathetic nod.

"But," said Agatha, "there will be an embargo on all acquaintance except the grandees at Clipstone."

"I shall never drop old friends," cried Vera. "I am a rock of crystal as regards them, whatever swells may require, if they burst themselves like the frog and the ox."

"Well done, crystal rock; but suppose the old friends slide off and drop you?" laughed Agatha.

Vera tossed her head; and Thekla ran in to say that Sister was ready.

The walk was shorter and pleasanter than that in the morning, over moorland, but with a good road; but all Magdalen discovered on the walk was that though the girls had attended botanical classes, they did not recognise spear-wort when they saw it, and Agatha thought the old catalogue fashions of botany were quite exploded. This was a sentiment, and it gave hopes of something like an argument and a conversation, but they were at that moment overtaken by the neighbouring farmer's wife, who wanted to give Miss Prescott some information about a setting of eggs, which she did at some length, and with a rapid utterance of dialect that amused, while it puzzled, Magdalen, and her inquiries and comments were decided to be "thoroughly good-wife" by all save Thekla, who hailed the possible ownership of a hen and chicken as almost equal to that of a bicycle.

Magdalen further discovered that Thekla's name in common use was "Tickle," or else "Tick-tick"; Paulina was, of course, Paula or Polly; Vera had her old baby title of Flapsy, which somehow suited her restless nervous motions, and Agatha had become Nag. Well, it was the fashion of the day, though not a pretty one; but Magdalen recollected, with some pain, her father's pleasure in the selection of saintly names for his little daughters, and she wondered how he would have liked to hear them thus transmuted. There had been something bordering on sentiment in her father's character, and something in Paulina's expression made her hope to see it repeated by inheritance. She saw the countenance brighten out of the morning's antagonistic air when they entered the little chapel at Clipstone, and saw the altar adorned and carefully decked with white narcissus and golden daffodils.

The little chapel was old and plain, very small, but reverently cared for. There was no choir, but the chairs of those who could sing were placed near the harmonium, which was played by one of the young ladies from the large gabled house to which the chapel was attached, and the singing had the refined tones that belong to the music of cultivated people. The congregation was evidently of poor folks from the hamlet, dependants of the great house, and the family itself, a grey-haired, fine-looking general, a tall dark-eyed lady, a tall youth, a schoolboy, and four girls—one of whom was musician, and the other presided over the school children. The service was reverent, the catechising good and effective, the sermon brief, and summing up in a spiritual and devotional manner; Magdalen was happy, and trusted that Paulina was so likewise.

She expected to hear some commendation as they walked home, but Vera alone kept with her, to examine her on the names and standing of the persons she had seen, on which there was as yet little to tell, for the first move towards acquaintance had not yet been made. All that was known was that there were Sir Jasper and Lady Merrifield, connections of Lord Rotherwood, who owned most of the Rockstone property, and who with his family had once been staying in the country house where Magdalen had been governess; but it was a long time ago, and she only recollected that there were some nice little girls. At least she said no more, but her friend thought the more.

"I suppose they will call?" said Vera.

"Most likely they will."

"Has nobody called?"

"Mr. Earl, the Vicar of Arnscombe. He has promised to tell me how we can be of use here. I believe there is great want of a lady at the Sunday school."

This did not interest Vera—and she went on asking questions about the neighbourhood, and whether any of the Rockstone people had left cards, and whether there were any parties, garden or evening, at Rockstone—more than Magdalen could yet answer, though she was glad to promote any sort of conversation with either of the girls who did not stand aloof fromher.

"I say, the M.A. (maiden aunt) knows nobody but that old clergyman, who wants her to teach his Sunday school."

"I'm out of that, thank goodness," said Agatha.

"And Sunday schools are a delusion, only hindering the children from going to church with their parents," said Paulina.

"And if nobody calls, and they all think her no better than an old governess, how awfully slow it will be," continued Vera.

"I do not suppose that will last," said Agatha. "There is Rockstone, remember."

"Ten miles off," said Vera disconsolately. "Oh, Nag, Nag, isn't it horrid! We shall be just smart enough to be taken for swells, and know nobody; and the swells won't have us because she is a governess. We might as well be upon a desert island at once."

Agatha could not help laughing and repeating—

"I am out of humanity's reach,
  I must finish my journey alone—
Never hear the sweet music of speech,
  I start at the sound of my own."

"But really, Nag," broke in Paulina, "it is horrid. Here we are equidistant from three or four churches, and condemned to the most behind the world of them all, and then to the one where there is this distant fragrance of swells, instead of the only Catholic one."

Agatha had a little more common sense than the other two, and she responded —

"After all, you know, you are better off than if you were still at school; and the M.A. is a good old soul at the bottom, and you may manage her, depend on it. Though I wish she had let me go to Girton."

Magdalen and Mrs. Best meantime were going over future prospects and old times. Mrs. Best's destination was Albertstown, in Queensland, where her son George had a good practice as a doctor, and where he assured her she would find church privileges—even a cathedral, so-called, and a bishop—though Bishop Fulmort was always out on some expedition among the colonists or the natives, but among his clergy there was always Sunday service. In fact, Magdalen thought the good old lady expected to find a town more like Filsted than the Goyle. There was a sisterhood located there too, which tried, mostly in vain, to train the wild native women—an attempt at which George Best laughed, though he allowed that the sisters were splendid nurses, especially Sister Angela, who had a wonderful way of bringing cases round.

Magdalen could feel secure that her old friend would be near kind people; and presently Mrs. Best, returning to the actual neighbourhood, observed—

"Merrifield! It is not a common name."

"No; but I do not think this is the same family. This is a retired general, living in a house of Lord Rotherwood's. I once met one of his little girls, who came to Castle Towers with the Rotherwood party, and though she had a brother of the name, he was evidently not the same person."

Mrs. Best asked no more, for tell-tale colour had arisen in Magdalen's cheeks; and she had been the confidante of an engagement with a certain Henry Merrifield, who had been employed in the bank at Filsted when Magdalen was a very young girl. His father had come down suddenly, had found debt and dissipation, had broken all off decidedly, and no more had been heard of the young man. It was many years previously; but those cheeks and the tone of the reply made her suspect that there was still poignancy in the remembrance.

CHAPTER IV—CYCLES

"What flowers grow in my field wherewith to dress thee."

—E. Barrett Browning.

Mrs. Best departed early the next morning. It was probably a parting for life between the two old friends; and Magdalen keenly felt the severance from the one person whom she had always known, and on whose sympathy she could rely. Their conversations had been very precious to her, and she felt desolate without the entire companionship. Yet, on the other hand, she felt as if she could have begun better with her sisters if Sophy Best had not come with them, to hand them over, as it were, when she wanted to start on the same level with them, and be more like their contemporary than their authority.

They all stood on the terrace, watching the fly go down the hill, and she turned to them and said—

"We will all settle ourselves this morning, and you will see how the land lies, so that to-morrow we can arrange our day and see what work to do. Thekla, when you have had a run round the garden, you might bring your books to the dining-room and let me see how far you have gone."

"Oh, sister, it is holidays!"

"Well, my dear, you have had a week, and your holiday time cannot last for ever. Looking at your books cannot spoil it."

"Yes, it will; they are so nasty."

"Perhaps you will not always think so; but now you had better put on your hat and your thick boots, for the grass is still very wet, and explore the country. The same advice to you," she added, turning to the others; "it is warm here, but the dew lies long on the slopes."

"We have got a great deal too much to do," said Agatha, "for dawdling about just now."

Really, she was chiefly prompted by the satisfaction of not being ordered about; and the other two followed suit, while Magdalen turned away to her household business.

They found the housemaid in possession of the bedrooms, so that the unpacking plans could not conveniently be begun; and while Agatha was struggling with the straps of a book box, Thekla burst in upon them.

"Oh, Nag, Nag, there is the loveliest angel of a bicycle in the stable, and a dear little pony besides! 'New tyre wheels,' he says."

"A bicycle! Well, if she has got it for us, she is an angel indeed," said Vera.

"It is a big one," said Thekla, "but the pony is a dear little thing; Pixy is his name, and I can ride him! Do come, Flapsy, and see! Earwaker will show you. It is he that does the oiling of Pixy and harnessing the bicycle. I mean —"

"Tick, Tick, which does he oil and which does he harness?" said Paula.

"That little tongue wants both," said Agatha.

"But do, do come and see," said Thekla, not at all disconcerted by being laughed at; and Vera came, only asserting her independence by not putting on either hat or boots.

Thekla led the way to the stable, tucked under the hill at the back, and presiding over a linhay, as she had already learnt to call the tiny farm-court, containing accommodation for two cows, a pig, and sundry fowls. There was a shed attached with a wicker pony carriage and the bicycle, a handsome modern one, with all the newest appendages, including the "Nevertires," as Thekla had translated them.

But disappointment was in store for Vera. Magdalen came out during the inspection, and was received with—

"Sister, you never told us of this beauty."

"It was a parting present from General Mansell," she said, "and he took great pains to get me a very good one."

"And you bike!"

"Oh, yes; I learnt to go out with the Colvins. But I do not venture to use it much here, unless the road is good. Those rocks, freshly laid towards Rockstone, would make regular havoc of the pneumatic tyres."

Vera saw that this was prohibitive, and felt too much vexed to mention Thekla's version of the same; but Magdalen asked, "Have you learnt?"

"They were always going to teach me at Warner Grange, but it always snowed, or rained, or skated, I mean we skated, or something, whenever Hubert had time; but I am perfectly dying to learn."

"Well, before you expire, we may teach you a little on these smoother paths; and hire one perhaps, by the time the stones are passable. Just at present, I think our own legs and Pixy's are safer for that descent."

Vera was pacified enough to look on with a certain degree of complacency, while Thekla was enraptured at being set to take out the eggs from the hens' nests.

But the conclave in the sitting-room on Vera's report decided, "Selfish old thing, it is only an excuse! Of course we should take care not to spoil it. It shows what will be the way with everything."

No one knew of a still more secret conclave within Magdalen's own breast, one of those held at times by many an elder, between the claims of loyalty to the keepsakes of affection and old association and the gratification of present desires. Magdalen thought of the rules of convents forbidding the appropriation of personal trifles, and wondered if it were wise, if stern; but for the present she decided that it could not be her duty to risk what had been carefully and kindly selected for her in unpractised and careless hands; and she further compromised the matter by reckoning whether her funds, which were not excessive, would admit of the hire or purchase of machines that might allay the burning aspirations of her young people.

The upshot of her reckoning was that when they all met at the early dinner, she announced, "I think we might go to Rock Quay this afternoon, between the pony carriage and Shanks's mare. I want to ask about some lessons, and we could see about the hire of a bicycle for you to learn upon."

It was only Agatha who answered, "Thank you, but it is not worth while for me, I shall be away so soon."

Thekla cried out, "Me too!"—and Paulina mumbled something. In truth, besides the thought of the bicycle in the stable, the other two had lived enough in the country-town atmosphere to be foolishly disgusted at being obliged to dine early. That they had always been used to it made them only think it beneath their age as well as their dignity, and, "What a horrid nuisance!" had been on their tongues when the bell was ringing.

Moreover, they had enough of silly prejudice about them to feel aggrieved at the sight of hash, nice as it was with fresh vegetables, and they were not disposed to good temper when they sat down to their meal. "They" perhaps properly means the middle pair, for Agatha had more notion of manners and of respect, and Thekla had an endless store of chatter about her discoveries.

The pony-carriage was brought round in due time, but just then another vehicle of the same kind, only prettier and with two ponies, was seen at the gate, too late for the barbarian instinct of rushing away to hide from morning visitors to be carried out, before Lady Merrifield and a daughter, were up the slope and on the levelled road before the verandah.

"I think this is an old acquaintance," said Lady Merrifield as she shook hands, "though perhaps Mysie is grown out of remembrance."

"Oh, yes," said an honest open-faced maiden, eagerly putting out her hand. "Don't you remember, Miss Prescott, our all staying at Castle Towers? I came with Phyllis Devereux, and she and I took poor Betty Bernard out after blackberries, and she thought it was a mad bull when it was a railway whistle, and ran into a cow-pond, and Cousin Rotherwood came and Captain Grantley and got her out."

Magdalen was smiling and nodding recollection, and added, "It was really one of the boys."

"Oh, yes."

"I thought it was a crazy bull
  Firing a blunderbuss—"

She paused for recollection, and Magdalen went on—

"I thought it was a crazy bull
  Firing a blunderbuss;
I looked again, and, lo, it was
  A water polypus.
'Oh, guard my life,' I said, 'for she
  Will make an awful fuss.'"

"Ah! do you remember that?" cried Mysie. "I have so often tried to recollect what it really was when she looked again. Captain Grantley made it, you know, when we were trying to comfort Betty."

"I remember you and Lady Phyllis said you would go and confess to Mrs. Bernard and take all the blame, and Lord Rotherwood said he would escort you!"

"Yes, and Betty said it was no good, for if her mother forgave her ten times over, still that spiteful French maid would put her to bed and say she had no *robe convenable*," went on Mysie. "But then you took her to your own room, and washed her and mended her, so that she came out all right at luncheon, and nobody knew anything, but she thought that horrid woman guessed and tweaked her hair all the harder for it."

"Poor child, she looked as if she were under a tyranny."

"Have you seen her since?"

"No; but Phyllis tells me she has burst forth into liberty, bicycles, and wild doings that would drive her parents to distraction if she dreamt of them."

"How is Lady Phyllis? Did I not hear that the family had gone abroad for her health?"

"Oh yes, and I went with them. They all had influenza, and were frightened, but it ended in our meeting with Franceska Vanderkist, the very most charming looking being I ever did see; and Ivinghoe had fallen in love with her when she was Miranda, and he married her like a real old hero. Do you remember Ivinghoe?"

"No; I suppose he was one of an indistinguishable troop of schoolboys."

"I remember Lord Rotherwood's good nature and fun when he met the bedraggled party," said Magdalen, smiling.

"That is what every one remembers about him," said Lady Merrifield, smiling. "You have imported a large party of youth, Miss Prescott."

"My young sisters," responded Magdalen; "but I shall soon part with Agatha; she is going to Oxford."

"Indeed! To which College? I have a daughter at Oxford, and a niece just leaving Cambridge. Such is our lot in these days. No, not this one, but her elder sister Gillian is at Lady Catharine's."

"I am going to St. Robert's," said Agatha, abruptly.

"Close to Lady Catharine's! Gillian will be glad to tell her anything she would like to ask about it. You had better come over to tea some afternoon."

The time was fixed, and then Magdalen showed some of the advertisements of tuition in art, music, languages, and everything imaginable, which had begun to pour in upon her, and was very glad of a little counsel on the reputation of each professor. Lady Merrifield saying, however, that her experience was small, as her young people in general were not musical, with the single exception of her son Wilfred, who was at home, reading to go up for the Civil Service, and recreating himself with the Choral Society and lessons on the violin. "My youngest is fifteen," she said, "and we provide for her lessons amongst us, except for the School of Art, and calisthenics at the High School, which is under superior management now, and very much improved."

Mysie echoed, "Oh, calisthenics are such fun!" and took the reins to drive away.

"Oh! she is very nice," exclaimed Mysie, as they drove down the hill.

"Yes, there is something very charming about her. I wonder whether Sam made a great mistake."

"Mamma, what do you mean?"

"Have I been meditating aloud? You said when you met her at Castle Towers, she asked you whether you had a brother Harry."

"Yes, she did. I only said yes, but he was going to be a clergyman, and when she heard his age, she said he was not the one she had known; I did not speak of cousin Henry because you said we were not to mention him. What was it, if I may know, mamma?"

"There is no reason that you should not, except that it is a painful matter to mention to Bessie or any of the Stokesley cousins. Harry was never like the rest, I believe, but I had never seen him since he was almost a baby. He never would work, and was not fit for any examination."

"Our Harry used to say that Bessie and David had carried off all the brains of the family."

"The others have sense and principle, though. Well, they put their Hal into a Bank at Filsted, and by and by they found he was in a great scrape, with gambling debts; and I believe that but for the forbearance of the partners, he might have been prosecuted for embezzling a sum—or at least he was very near it; besides which he had engaged himself to an attorney's daughter, very young, and with a very disagreeable mother or stepmother. The Admiral came down in great indignation, thought these Prescotts had inveigled poor Henry, broke everything hastily off, and shipped him off to Canada to his brothers, George and John. They found some employment for him, but Susan and Bessie doubt whether they were very kind to him, and in a few years more he was in fresh scrapes, and with worse stains and questions of his integrity. It ended in his running away to the States, and no trace has been found of him since. I am afraid he took away money of his brothers."

"How long ago was it, mamma?"

"At least twenty years. It was while we were in Malta."

"Who would have thought of those dear Stokesley cousins having such a skeleton in their cupboard?"

"Ah! my dear, no one knows the secrets of others' hearts."

"And you really think that this Miss Prescott was his love?"

"I know it was the same name, and Bessie told me that he used to talk to her of his Magdalen, or Maidie; and when I heard of your meeting her at Castle Towers I wondered if it were the same. And now I see what she is, and what she is undertaking for these young sisters; I have wondered whether your uncle was wise to insist on the utter break, and whether she might not have been an anchor to hold him fast to his moorings."

"Only," said Mysie, "if he had really cared, would he have let his father break it off so entirely?"

"I think your uncle expected implicit obedience."

"But—," said Mysie, and left the rest unsaid, while both she and her mother went off into meditations on different lines on the exigencies of parental discipline and of the requirements of full-grown hearts.

And, on the whole, the younger one was the most for strict obedience, the experienced parent in favour of liberty. But then Mysie was old-fashioned and dutiful.

CHAPTER V—CLIPSTONE FRIENDS

"What idle progeny succeed
To chase the rolling circle's speed,
Or urge the flying ball."—Gray.

The afternoon at Clipstone was a success. Gillian was at home, and every one found congeners. Lady Merrifield's sister, Miss Mohun, pounced upon Miss Prescott as a coadjutor in the alphabet of good works needed in the neglected district of Arnscombe, where Mr. Earl was wifeless, and the farm ladies heedless; but they were interrupted by Mysie running up to claim Miss Prescott for a game at croquet. "Uncle Redgie was so glad to see the hoops come into fashion again," and Vera and Paula hardly knew the game, they had always played at lawn tennis; but they were delighted to learn, for Uncle Redgie proved to be a very fine-looking retired General, and there was a lad besides, grown to manly height; and one boy, at home for Easter, who, caring not for croquet, went with Primrose to exhibit to Thekla the tame menagerie, where a mungoose, called of course Raki raki, was the last acquisition. She was also shown the kittens of the beloved Begum, and presented with Phœbus, a tabby with a wise face and a head marked like a Greek lyre, to be transplanted to the Goyle in due time.

"If Sister will let me have it," said Thekla.

"Of course she will," said Primrose. "Mysie says she is so jolly."

"Dear me! all the girls at our school said she was a regular Old Maid."

"What shocking bad form!" exclaimed Primrose. "Just like cads of girls," muttered Fergus, unheard; for Thekla continued—"Why, they said she must be our maiden aunt, instead of our sister."

"The best thing going!" said Fergus.

"Maiden aunts in books are always horrid," said Thekla.

"Then the books ought to be hung, drawn, and quartered, and spifflicated besides," said Fergus.

"Fergus doesn't like anybody so well as Aunt Jane," said Primrose, "because nobody else understands his machines."

Thekla made a grimace.

"Ah!" said Primrose. "I see it is just as mamma and Mysie said when they came home, that Miss Prescott was very nice indeed, and it was famous that she should make a home for you all, only they were afraid you seemed as if—you might be—tiresome," ended Primrose, looking for a word.

"Well, you know she wants to be our governess," said Thekla.

"Well?" repeated Primrose.

"And of course no one ever likes their governess."

This aphorism, so uttered by Thekla, provoked a yell from Primrose, echoed by Fergus; and Primrose, getting her breath, declared that dear Miss Winter was a great darling, and since she had gone away, more's the pity, mamma was real governess to herself, Valetta, and Mysie, and she always looked at their translations and heard their reading if Gillian was not at home.

"And they are quite grown-up young ladies!"

"Mysie is; but I don't know about Val. Only I don't see why any one should be silly and do nothing if one is grown up ever so much," said Primrose.

"As the Eiffel Tower," put in Fergus.

"Nonsense!" said Primrose, bent on being improving. "Don't you know what that old book of mamma's says, 'When will Miss Rosamond's education be finished?' She answered 'Never.'"

Thekla gave a groan, whether of pity for Rosamond or for herself might be doubted; and a lop-eared rabbit was a favourable diversion.

There was a triad who seemed to be of Rosamond's opinion regarding education, for Agatha was eagerly availing herself of the counsel of Gillian, and the books shown to her; with the further assistance of the cousin, Dolores Mohun, now an accredited lecturer in technical classes, though making her home and headquarters at Clipstone.

Thekla's views of young ladyhood were a good deal more fulfilled by the lessons on cycling which were going on among the other young people after the game of croquet had ended. Every size and variety seemed to exist among the Clipstone population, under certain regulations of not coasting down the hills, the girls not going out alone, and never into the town, but always "putting up" at Aunt Jane's.

Vera and Paulina were in ecstasy, and there was a continual mounting, attempting and nearly falling, or turning anywhere but the right, little screams, and much laughter, Jasper attending upon Vera, who, in spite of her failures, looked remarkably pretty and graceful upon Valetta's machine; while Paula, whom Mysie and Valetta were both assisting, learnt more easily and steadily, but looked on with a few qualms as to the entire crystal rock constancy that Vera had professed, more especially when Jasper volunteered to come over to the Goyle and give another lesson.

Magdalen, after her game at croquet, had spent a very pleasant time with Lady Merrifield and her brother and sister, till they were imperiously summoned by Primrose to come and give consent to the transfer of Phœbus, or to choose between him and the Mufti, to whom Thekla had begun to incline.

The whole party adjourned to the back settlements, where Magdalen was edified by the antics of the mungoose, and admired the Begum and her progeny with a heartiness that would have won Thekla's heart, save that she remembered hearing Vera say, over the domestic cat in the morning, that M.A.'s were always devoted to cats. But, on the whole, the visit had done much to reconcile the young sisters to their new surroundings; books, bicycles, and kitten had reconciled them even to the intimacy with "swells."

The hired bicycle and tricycle had arrived in their absence, and the moment breakfast was over the next morning, the three younger ones all rushed off to the enjoyment, and, at ten minutes past the appointed hour for the early reading and study, Agatha felt obliged to go out and tell them that the M.A. was sitting like Patience on a monument, waiting for them; on which three tongues said "Bother," and "She ought to let us off till the proper end of the holidays."

"Then you should have propitiated her by asking leave after the Scripture was done," said Agatha; "you might have known she would not let you off that."

"Bother," said Vera again; "just like an M.A."

"I did forget," said Paula; "and you know it was only just going through a lesson for form's sake, like the old superlative."

They had, in fact, read the day before; when Thekla had made such frightful work of every unaccustomed word, and the elders by one or two observations had betrayed so much ignorance alike of Samuel's history and of the Gospel of St. Luke, that she had resolved to endeavour at a thorough teaching of the Old and New Testaments for the first hour on alternate days, giving one day in the week to Catechism and Prayer Book.

She asked what they had done before.

"Mrs. Best always read something at prayers."

"Something?"

"Something out of the Bible."

"No, the Testament."

"I am sure it was the Bible, it was so fat."

"And Saul was in it, and we had him yesterday."

"That was St. Paul before he was converted," said Paula.

There their knowledge seemed to end, and it further appeared that Mrs. Best heard the Catechism and Collect on Sundays from the unconfirmed, and had tried to get the Gospel repeated by heart, but had not succeeded.

"We did not think it fair," said Vera. "None of the other houses did."

"Yes," said Agatha, "Miss Ferris's did."

"Oh, she is a regular old Prot," said Paula, "almost a Dissenter, and it is not the Gospel either, only texts out of her own head."

"Polly!" said Agatha. "Texts out of her own head!"

"It is Bible, of course, only what she fancies; and they have to work out the sermon, and if they can't do the sermon, a text. They might as well be Dissenters at once!" said Paula.

"Janet M'Leod is," said Vera. "It was really Dissentish."

Magdalen could not help saying, "So you would not learn the Gospel because Dissenters learnt pieces of Scripture! You seem to me like the Roman Catholic child, who said there were five sacraments, there ought to be seven, but the Protestants had got two of them."

She was sorry she had said it, for though Agatha laughed, the other two drew into themselves, as if their feelings were hurt. "These are the boarding-house habits," she said. "What is done at the High School itself?"

"The Vicar comes when he has time, and gives a lecture on an Epistle," said Agatha, "or a curate, if he doesn't; but I was working for the exam., and didn't go this last term. What was it, Polly?"

"On the—on the Apollonians," answered Paulina, hesitating.

"My dear, where did he find it?"

"I know it was something about Apollo," said Vera.

"It was Corinthians," said Paula. "I ought to have recollected, but the lectures are very dull and disjointed; you said so yourself, Nag, and the Rector is very low church."

"So you could not learn from him!"

"Really, sister," said Agatha, "the lectures are not well managed, they are in too many hands, and too uncertain, and it is not easy to learn much from them."

"Well, that being the case, I think we had better begin at the beginning. Suppose I ask you to say the first answer in the Catechism."

On which Vera said they had all been confirmed except Thekla, and passed it on to her.

However, the endeavours of that half-hour need not be recounted, and the moment half-past ten chimed out the young ladies jumped up, and would have been off to the bicycles, if Magdalen had not felt that the time was come for asserting authority, and said, "Not yet, if you please. We cannot waste whole days. You know Herr Gnadiger is coming to-morrow, and it would be well to practise that sonata beforehand; you ought each to practise it; Paula, you had better begin, and Vera, you prepare this first scene of Marie Stuart to read with me when Thekla's lessons are over. Change over when Paula has done."

"It is of no use my doing anything while anyone is playing," said Vera.

"Nonsense," Agatha muttered; but Magdalen said, "You can sit in the drawing-room or your own room. Come, Tick-tick, where's your slate? Come along."

"Don't sulk, Flapsy," said the elder sister, "it is of no use. The M.A. means to be minded, and will be, and you know it is all for your good."

"I hate my good," said naughty Vera.

"So does every one when it is against the grain," said Agatha; "but remember it is a preparation for a free life of our own."

"It is our cross," said Paula, as she placed herself on the music stool with a look of resignation almost comical.

Nor did her performance interfere with the equations which Agatha was diligently working out; but Vera, though refusing to take refuge from the piano, to which, in fact, she was perfectly inured, worried her elder as much as she durst, by inquiries after the meaning of words, or what horrid verb to look out in the dictionary; and it was a pleasing change when Paula proceeded to work the same scene out for herself without having recourse to explanations, so that Agatha was undisturbed except by the careless notes, which almost equally worried Magdalen in the more distant dining-room.

This was really the crisis of the battle of study. As the girls were accustomed to it, and knew that they were of an age to be ground down, they followed Agatha's advice, and submitted without further open struggle, though there was a good deal of low murmur, and the foreman's work was not essentially disagreeable, even while Vera maintained, what she believed to be an axiom, that governesses were detestable, and that the M.A. must incur the penalty of acting as such.

Very soon after luncheon appeared three figures on bicycles. Wilfred Merrifield, with Mysie and Valetta, come to give another lesson on the "flying circle's speed."

Magdalen came out with her young people to enjoy their amusement, as well as to watch over her own precious machine, as Vera said. It was admired, as became connoisseurs in the article; and she soon saw that Wilfred was to be trusted with the care of it, so she consented to its being ridden in the practice, provided it was not taken out into the lanes.

Mysie turned off from the practising, where she was not wanted, and joined Miss Prescott in walking through the garden terraces, and planning what would best adorn them, talking over favourite books, and enjoying themselves very much; then going on to the quarry, where Mysie looked about with a critical eye to see if it displayed any fresh geological treasures to send Fergus in quest of. She began eagerly to pour forth the sister's never-ending tale of her brother's cleverness, and thus they came down the outside lane to the lower gate, seeing beforehand the sparkle of bicycles in its immediate proximity.

It was not open, but Vera might be seen standing with one hand on the latch, the other on Magdalen's bicycle, her face lifted with imploring, enticing smiles to Wilfred, who had fallen a little back, while Paula had decidedly drawn away.

None of them had seen Magdalen and Mysie till they were round the low stone wall and close upon them. There was a general start, and Vera exclaimed, "We haven't been outside! No, we haven't! And it is not the Rockquay Road either, sister! I only wanted a run down that lane up above."

Wilfred laughed a little oddly. It was quite plain that he had been withstanding the temptress, only how long would the resistance have lasted?

Downright Mysie exclaimed, "It would have been a great shame if you had, and I am glad Wilfred hindered you."

"Thank you," said Magdalen, smiling to him. "You know better than my sisters what Devon lanes and pneumatic tyres are!"

Perhaps Wilfred was a little vexed, though he had resisted, for he was ready to agree with Mysie that they could not stay and drink tea.

But he did not escape his sister's displeasure, for Mysie began at once, "How lucky it was that we came in time. I do believe that naughty little thing was just going to talk you over into doing what her sister had forbidden."

"A savage, old, selfish bear. It was only the lane."

"Full of crystals as sharp as needles, enough to cut any tyre in two," said Mysie.

"Like your tongue, eh, Mysie?"

"Well, you did not do it! That is a comfort. You would not let her transgress, and ruin her sister's good bicycle."

"She is an uncommonly pretty little sprite, and the selfish hag of a sister only left orders that I was to take care of the bike! I could see where there was a stone as well as anybody else."

"Hag!" angrily cried Mysie, "she is the only nice one of the whole lot. Vera is a nasty little thing, or she would never think of meddling with what does not belong to her, or trying to persuade you to allow it."

"I call it abominable selfishness, dog in the mangerish, to shut up such a machine as that, and condemn her sisters to one great lumbering one."

"That's one account," said Valetta. "Paula said it was only till they had learnt to ride properly, and till the stones have a little worn in."

"Yes," said Mysie, "I could see Vera is an exaggerating monkey, just talking over and deluding Will, just as men like when they get a silly fit."

By this time Wilfred had thought it expedient to put his bicycle to greater speed, and indulge in a long whistle to show how contemptible he thought his sisters as he went out of hearing.

"Paulina is nice and good," said Valetta, "she has heard all about St. Kenelm's, and wants to go there. Yes, and she means to be a Sister of Charity, only she is afraid her sister is narrow and low church."

"That is stuff and nonsense," said Mysie. "I have had a great deal of talk with Miss Prescott. She loves all the same books that we do. She is going to have G. F. S. and Mothers' Union, and all at poor Arnscombe, and she told me to call her Magdalen."

With which proofs of congeniality Valetta could not choose but be impressed.

CHAPTER VI—THE FRESCOES OF ST. KENELM'S

Earn well the thrifty months, nor wed
Raw Haste, half-sister to Delay.—Tennyson.

The deferred expedition to Rockquay also began, Magdalen driving Vera and Thekla. She was pleased with her visitors, and hoped that the girls would feel the same, but Vera began by declaring that *that* Miss Merrifield was not pretty.

"Not exactly, but it is an honest, winning face."

"So broad, and such a wide mouth, and no style at all, as I should have expected after all that about lords and ladies! An old blue serge and sailor hat!"

"You don't expect people to drive about the country in silk attire?"

"Well, perhaps she is not out! Sister, do you know I am seventeen?"

"Yes, my dear, certainly."

"Oh, look, look, there's a dear little calf!" broke in Thekla, "and, oh! what horns the cows have. I shall be afraid to go near them! Was it only a sham mad bull when the little girl ran into the pond?"

"It was the railway whistle, and she had never heard it in the fields. She rushed away in a great fright and ran into the pond, full of horrible black mud. The gentlemen heard the scream and dragged her out, and it would have all been fun and a good story if she had not been so much afraid of the French lady's maid. It is curious how the sight of those brown eyes brought the whole scene back to me. We all grew so fond of Mysie Merrifield in the few days we spent together, and she is very little altered."

"Is she out?" asked Vera once more.

"Oh, yes, she cannot be less than twenty."

"And I am seventeen," said Vera, returning to the charge. "I ought to be out."

"If there are nice invitations, I shall be quite ready to accept them for you."

"But I am too old for the schoolroom and lessons and masters."

"Too old or too wise?" said Magdalen laughing.

"I have got into the highest form in everything. Every one at Filston of my age is leaving off all the bother."

"Not Agatha."

"Oh, but Agatha is—!"

"Is what?

"Agatha is awfully clever, and wants to be something!"

"Something? But do you want to evaporate? To be nothing at all, I mean," said Magdalen, seeing her first word was bewildering, and Thekla put in—

"Flapsy couldn't go off in steam, could she? Isn't that evaporating?"

"I think what she wants is to be a young lady at large! Eh, Vera? Only I don't quite see how that is to be managed, even if it is quite a worthy ambition. But we will talk that over another time. Do you see how pretty those sails are crossing the bay?"

Neither girl seemed to have eyes for the lovely blue of the sea in the spring sunshine, nor the striking forms of ruddy peaks of rock that enclosed it. Uneducated eyes, she thought, as she slowly manœuvred the pony down the steep hill before coming to the Rockstone Cliff Road. The other two girls were following her direction across field and road, and making their observations.

"A dose of lords and ladies," said Agatha.

"I thought they were rather nice," said Paula.

"I see how it will be," said Agatha. "They will patronise the M.A. as Lady Somebody's old governess, and she will fawn upon them and run after them, and we shall be on those terms."

"But I thought you meant to be a governess?"

"I shall make my own line. I know how swells look on a governess of the *ancien régime*, and how they will introduce her as the kindly old goody who mends my little lady's frock!"

"The girl had not any airs," said Paula. "She told me about the churches down there in the town—not the ones we went to on Sunday; but there's one that is very low indeed, and St. Andrew's, which is their parish church, was suiting the moderate high church folk; and there is St. Kenelm's, very high indeed, Mr. Flight's, I think I have heard of him, and it is just the right thing, I am sure."

"Don't flatter yourself that the M.A. will let you have much pleasure in it. It is just what people of her sort think dangerous."

"But do you know, Nag, I do believe that it is the church that Hubert Delrio was sent down to study and make a design for."

"Whew! There will be a pretty kettle of fish if he comes down about it! That is, if he and Flapsy have not forgotten all about the ice and the forfeits at Warner's Grange, as is devoutly to be hoped."

"Do you hope it really, Nag, for Flapsy really was very much—did care very much."

"I have no great faith in Flapsy's affections surviving the contact with greater swells."

"Poor Hubert!"

"Perhaps his will not survive common sense. I am sure I hope not for both their sakes."

"But, Nag, it would be very horrid of them if they had no constancy," declared the more romantic Paula.

"It will be a regular mess if they do have it, and bring on horrid scrapes with the M.A. Just think. It is all very well to say she has known Hubert all his life; but she can't treat him as a gentleman, or she won't. She has a position to keep up with all these swells, and he will be only the man who paints the church! I only hope he will not come. There will be nothing but bother if he does, unless they both have more sense and less constancy than you expect. Well, this really is a splendid view. Old Mr. Delrio would be wild about it."

Here the steep and stony hill brought them into contact with the pony carriage, nor were there any more confidential conversations. The pony was put up at the top of the hill leading from Rockstone to Rockquay, and thence the party walked down for Miss Prescott to make a few purchases, and, moreover, to begin by gratifying Thekla's reiterated entreaty for a bicycle, though, as she was unpractised and growing so fast, it was decided to be better to hire a tricycle for practice, and one bicycle on which Vera and Paula might learn the art.

The choice was a long one, and left only just time for a peep into the two churches and a study of the hours of their services. St. Kenelm's was decided to be a "perfect gem," ornaments, beauty, and all, a little overdone, perhaps, in Magdalen's opinion, but perfectly "the thing" in her sisters'.

This St. Andrew's fulfilled to her mind, being handsome, reverent, and decorous in all the arrangements, while to the younger folk it was "all very well," but quite of the old times. Little did they know of "old times" beyond the quarter century of their birth! Poor old Arnscombe might feebly represent them, but even that had struggled out of the modern "dark ages." Magdalen had decided on talking to Agatha and seeing how far she understood the situation, and she came to her room to put her in possession now that Mrs. Best had left the guest chamber free.

"This is your home when you are here. You must put up any belongings that you do not want to take to St. Robert's."

"Thank you; it is a nice pleasant room."

"And, my dear, may I stay a few minutes? I think we had better have a talk, and quite understand one another."

"Very well."

It was not quite encouraging, but Agatha really wished to hear, and she advanced a wicker chair for her elder sister, and sat down on the window seat.

"Thank you, my dear; I do not know how much Mrs. Best has told you."

"She told us that you had always been very good to us, and that you had been our guardian ever since we lost our mother."

"Did she tell you what we have of our own that our father could leave us?"

"No."

"What amounts to about £40 a year apiece. Mrs. Best in her very great goodness has taken you four for that amount, though her proper charge is eighty."

"And she never let any one guess it," said Agatha, more warmly, "for fear we might feel the difference. How very good of her."

She seemed more impressed by Mrs. Best's bounty than by Magdalen's, but probably she took the latter as a matter of course and obligation; besides, the sense of it involved a sum in subtraction. However, this was not observed by her sister, who did not want to feel obliged.

"Now that this property has come in," continued Magdalen, "we can live comfortably together upon it for the present, and your expenses at Oxford can be paid, as well as masters in what may be needful for the others, and an allowance for dress. I suppose you will want the £40 while you are at St. Robert's, besides the regular expenses?"

"Thank you," warmly said.

"But I want you to understand, as I think you do, about the future, for you must be prepared to be independent."

"I should have wished for a career if I had been a millionaire," said Agatha.

"I believe you would, and it is well that you should have every advantage. But the others. If I left you all this property, it would not be a comfortable maintenance divided among four; and you would not like to be dependent, or to leave the last who might not marry to a pittance alone."

"Certainly not," said Agatha, with flashing eyes.

"Then you see that it is needful that you should be able to do something for yourselves. I can give one of you at a time the power of going to the University."

"I don't think Vera or Polly would wish for that," said Agatha.

"Well, what would they wish for? I can do something towards preparing them, and I can teach Thekla, but I should like to know what you think would be best for them."

"Vera's strong point is music," said Agatha. "She cares for that more than anything else, and Mr. Selby thought she had talent and might sing, only she must not strain her voice. I don't believe she will do much in any other line. And Polly—she is very good, and always does her best because it is right, but I don't think anything is any particular pleasure to her, except needlework. She is always wanting to make things for the church. She really has a better voice than Flapsy, and can play better, but that is because she is so much steadier."

"Seventeen and sixteen, are they not?"

"Yes; but Polly seems ever so much older than Flapsy."

"Mrs. Best showed me that she had higher marks. She must be a thoroughly good girl."

"That she is," cried Agatha, warmly. "She never had any task for getting into mischief."

"Well, they are both so young that a little study with me will be good for them, and there will be time to judge what they are fit for. In art I think they are not much interested."

"Paula draws pretty well, but Vera hates it. Old Mr. Delrio is always cross to her now; but—" Agatha stopped short, remembering that there might be a reason why the drawing master no longer made her a favourite pupil.

"Do you think him a good judge?"

"Yes; Mrs. Best thinks much of him. He had an artist's education, and sometimes has a picture in the Water Colour Exhibition; but I believe he did not find it answer, and so he took our school of art."

Agatha had talked sensibly throughout the conference, but not confidentially; much, in fact, as she would have discussed her sisters with Mrs. Best. She was glad that at the moment the sound of the piano set them listening. She did not feel bound to mention to "sister" any more than she would to the head mistress, that when staying at Mr. Waring's country house a sort of semi-flirtation had begun with Hubert Delrio, a young man to whose education his father had sacrificed a great deal, and who was a well-informed and intelligent gentleman in all his ways. He had engaged himself to the great firm of Eccles and Beamster, ecclesiastical decorators, and might be employed upon the intended frescoes of St. Kenelm's Church.

Ought "Sister" to be told?

But Agatha thought it would be betraying confidence to "set on the dragon"; and besides nobody ever could tell how much Vera's descriptions meant. She knew already that the sweetest countenance in the world and the loveliest dark eyes belonged to a fairly good-looking young man, and she could also suspect that the "squeeze of my hand" might be an ordinary shake, and the kneeling before the one he loved best might have been only the customary forfeit. On the whole, it would be better to let things take their course; it was not likely that either was seriously smitten, and it was more than probable that Hubert Delrio would be too busy to look after a young lady now in a different stratum, and that Vera would have found another sweetest countenance in the world.

All this passed through her mind while Magdalen listened, and pronounced—

"That is brilliant—a clever touch—only—"

"Yes, that is Vera—I know what you are noticing, but this is only amusement; she is not taking pains."

"It is very clever—especially as probably she has no music. But there—"

"Polly's? Oh, yes; she is really steady-going. That is just what you will find her. This is a charming room, sister; thank you very much."

"Make it your home, my dear."

But in reality they were not much nearer together than before the conference.

CHAPTER VII—SISTER AND SISTERS

"Have we not all, amid earth's pettystrife,
Some pure ideal of a nobler life?
We lost it in the daily jar and fact,
And now live idly in a vain regret."

ADELAIDE PROCTER.

AGATHA was so much absorbed in her preparation for St. Robert's that she did not pay very much heed to her younger sisters or their relations with Magdalen. She had induced them to submit to the regulation of their studies with her pretty much as if she had been Mrs. Best, looking upon her, however, as something out of date, and hardly up to recent opinions, not realising that, of late, Magdalen's world had been a wide one.

Perhaps, in Agatha's feelings, there was an undercurrent inherited from her mother, who had always felt the better connected, better educated step-daughter, a sort of alien element, exciting jealousy by her companionship to her father, and after his death, apt to be regarded as a scarcely willing, and perhaps censorious pay-master.

"Your sister might call it too expensive." "I must ask your sister." "No, your sister does not think she can afford it. I am sure she might. Her expenses must be nothing." All this had been no preparation for full sisterly confidence with "Sister," even when a sort of grudging gratitude was extracted, and Agatha had been quite old enough to imbibe an undefined antagonism, though, being a sensible girl, she repressed the manifestations, kept her sisters in order and taught them not to love but to submit, and herself remained in a state of civil coolness, without an approach beyond formal signs of affection, and such confidence.

It was the more disappointing to Magdalen, because Agatha and Paulina both showed so much unconscious likeness to their father, not only in features, but in little touches of gesture and manner. She longed to pet them, and say, "Oh, my dears, how like papa!" but the only time she attempted it, she was met by a severe, uncomprehending look and manner.

And Agatha went away to Oxford without any thawing on her part.

The only real ground that had been gained was with little Thekla, who was soon very fond of "Sister," and depended on her more and more for sympathy and amusement. Girls of seventeen and sixteen do not delight in the sports of nine-year-olds, except in the case of special pets and *protégées*, and Thekla was snubbed when a partner was required to assist in doll's dramas, or in evening games. Only "Sister" would play unreservedly with her, unaware or unheeding that this was looked on as keeping up the *métier* of governess. Indeed, Thekla's reports of schoolroom murmurs and sneers about the M.A. had to be silenced. Peace and good will could best be guarded by closed ears. Yet, even then, Thekla missed child companionship, and, even more, competition, the lack of which rendered her dull and listless over her lessons, and when reproved, she would beg to be sent to school, or, at least, to attend the High School on her bicycle. Not admiring the manners or the attainments of the specimens before her, Magdalen felt bound to refuse, and the sisters' pity kept alive the grievance.

She had, however, decided on granting the bicycles. She had found plenty of use for her own, for it was possible with prudent use of it, avoiding the worst parts of the road, to be at early celebration at St. Andrew's, and get to the Sunday school at Arnscombe afterwards; and Paulina, with a little demur, decided on giving her assistance there.

At a Propagation of the Gospel meeting at the town hall, the Misses Prescott were introduced to the Reverend Augustine Flight, of St. Kenelm's, and his mother, Lady Flight, who sat next to Magdalen, and began to talk eagerly of the designs for the ceiling of their church, and the very promising young artist who was coming down from Eccles and Beamster to undertake the work.

The church had not yet been seen, and the conversation ended in the sisters coming back to tea, at which Paula was very happy, for the talk had something of the rather exclusive High Church tone that was her ideal. She had seen it in books, but had never heard it before in real life, and Vera was in a restless state, longing to hear whether the promising young artist was really Hubert Delrio, and hoping, while she believed that she feared, that she should blush when she heard his name. However, she did not, though Mr. Flight unfolded his rough plans for the frescoes, which were to be of virgin and child martyrs, Magdalen hesitating a little over those that seemed too legendary; while old Lady Flight, portly and sentimental, declared them so sweet and touching. After tea, they went on to the church. Just at the entrance of the porch, Vera clutched at Paula, with the whisper, "Wasn't that Wilfred Merrifield? There, crossing?"

"Nonsense," was Paula's reply, as she lingered over the illuminated list of the hours of services displayed at the door, and feeling as if she had attained dreamland, as she saw two fully habited Sisters enter, and bend low as they did so.

The church was very elaborately ornamented, small, but showing that no expense had been spared, though there was something that did not quite accord with Magdalen's ideas of the best taste; so that when they went out she answered Paula's raptures of admiration somewhat coldly, or what so appeared to the enthusiastic girl.

The next day, meeting Miss Mohun over cutting out for a working party, Magdalen asked her about the Flights and St. Kenelm's.

"He is an excellent good man," said Jane Mohun, "and has laid out immense sums on the church and parish."

"All his own? Not subscription?"

"No. He is the only son of a very rich City man, a brewer, and came here with his mother as a curate, as a good place for health. They found a miserable little corrugated-iron place, called the Kennel Chapel, and worked it up, raising the people, and doing no end of good till it came to be a district, as St. Kenelm's."

"Very ornamental?"

"Oh, very," said Jane, warming out of caution, as she felt she might venture showing city gorgeousness all over. "But it is infinitely to his credit. He had a Fortunatus' purse, and was a spoilt child—not in the bad sense—but with an utterly idolising mother, and he tried a good many experiments that made our hair stand on end; but he has sobered down, and is a much wiser man now—though I would not be bound to admire all he does."

"I see there are Sisters? Do they belong to his arrangements?"

"Yes. They are what my brother calls Cousins of Mercy. The elder one has tried two or three Sisterhoods, and being dissatisfied with all the rules, I fancy she has some notion of trying to set up one on her own account atMr. Flight's. They are both relations of his mother, and are really one of his experiments—fancy names and fancy rules, of course. I believe the young one wanted to call herself Sister Philomena, but that he could not stand. So they act as parish women here, and they do it very well. I liked Sister Beata when I have come in contact with her, and I am sure she is an excellent nurse. They will do your nieces no harm, though I don't like the irregular."

Of this assurance Magdalen felt very glad, when at the door of the parish room, where the ladies were to hold a working party for the missions, Carrigaboola Missions at Albertstown, she and her nieces were introduced to the two ladies in hoods and veils; and Paula's eyes sparkled with delight as she settled into a chair next to Sister Mena. She looked as happy as Vera looked bored! Conversation was not possible while a missionary memoir was being read aloud, but the history of Mother Constance, once Lady Herbert Somerville, but then head at Dearport, and founder of the Daughter Sisterhood at Carrigaboola. To the Merrifields it was intensely interesting, and also to Magdalen; but all the time she could see demonstrations passing between Paula and Sister Mena, a nice-looking girl, much embellished by the setting of the hood and veil, as if the lending of a pair of scissors or the turning of a hem were an act of tender admiration. So sweet a look came out on Paula's face that she longed to awaken the like. Vera meantime looked as if her only consolation lay in the neighbourhood of a window, whence she could see up the street, as soon as she had found whispers to Mysie Merrifield treated as impossible.

The party at the Goyle had begun to fall into regular habits, and struggles were infrequent. There was study in the forenoon, walks or cycle expeditions in the afternoon, varied by the lessons in music and in art, which Vera and Paula attended on Wednesdays and Fridays, the one in the morning, the other after dinner. It was possible to go to St. Andrew's matins at ten o'clock before the drawing class, and to St. Kenelm's at five, after the music was over. Magdalen, whenever it was possible, went with her sisters on their bicycles to St. Andrew's, and sometimes devised errands that she might join them at St. Kenelm's, but neither could always be done by the head of the household. And she could perceive that her company was not specially welcome.

Valetta, the only one of the Clipstone family whose drawing was worth cultivating, used to ride into Rockstone, escorted by her brother Wilfred, who was in course of "cramming" with a curate on his way to his tutor, and Vera found in casual but well-cultivated meetings and partings, abundant excitement in "nods and becks and wreathed smiles," and now and then in the gift of a flower.

Paula on the other hand found equal interest and delight in meetings with Sister Mena, especially after a thunderstorm had driven the two to take refuge at what the Sisters called "the cell of St. Kenelm," and tea had unfolded their young simple hearts to one another! Magdalen had called on the Sisters and asked them to tea at the Goyle, and there had come to the conclusion that Sister Beata was an admirable, religious, hardworking woman, of strong opinions, and not much cultivated, with a certain provincial twang in her voice. She had a vehement desire for self-devotion and consecration, but perhaps not the same for obedience. She sharply criticised all the regulations of the Sisterhoods with which she was acquainted, wore a dress of her own device, and with Sister Mena, a young cousin of her own, meant to make St. Kenelm's a nucleus for a Sisterhood of her own invention.

Sister Mena had been bred up in a Sisterhood's school, from five years old and upwards, and had no near relatives. Mr. Flight was Saint, Pope and hero to both, and Mena knew little beyond the horizon of St. Kenelm's, but she and Paula were fascinated with one another; and Magdalen saw more danger in interfering than in acquiescing, though she gave no consent to Paulina's aspirations after admission into the perfect Sisterhood that was to be.

CHAPTER VIII—SNOBBISHNESS

"Why then should vain repinings rise,
That to thy lover fate denies
A nobler name, a wide domain?"—Scott.

The friendship with the Sisters was about three weeks old when, one morning, scaffold poles were being erected in the new side aisle of St. Kenelm's Church, and superintending them was a tall dark-haired young man. There was a start of mutual recognition; and by and by he met Paula and Vera in the porch, and there were eager hand-clasps and greetings, as befitted old friends meeting in a strange place.

"Mr. Hubert! I heard you were coming!"

"Miss Vera! Miss Paula! This is a pleasure."

Then followed an introduction of Sister Mena, whose elder companion was away, attending a sick person.

"May I ask whether you are living here?"

"Two miles off at the Goyle, at Arnscombe, with our sister."

"So I heard! I shall see you again." And he turned aside to give an order, bowing as he did so.

"Is he the artist of those sweet designs?" asked Sister Mena.

"Did we not tell you?"

"And now he is going to execute them? How delicious!"

"I trust so! We must see him again. We have not heard of Edie and Nellie, nor any one."

"He will call on you?" said Sister Mena.

"I do not think so," said Paula. "At least his father is really an artist, but he is drawing-master at the High School, and Hubert works for this firm. They are not what you call in society, and our sister is all for getting in with Lady Merrifield and General Mohun and all the swells, so it would never do for him to call."

"She would first be stiff and stuck up," said Vera, "and I could not stand that."

"I thought she was so kind," said Mena.

"You don't understand," said Vera. "She would be kind to a workman in a fever; but this sort—oh, no."

"To be on an equality with the man painting the church?" said Paula. "No, indeed! not if he were Fra Angelico and Ary Scheffer and Michelangelo rolled into one."

At that moment the subject referred to in that mighty conglomeration reappeared. He was a handsome young man, his touch of Italian blood showing just enough to give him a romantic air; and Sister Philomena listened, much impressed by the interchange of question and answer about "Edie and Nellie," and the dear Warings, and the happy Christmas at the Grange; and Vera blushed again, and Paula coloured in sympathy, as it appeared that Mr. Delrio had never had such a splendid time.

The colloquy was ended by Mr. Flight being descried, approaching with his mother, whereupon the two girls fled away like guilty creatures.

Presently Vera exclaimed, "Oh, Polly dear, what a complication! Poor dear fellow! he cares for me as much as ever."

"And you will be staunch to him in spite of all the worldly allurements," said Paula.

"Well, I mean Mr. Wilfred Merrifield is not half so handsome," returned Vera.

"Nor is he engaged in sacred work; only bent on frivolity," said Paula; "yet see how the M.A. encourages him with tennis and games and nonsense."

Poor M.A., when the encouragement had only been some general merriment, and a few games on the lawn Paulina, who had heard many confidences when Vera returned from Waring Grange, believed altogether in the true love of the damsel and Hubert Delrio, who had been wont to single out the prettiest of the girls at Filstead, and she was resolved to do all she could in their cause, being schoolgirl enough to have no scruple as to secrecy towards Magdalen, though on the next opportunity she poured out all to Sister Philomena's by no means unwilling ears.

Lovers had never fallen within the young Sister's experience, either personally or through friends; and they had only been revealed to her in a few very carefully-selected tales, where they were more the necessary machinery than the main interest, for she had been bred up in an orphanage by Sister Beata, and had never seen beyond it. So to her Paula's story, little as there was of it, was a perfect romance, and it gained in colour when she related it to her senior.

Sister Beata hesitated a little, having rather more knowledge of the world, remembering that Vera Prescott was not eighteen years old, and doubting whether an underhand intimacy ought to be encouraged; but then Mr. Flight had spoken of Mr. Delrio as a highly praiseworthy young man, of decided Catholic principles; he was regular at Church services, and had dined or supped at the Vicarage. The intercourse, as the girls had explained, had been sanctioned by Mrs. Best in their native town, where all parties were well known, and thus there could be no harm in letting it continue. While as to the elder Miss Prescott, she was understood to be unduly bent on county and titled society, and to be exclusive towards inferiors. Moreover, she was an attendant at St. Andrew's Church, and thus regarded as out of the pale of sympathy of the St. Kenelm's flock.

So no obstacle was put in the way of the gossips, for they were really nothing more, except that there was admiration of the designs for the side chapel, which were of the Scripture children on one side, and on the other of child martyrs. Now and then there was a reference to the chilliness and hardship of living with an unsympathising sister, and being obliged to go to churches of which they did not approve. Sometimes too there were airy castles of a distant future to be shared by the magnificent architect, together with Vera, while Paula nursed in the convent with Mother Beata and Sister Philomena.

But all this did not prevent an excitement and eager laughter and chatter whenever Wilfred Merrifield came in the way, and he certainly was enough attracted by Vera's pretty face and lively graces to make his sisters think him very absurd; but his mother had seen so many passing fancies among her elder sons as to hold that blindness was better than serious treatment.

There was the further effect that Magdalen had no suspicion that the vehement attraction to St. Kenelm's went beyond the harmless quarter of the two nursing Sisters and some hero worship of Mr. Flight. Miss Mohun, who knew everything, had indeed hinted that something foolish might be going on there; but Magdalen had not decided on the mutual fairness of the two congregations, and deferred investigation till Agatha should come home, when she would have a reasonable, if cold, person to deal with. Nor did Thekla's chatter excite any suspicion; for the only time when she had been present at a meeting with Mr. Delrio, she had been half bribed, half threatened into silence, and she was quite schoolgirl enough to feel that such was the natural treatment of authority, though she had become really fond of "sister."

CHAPTER IX—GONE OVER TO THE ENEMY

"Can I teach thee, my beloved? can I teach thee?"

E. B. Browning.

Agatha came home in due time, and Magdalen sent her sister to meet her at the station, where they found a merry Clipstone party in the waggonette waiting for Gillian, who was to come home at the same time. There was so much discussion of the new golf ground, that Vera had hardly a hand or a glance to bestow on Mr. Delrio, who jumped out of the same train, shook hands with Agatha, and bestirred himself in finding her luggage and calling a cab.

"How he is improved! What a pleasing, gentlemanly fellow he looks!" she exclaimed, as she waved her thanks, while driving off in the cab.

"Is he not?" said Paula, while Vera bridled and blushed. "You will be delighted with his work. I never saw anything more lovely than little St. Cyriac the martyr."

"He is taken from Mrs. Henderson's little boy," added Vera; "such a dear little darling."

"And his mother is to be done; indeed, he has sketched her for St. Juliet."

"Flapsy! St. Romeo, too, I suppose?"

"Nonsense, Nag! There really was a St. Juliet or Julitta, and she was his mother, and they both were martyrs. I will tell you all the history," began Paula; but Agatha interposed.

"You must like having him down here. Sister must be much pleased with him. She used to like old Mr. Delrio."

"Well, we have not said much about him," owned Paula. "He does not seem to wish it, or expect to be in with swells."

"We could not stand his being treated like a common house-painter and upholsterer," added Vera.

"Surely no one does so," said Agatha.

"Not exactly," said Paula; "at least, he has had supper at St. Kenelm's Vicarage with Lady Flight, and luncheon at Carrara with Captain and Mrs. Henderson."

“Because he was *doing* the child,” interposed Vera; “and Thekla says that Primrose Merrifield says that her Aunt Jane—that is, old Miss Mohun—says that Lady Flight is not a gentlewoman.”

“What has that to do with Magdalen?”

“Why, she is so taken up with those swells of hers, especially now that there is a talk of Lord Somebody’s yacht coming in, that she would never treat him as on equal terms, but just keep him at a distance, like a mere decorator.”

“That seemed to me just what you were doing,” said Agatha, “when he was so kind and helpful about my box.”

“Oh, *they* were all there, and we did not want to be talked of,” said Vera, blushing. “He understands.”

“He understands,” repeated Paula. “We do see him at the church and at the Sisters’. Those dear Sisters! There is no nonsense about them. You will love them, Nag.”

“Well, it does not seem to me to be treating our own sister Magdalen fairly.”

“The M.A.!” said Vera, in a tone of wonder.

“No; not to be intimate with a person you do not introduce to her, because you do not think she would consider him as on equal terms.”

“Sister Beata quite approves,” added Paula, sincerely, not guessing how little Sister Beata knew of the situation, of which she only heard through the medium of her own representations to Sister Mena.

The two girls rushed into the charms of these two Sisters, and the plan for an entertainment for the maidens of the Guild of St. Milburgha, at which they were to assist. It lasted up to the gate of the Goyle, where Magdalen and Thekla were ready to meet them; and they trooped merrily up the hill, Agatha keeping to Magdalen’s side in a way that struck her as friendly and affectionate. It seemed to be more truly coming *home* than the elder sister had dared to anticipate; nor, indeed, did she feel the veiled antagonism to herself that had previously disappointed her.

The talk was about St. Robert’s, about Oxford in general, the new friends, the principal, the games, the debates, the lectures, the sermons, the celebrities, the undergraduates, the concerts, the chapels, the boats, the architecture; all were touched on for further discussion by and by as they sat at the evening meal, and then on the chairs and cushions in the verandah; and through all there was no exclusion of the elder sister, but rather she was the one who could appreciate the interest of what Agatha had seen and heard; and even she was allowed to enter into the amusement of an Oxford *bon mot*, sometimes, indeed, when it was far beyond Paula and Vera.

There was no doubt that the term had much improved Agatha even in appearance and manner. She held herself better, pronounced better, uttered no slangish expressions, and twice she repressed little discourtesies on the part of her sisters, and neglects such as were not the offspring of tender familiarity, but of an indifference akin to rudeness. Magdalen had endured, knowing how bad it was for their manners, but unwilling to become more of an annoyance than could be helped. The indescribable difference in Agatha's whole manner sent Magdalen to bed happier than she had been since the arrival of her sisters, and feeling as if Agatha had come to her own side of a barrier.

Perhaps it was quite true; for the last two months had been a time of growth with the maiden, changing her from a schoolgirl to a student, from the "brook to the river." She had, indeed, studied hard, but that she had always done, as being clever, intellectual and ambitious. The difference had been from her intercourse with persons slightly her elders, but who did not look on authorities as natural enemies, to be tolerated for one's own good. There had been a development of the conscience and soul even in this first term that made her regard her elder sister not merely with a sense of compulsory gratitude and duty, but with sympathy and fellow feeling, which were the more excited when she saw her own chilliness of last spring carried further by the two young girls.

So breakfast went off merrily; and after the round of the garden and the pets, Agatha promised to come, when summoned, to hear how well Thekla could read French. In the meantime she waited in the morning-room, looking at her sisters' books; Vera pushed aside the Venetian blind.

"Don't come in that way, Flapsy!" called Paula. "You'll be heard in the dining-room, and the M.A. will tremble at your dusty feet."

"They aren't dusty," said Vera, pulling up the blind with a clatter.

"Aren't they?" laughed Paula, pointing.

"You had better go and wipe them," said Agatha.

"I don't believe in M.A.'s fidgets," returned Vera.

"But I do, in proper deference to the head of the house," said Agatha, gravely.

"Murder in Irish!" cried Vera, bouncing away, while Paula argued, "Really, Nag, life is not long enough to attend to all the M.A.'s little worries."

"Polly, dear, I am afraid we have been on a wrong tack with our sister. I don't like calling her by that name."

"You began it!" exclaimed Vera, dashing in by the door as she spoke.

"I could not have meant it as a nickname to be always in use."

"Oh yes, you did, I remember"—and an argument was beginning, which Agatha cut short by saying, "Any way, it is bad taste."

"Nag has been so much among the real M.A. that she is tender about their title."

"She wants to be one herself," said Vera; "and so she will if she goes on getting learned and faddy."

"In both senses?" said Paula.

Agatha laughed a little, but added, "No, Polly, the thing is that it is hardly kind or right to put that sort of label upon a person like Magdalen—who has done so much for us—and—"

The perverse young hearts could not bear a touch on the chord of gratitude; and Paula burst in, "Label or libel, do you mean?"

"It becomes a libel as you use it."

"Do you want us to call her sister or Magdalen, the whole scriptural mouthful at once?"

"I believe that to call her Magdalen or Maidie, as my father did, would make her feel nearer to us than the formal way of saying 'Sister.'"

"I don't mind about changing," said Paula. "She can never be the same to us as dear Sister Mena."

"She is so tiresome," added Vera. "She bothers so over my music; calling out if I make ever so small a slip, and making me go over all again."

"Well she may," said Paula. "She is making little Tick play so nicely. Just listen! But I can't bear her dragging us off to that horrid old Arnscombe Church and the nasty stuffy Sunday school."

"That reminds me," said Agatha; "Gillian Merrifield met a relation of Mr. Earl's, who said that Miss Prescott had brought quite new life and spirit to the poor old man, who had been getting quite out of heart for want of any one to help and sympathise with him."

"Then he ought to make his services more Catholic," said Paula. "But nothing will wean her from the old parochial idea. Why, she would not let me give my winter stockings to Sister Beata's poor girls, but made me darn them and put them by."

"Yes, and mine, which were bad enough to give away, she made me darn first," cried Vera. "She is ever so much worse than the superlative about mending one's clothes."

"There ought to be another degree of comparison," said Paula, —"Botheratissima!"

"For, only think!" said Vera. "She won't let us have new hats, but only did up the old ones, and not with feathers, though there is such a love at Tebbitts's at Rockstone."

"She says it is cruel," said Paula.

"Cruel to me, I am sure; and what difference does it make when the birds are once killed?"

"Well, she did give us those lovely wreaths of lilies," said Paula.

"Of course, but nothing to make them stylish! What's the good of being out if one is to have nothing *chic*? And she won't let me have a hockey outfit. She says she must see more of it to be able to judge whether to let us play!"

"That just means seeing whether her dear Merrifields do," said Paula.

"Gillian did at St. Catherine's. But you will know soon. Did I not hear something about a garden party?"

"Oh, yes; she is talking of one, but it will be all swells and croquet, and deadly dull."

"I thought you seemed to be getting on well with the swells, if you mean the Merrifields, especially Wilfred, if that is his name."

"Bil—Bil! Oh, he is all very well," said Vera, "if he would not be always so silly and come after me! As if I cared!"

"And only think," said Paula, "that she was going to have it on the very day that St. Milburga's Guild has their festival! Just as if it was on purpose!"

"Did you ask her to keep clear of your engagements?"

"I told her, but I don't think she listened." And as another grievance suggested itself to Vera, she declared, "And she won't let us join the Girls' Magazine Club, because she saw one she didn't like on somebody's table. As if we were little babies!"

"She won't let us order books at the library, but gets such awfully slow ones," chimed in Paula, "or only baby stories fit for Thekla. She made me return that book dear Sister Mena lent me, because she said it was Roman Catholic."

"And hasn't she got Thomas à Kempis on her table? and I'm sure he was Roman Catholic. There's consistency!"

"You don't understand," began Agatha. "He was a great Saint before the Catholics became so Roman."

"Oh, never mind! It is anything to thwart us," cried Vera. "It is ever so much worse than school."

"But," began Agatha, and the tone of consideration to that one conjunction caused an outburst. "Oh, Nag, Nag, if you are gone over to the enemy, what will life be worth?"

As that terrible question was propounded, in burst Thekla with, "Oh, Nag, Nag, they are cutting the hay in the high torr field, and sister says we may go and see them before I read my French."

"Oh!" cried Vera, with a prolongation into a groan, "is she going to be tiresome?"

"She has come to be quite a don," said Paula; "but never mind, we will soon make her all right again."

The two sisters had to go to their different classes in the afternoon, and wanted Agatha to go with them; but it was a very warm day, and she preferred resting in the garden, and, to Magdalen's surprise and pleasure, conversation with her. At first it was about Oxford matters, very interesting, but public and external to the home, and it did not draw the cords materially closer; but when Thekla had privately decided that even hanging upon the newly recovered Nag was not worth the endurance of anything so tedious, and had gone off to assist her beloved old gardener in gathering green gooseberries, Magdalen observed that she was a very pleasant little pupil, and was getting on very well, especially with arithmetic.

"That was the strong point in the junior classes," said Agatha; "better taught than it was in my time."

"I wish she could have more playfellows," said Magdalen. "She would like to go to the High School at Rockquay, but there are foundations I should wish to lay before having her out of my own hands."

"I should think you were her best playfellow. She seems very fond of you, and very happy."

"Yes," said Magdalen, rather wistfully. "I think she generally is so."

"Maidie! may I call you by the old home name?" And as Magdalen answered with a kiss and tearful smile, "Do tell me, please, if Polly and Flapsy are nice to you?"

Magdalen was taken by surprise at the pressure of the hand and the eyes that gazed into her face full of expression.

She could not keep the drops from rushing to her own eyes, though she smiled through them and said, "As nice as they know how."

"I am afraid I know what that means," said Agatha.

"If I only knew how to prevent their looking on me as their governess," continued Magdalen; "but I must have got into the groove, and I suppose I do not always remember how much must be tolerated if love has to be won; and Paula is a thoroughly good girl."

"Yes, I am sure she wishes to be," said Agatha. "Are those Sisters nice that she talks of so eagerly?"

"They are very excellent women, but somehow I should have had more confidence in them if they were not unattached, or belonged to some regular Sisterhood. I wish she had taken instead to Mysie Merrifield, who is more of my sort; but no one can control those likings."

"I don't think Gillian very attractive; she is so wrapped up in her work," confessed Agatha.

"You will see them all, I hope, for I am giving a garden party next week, perhaps. Have not they told you?"

"Oh, yes; but Polly seemed bent on its not clashing with some festival at St. Kenelm's."

"Therefore I had not fixed the day till I had heard what is settled. I have invited people for Thursday, which will hardly interfere."

"Did you know that the young man who is painting the ceiling at St. Kenelm's Church is old Mr. Delrio's son Hubert?"

"Indeed! Is he staying here? We must ask him to come up to luncheon or to tea. I am glad he is doing so well. I heard Eccles and Beamster were to do the decorations; I suppose they employ him. I should think it was a very good line to get into."

This was on a Friday; and the next day Magdalen proposed driving down in the cool of the evening to see the decorations at St. Kenelm's and their artist; but it turned out that he was gone to spend Sunday at the Cathedral city, and all that could be done was to admire the designs, and listen to Paula's enthusiastic explanation.

Magdalen consulted Agatha whether to send young Delrio a card for the garden party; but they decided that it was too late for an invitation to be sent, though a spoken one might have been possible. Besides, it was not likely to be pleasant to a stranger who knew no one but the Flights and Hendersons, and those professionally. Agatha told her sisters, and with one voice they declared that they would not see him patronised; while Agatha's acute senses doubted whether Vera's objection was not secretly based on the embarrassment of a double flirtation with him and with Wilfred Merrifield.

Indeed, Vera told her gaily: "Only think, Nag, I did have a jolly ride on the M.A.'s bike after all."

"Indeed! Then she lent it to you."

"Not she! But she and the little kid were safe gone to Avoncester, and Paula was with her dear Sisters, so Will and I took a jolly spin along the cliff road; and it was such screaming fun. Only once we thought we saw old Sir Jasper coming, and we got behind a barn, but it turned out to be only a tripper, and we had such a laugh."

"Paula does not know?"

"What would be the good of telling her, with her little nun's schoolgirl mind? She would only make no end of a fuss about a mere bit of fun and nonsense."

"I think if Wilfred Merrifield was afraid to meet his father, it showed a sense of wrong."

"Sir Jasper is a horrid old martineau, who never gives them any peace at home, but is always after them."

"A martinet, I suppose you mean. I don't think that makes it any better. I should not be happy till Magdalen knew."

"Why, no harm was done! There's her precious machine all safe! It was just for the fun of the thing, and to try how it goes. One can't be kept in like a blessed baby! She never has guessed it. That's the fun of it."

"I would not return her kindness in such an unladylike way when she is trusting you, Vera."

Did Magdalen know what had been done? She did guess, for there was a mark on the wheel that she did not remember to have known before, and it cost her a bitter pang of mistrust; but she abstained from inquiries, thinking that they might only do harm. But she bought a chain for her bicycle; and Agatha felt more shame than did Vera, who tried to believe herself amused by her tacit sense of emancipation.

CHAPTER X—FLOWN

"Till now thy soul hath been all glad and gay,
Bid it arise and look on grief to-day."

ADELAIDE PROCTOR.

THERE was a Guild at St. Kenelm's which was considered by the promoters to be superior to the Girls' Friendly Society, and which comprised about a dozen young women, who attended classes held by Sister Beata, and occasional modest entertainments given by Lady Flight.

One of these was to take place the day before Miss Prescott's garden party. It was to be given at Carrara, the very pretty grounds on the top of the cliff, belonging to Captain Henderson, the managing partner in the extensive marble works of Mr. White, who lived at Rocca Marina, in the Riviera. Mrs. Henderson had resided in Mr. Flight's parish, and been a member of his congregation, and while he was absent for a day or two she had put her garden at the service of the Guild of St. Milburga's for the day.

Of course Vera and Paula were delighted to assist; but Thekla was too young for the amusements of grown-up maidens, and was much better pleased to help her two elder sisters in preparations for the next day, placing tennis nets, arranging croquet hoops, mustering chairs by the verandah, and adorning tables with flowers. Agatha's assistance was heartily given, as making it her own concern, and, for that reason above all others, it was a happy day, though a very tiring one, to Magdalen, in spite of the sultry atmosphere and the sight of lurid-looking clouds over the moors, which did not augur well for the next day's weather, and caused all the arrangement of chairs and rugs to be prudently broken up and deposited under the verandah.

This was done, and the evening meal had been taken, and Thekla had gone to bed before some flashes of lightning made the two sisters wish to see the other pair at home, especially as Vera was much afraid of lightning, and Paula apt to be made quite ill by it.

The storm rolled on, bringing violent gusts of wind and hail, though not at the very nearest, and such a hurricane of wind and rain ensued that the two watchers concluded that the two girls must have been housed for the night by some of the friends at Rock Quay, and it was near midnight, when just as they had gone to their rooms, a carriage was heard ascending the hill, and they had reached the door before Paulina sprang out with the cry, "Is she come home?" Then at sight of the blank faces of dismay, she seized hold of Agatha's hands and began to sob. Mr. Flight had stepped out of the car at the same moment, and answered the incoherent questions andexclamations.

"Young Delrio offered to take photographs of the party, and that was the last time she was seen."

"Yes," sobbed Paula, "Sister Mena saw her there. We were trying to get up croquet, and then I missed her. I tried to find her when the lightning began, but I could not find her anywhere, though I looked in all the summer-houses!"

"At Mrs. Henderson's? or Miss Mohun's? or the Sisters'?" asked Magdalen, catching alarm from each denial. "She might have gone home with one of the girls."

"She would be wild in such a storm," said Agatha, "and not know what she was about."

"Sister Beata and I have gone to each house," said Mr. Flight.

"When did you say you saw her last?"

"I saw her when we were grouped," said Paula; "Sister Mena, when she was helping him to put up his photos."

"The strange thing is," said Mr. Flight, "though no doubt it will be explained, that Delrio is missing too."

"Hubert Delrio!" exclaimed Agatha. "Impossible! He must have taken her into the church to be out of the storm."

"We have tried," said the clergyman. And as the round of suggestions began to be despairingly reiterated, he said, hesitating, "Miss Mohun told me that she thought she had seen a boat, Captain Henderson's, she believed, in the cave with some one rocking in it; and certainly that little boat was there, when on the hope, if it can be called a hope, I ran down the steps tolook."

"Would it not have been put into the boathouse out of the rain?" said Agatha.

"The gardener was gone home, out of reach round the point, but we shall know to-morrow."

"He thinks they may have rowed out and been caught in the storm," cried Paula, bursting into fresh weeping; and Magdalen saw the conjecture confirmed by Mr. Flight's countenance.

"I am afraid it is the least distressing—the least unsatisfactory idea," said he, in much agitation. "I thought Mr. Delrio an excellent young man; and she," indicating his companion, "tells me you know him and his family well."

“Oh, yes,” said Agatha and Magdalen in one breath. “We have known his father all our lives. Nothing can be more respectable.”

“And Hubert is as steady and good as possible,” continued Agatha. “His mother used to come to Mrs. Best and praise him, till we were quite tired of his name; I am sure he is all right.”

“Or I should be much deceived in him,” said the clergyman.

Yet there was an idea in Paulina’s mind. Could Vera have poured out such an exaggerated tale of oppression and unhappiness as to have induced her old playfellow to carry her off to his mother at Filsted? She had given some such hint to Mr. Flight on the way; but he had not seemed to hear or attend, and he was now promising to let the sisters know as soon as possible in the morning whether anything had been discovered, and to telegraph to Filsted and to the office in London if he should see occasion.

Then he drove off, in what would have been almost daylight but for the pelting of the storm; and after a vain attempt to make Paula swallow some nourishment, Magdalen thought it kinder to let Agatha carry her off to bed, and then she confessed, what really gave a certain hope, that the pair had been in the habit of murmuring against “sister” so much that, considering poor Vera’s propensity to strong language, it was quite possible that Hubert might think her cruelly oppressed, and for a freak carry her off to his mother to be consoled.

Agatha tried to believe it, for the sake of hushing the exhausted Paula, who almost went into hysterics, as she laughed at the notion of to-morrow’s telegram that Vera was safe at Filsted; and then allowed herself to be calmed enough to sleep, while Agatha revolved the notion, but found herself unable seriously to believe, that sufficient grievance could be brought against sister to induce any man in his senses to take such a step. But then Paula had inferred that he was a lover, and Agatha did not know of what lovers might be capable, and she could not but blame herself for not having given more importance to the semi-confidences of her sisters on the first day of her arrival. It was all misery; and the two poor girls could find no solace in the morning, save in talking to Magdalen, though that involved the confession of all the murmurs against her, the distrust of her kindness, and the explanation of the interviews, which, as far as Paula had ever witnessed them, were absolutely harmless, the only pity being in their concealment.

Magdalen was manifestly as wretched as they, or even more so, being convinced of her own shortcoming in not having won the affection or confidence that would have made all open between them. She could not understand why Hubert Delrio should not have been made known to her.

“We thought,” said Paula, “we thought you might not think him enough—enough—of a gentleman for your sort of society.”

“I think you might have trusted me to know what was due to an old friend,” said Magdalen “but, oh, I ought to have made you feel that we could think together.”

“Perhaps,” said Agatha, “there was a little consciousness on poor dear Vera’s part that she did not want you to know the terms she was on.”

They had tried only to let Thekla know that they were much alarmed because Vera had gone out in a boat and not returned. It was observable that, on the principle that where there is life there is hope, Paula clung to the notion that Vera’s having fled to Filsted; while the two elder sisters, perhaps because they better knew what such a flight might seem to others, would almost have preferred to suppose there had been a fatal accident in the midst of youthful, innocent sport.

The two were lingering sadly over their uneaten breakfast, talking more freely when they had sent Thekla to feed her pets, when Mr. Flight came up on his bicycle; but it was plain at the first moment that he had no good news.

Nothing had been heard. It only appeared that one of the young gardeners at Carrara had taken Captain Henderson’s boat without leave, to fetch one of the girls, but on entering the cove had found the boathouse locked. He had moored the boat to a stake for want of the ring that secured it within. When the storm threatened he ran down to recover it, but it was gone, and he had concluded that the gardeners had put it into the boathouse. It now appeared that they had not seen it, and were very angry at its having been meddled with. An oar had drifted up with the morning tide, and had been recognised as belonging to the boat; but such a gale was blowing that it was impossible to put out to sea or make any search round the coast. Words could hardly describe the distress of Mr. Flight or of his ladies at not having better looked after the young girl; Sister Beata for never having thoroughly attended to the matter; and Sister Mena for having accepted confidences which, if she had only guessed it, told her more than there really was to be known. Both these two were inclined to the elopement idea, partly because it was the least shocking, and partly because they had looked at Vera’s grievances through her own spectacles, and partly from their unlimited notions of young men’s wickedness. Their vicar was not of the same opinion, knowing Hubert better, and besides having found his work, his orders to his subordinates, and the belongings at the lodgings in a state that showed that whatever he had done had been unpremeditated. Sending off notes to stop the garden party was a sort of occupation, broken by many signs, much listening, and much sorrowful discussion, not quite vain, since it made Paulina more one with

Magdalen than ever before. Poor old Mr. Delrio arrived in the afternoon, a thin, grey-haired and bearded old man, who could only make it too certain that Paula's theory of the innocent flight to Filsted was impossible. Moreover, he was as certain as a father could be, intimate with, and therefore confident of, his eldest son, that though Hubert might indulge in a little lively flirtation, it could never be otherwise than perfectly harmless. In the terrible suspense and restlessness, he went vibrating about in the torrents of moorland rain between Rock Quay and the Goyle, on the watch for telegrams from the office in London or his wife at home, or for the discovery of anything from the sea, or searching in his son's lodgings, where nothing was found that did not show him to have been a pure-hearted young man, devoted to his art, and fond of poetry. Sundry compositions were in the blotting-book, one, indeed, to Vera's name, under the supposition (a wrong one) [100] that it meant "true," but mostly rough copies of a poem about the Saints Julitta and her child Cyriac. Hope sank as another stormy day rose; and still the poor old artist lingered in hopes of news by some returning craft which might have picked up the derelict. His chief comfort was in walking about between the showers with Magdalen, as an old friend, and trying to think of the two as innocent creatures, engulfed like mayflies in the stream.

Sister Mena came over, wanting to join Paula in bewailing entreaties; but Paula, in youthful hard-hearted wilfulness, declared that it was impossible to see her; and it fell to Magdalen to try to discuss the grief with her.

It turned out that Mr. Flight had spoken severely to her and to the far less implicated Sister Beata, declaring his confidence in them destroyed, so that they had begun to consider of throwing up their work in his parish. "And it was all my fault," said Mena; "Sister Beata really knew nothing, or hardly anything of what Vera told me."

"Indeed, I can quite understand that you had hardly experience enough to know that it might be wiser not to encourage what was not quite open."

"But I thought,—I thought you—"

"That I was unkind and unsympathising."

"Oh, you never could have been—"

"Indeed I never meant to be, but I am afraid it seemed so to my young sisters. I can quite see how you thought you were acting kindly."

"Oh, that is so good of you."

"And perhaps I, being only an elder sister, you would not feel that I was the only authority the poor girls have to look to; and that it would have been kinder to help them to be content with me."

“I did not know what you could be,” said Mena, greatly soothed and surprised by her caresses.

“We often do go on in ignorance, and get on a wrong tack; but you know God pardons our mistakes, and I do believe that you will be wiser for all this sorrow, and better able to rise to your work. I am sure, however it ends, that is the reason that such blows are sent to us.”

Mena went back sorrowful and chastened, but tenderly hopeful. If Miss Prescott could forgive, surely Mr. Flight could, and One still greater.

CHAPTER XI—ADRIFT

"She splashed, and she dashed, and she turned herself round,
And heartily wished herself safe on the ground."

JANE TAYLOR.

AND where were the missing pair?

Vera had lingered about, fancying she was helping to pack the photographic apparatus, while the others dispersed. Presently, seeing no one near, Hubert Delrio said, in a gentle diffident voice, "It would be a great pleasure to me if I might ask you to listen to the verses on St. Cyriac and his mother that the design brought with it."

"I should love it better than anything," said Vera, highly flattered.

"If you would come down this way, there is a charming secluded cove, where we should be free from interruption."

"How deliciously romantic! Quite stunning!" cried Vera, as her cavalier conducted her down a steep path along the side of the cliff to the stony beach, where a few red rocks had been manipulated into a tiny harbour, with a boathouse for the little skiff in which Captain Henderson was wont to go round to the marble works on the other side of the headland. The boat looked very inviting as it lay swinging gently in the sluggish waves in the advancing shade of the tall cliff; and Vera exclaimed with delight as she was assisted into it, and placed herself comfortably on the cushion, with one hand dabbling in the cool translucent wave. Hubert Delrio opened his manuscript and began to read his ballad, if so it was to be called, being the history of the little boy of four years old, who, being taken with his mother before the tribunal at Tarsus, was lifted on the proprætor's knee, but struggled, crying out, "I am a Christian!" till the proprætor, in a rage, hurled him down. His skull was fractured on the marble pavement, and his mother gave thanks for his soul's safety, when she too was sentenced to be beheaded. Great pains had been taken with the noble-minded tale; and the verses had considerable merit, more, perhaps, than Vera could appreciate. But to read such a production of his own, in such surroundings, to the auditor whom youthful fancy most preferred, was such luxury to both that it was no wonder that under the broad shady hat with the lily wreath she was nodding in the gentle breeze, the lapping of the waves, and the soft cadence of the poetry, till at an effective passage on the mother's death, the poet looked up, expecting to receive a responsive glance from those blue eyes.

Not only were they hidden, but the cliff was farther off. The mooring rope and the stake were dragging behind in the water. The tide had turned, and the boat was already out of reach of the rock where it had been drawn up. His exclamation of dismay awoke Vera, who would have started up with a little shriek, but for his, "Don't! Don't! I'll row back."

But he was a landsman, whose only knowledge of the water was in an occasional bathe, or in a river steamer; and his first attempt at placing the oars in the rowlocks resulted in one falling overboard, while he helplessly grasped the other; and Vera screamed again.

"Don't be frightened, my dear! Dearest, don't! We must be seen. Some one will come out and help us."

"Can't you get on with one oar? They do in pictures."

"Punting? Yes, but there must be a bottom. No, don't move, whatever you do. There can't be any danger. Fishermen must be about. Or we shall be seen from the cliffs."

"They are getting farther off! Can't you shout?"

Hubert shouted, and Vera added her shriller cries; but all in vain, and the outgoing tide was carrying them, not towards the quay and marble rocks, but farther to sea. The waves grew rougher and had crests of foam, and discomfort began. Once the feather of a steamer was seen on the horizon. They waved handkerchiefs and redoubled their shouts, and Hubert had to hold his companion to prevent her from leaping up; but they never were within the vessel's ken, and she went on her way, while the sea bore them farther and farther.

The shore was growing dim and indistinct, the sun was sinking, and the cloud, that had at first shown only a golden border, was lifting tall perpendicular masses, while the tossing of the little boat became more and more distressing. Anxiety and sense of responsibility kept Hubert from feeling physical discomfort; but Vera began to cry, and to declare that it would be the death of her if she were not landed immediately.

"If it were only possible!" sighed Delrio.

"There must be some way! You are so stupid! Oh! There was a flash of lightning."

"Summer lightning."

"No such thing! There will be a storm, and we shall be drowned. Oh, I wish I had never listened to your nonsense, and got into this horrible boat." She was in a state for scolding, and scold she did, as the clouds rose higher, and sheets of lightning more decided. "How could you? You, who know nothing about boats, and going on, on, with those horrid tiresome verses—not minding anything—I wish I had never come near you!"

Vainly the poor young fellow tried to get in a word of consolation; it only made her scold the more, till there was no question that the storm was raging overhead; the hail rattled and splashed, the waves raised them to a height, then subsided into endless depths; the thunder pealed, and she clung to Hubert, too frightened for screaming. His fear was that the cockleshell of a boat should fill and founder; he tried to bale out the water with his hat, and to make her assist, but she seemed incapable, and he could only devise laying her down in the bottom of the boat with his coat over her, hiding her face in terror. Her hat had long ago been blown away, and her hair was flapping about. Ejaculations were in his heart, if not on his lips, and once or twice she cried out something like, "Save me!" but in general it was, "We are sinking! Hold me! We are going! Paula! Nag!" clutching at his legs, so as to hamper him in the baling out the water.

The hail passed, but there was a solid sheet of rain descending on them, undistinguishable from the foam that rushed over them as they went down, down, down. Vera was silenced; and Hubert, drenched and nearly beaten out of life, almost welcomed every downward plunge as the last, tried to commend his spirit, and was amazed to find his little boat lifted up again, and the black darkness not so absolute.

CHAPTER XII—"THE KITTIWAKE"

"Good luck to your fishing! Whom watch ye to-night?
A man of mean, or a man of might?"—Scott.

Something black was before the tossed boat! Yes, and light, not lightning. A human voice seemed to be on the blast. Hubert Delrio essayed to shout, but his voice was gone, or was blown away. He understood that a vessel must be above him. Would it finish all by running him down? He perceived that he was bidden to catch something. A rope! His benumbed hands and the heaving of the boat made him fail once, twice, and he was being swept away as at last he did grasp a rope, and was drawn, as it ground his hands, close to the dark wall that rose above, with lights visible.

"Cheer up! cheer up!" he cried to Vera. "Thank God, we are saved!"

Response from her there was none; but he could hear the yell of inquiry from ahead, and answered, "Here! Two! A woman!"

A second rope was lowered. "Lash her to it." But as it was evident that Delrio could do nothing but hold on, and that his companion was helpless, a sailor descended from no great elevation, and, in another moment, the senseless girl was hoisted up and received on deck; and, with some assistance, Hubert was also on board, thinking of nothing but the breathless question, "Is she safe?"

"Oh, yes! She will soon come round! Here! They will see to her." As she was carried away, and Hubert had a perception that she was received by female hands, but he was utterly exhausted, and unable to see or speak, till some stimulant had been poured down his throat, and even then he could hardly ask, "Is she safe?

"Yes, yes! All right! Reviving fast! Here! Take some more! Bed is ready! Get rid of those clothes!" It was an elderly, grey-haired man who spoke, and Hubert was in no condition to resist, as the yacht was pitching considerably, though after the boat the motion was almost rest. He instinctively shook his head at the glass, but swallowed what was forced upon him, and managed to say, "Thanks—sitting in boat—drifted off—Rock Quay."

"All right! Never mind. Take him down. My berth, Ivy—Jephson. Tuck him in. Don't let him speak! Never mind, my lad! We will hear all about it to-morrow!"

Meantime, Vera, though reviving, was conscious of very little, save a soft pillow, tender hands, and warm drink that choked her; and then she fell asleep, though still she was aware of a strange tossing going on all night, and by and by she found herself secured into a sort of narrow shelf, and murmuring female voices were at hand. As she moved, she heard, "There, you are better now. You can take this, then you will be more comfortable."

Her eyes had opened to a curious sort of twilight, and there was a fair girlish head over her, with a sweet smiling face. An elderly weather-beaten face in a hood next appeared, and a brown hand holding a cup closed over the top, in invalid fashion, and a kind strong arm slightly raised her with, "There, there, poor dear! The spirit, my lady dear, the spirit! That's right, now then."

"You *must* be a baby;" and a merry reassuring smile broke out as the draught was administered. Vera tasted, thanked, swallowed, felt giddy, and lay down, hearing a lively bit of self-gratulation. "There, Mrs. Griggs, I'm getting my sea legs!" followed by an ignominious stumble as Mrs. Griggs caught the cup in good time as the vessel gave a lurch which completed Vera's awakening in the fear of being shaken out on the floor.

She looked round to find herself in a tiny room, cushioned throughout, with strange dancing confused light coming in, and the few articles of furniture carefully secured. Two young figures were there, both dressed in stout blue serge, with white trimmings; one, the darker, beside her bed, had a face full of kindness and solicitude, yet of fun dimpling over continually; the other, even in that dim light, striking Vera as something out of the loveliest visions of romance, so fair and beautiful was the countenance.

A man's voice was at the door. "Fly! Francie! How is she?"

"Much better! Nearly well! Good morning, Papa dear. Is he all right?"

"As sound as a bell! Ha!" As the door escaped, the curtain over it shook, and he nearly fell against it, saving himself with his hands. "That was exercise!" As the young girls came tumbling up and disappeared behind the curtain, where, however, the voices could be plainly heard, "Had any sleep to-night or this morning?"

"Between whiles! O yes! All our bones are still whole, as I hope yours and Ivy's are."

"Come and see. Griggs is getting breakfast under difficulties insurmountable to any one but a sea-grasshopper! I came to call you damsels, and present my inquiries to Miss Prescott."

"She will soon be all right! Francie and I are so proud of having had a real downright adventure."

"I trust she will not be the worse, and will—excuse me, and regard me as incognito."

This was said as another lurch drove the grizzled head into the cabin; and recovering in another upheaval they all disappeared, leaving Vera in a dreaming state, whence she was only half roused when Mrs. Griggs returned to administer breakfast, so far as she could taste it, under exhortations, pettings, and scoldings; and she very soon fell asleep again, and was thus left, sensible all the time of tossings and buffetings, but so worn out by the five hours of the boat, and so liable to be made ill by the motion of the vessel, that it was thought best to leave her to sleep in her berth.

She was only aware of voices above talking and laughing, or sailor calls being shouted out, or now and then of some one coming to look at her, and insisting on her taking food.

It was not till late in the afternoon that she awoke from what seemed like a strange long uneasy dream, and found one of the girls sitting by her and telling her she was better now.

"Yes," said Vera, trying to raise herself, finding something over her head, and falling back on the pillow; "but what is it? Where is this?"

"*This* is somewhere out in the Channel, near off Guernsey, Griggs says, but we cannot put in anywhere till the gale goes down."

"What is it? Is it a ship, then?"

"O yes," said the girl, laughing; "a yacht, the *Kittiwake*. Sir Robert Audley has lent it to my brother, and we are all going to see the Hebrides and Staffa and Iona."

"Not to take me all up there?" groaned poor Vera, in horror. "Can't you put me out somewhere, anywhere?"

"Don't be afraid," was the much-amused reply. "As soon as ever we can put in anywhere, we can telegraph to Rock Quay and put you ashore to go home; but we can only run before the wind while the sea is so high. I wish you could come on deck, it is so jolly!"

"Oh! it was too dreadful!"

"Beating about in the boat! It must have been, Mr. Delrio told us."

"It was so stupid in him never to see that we had got loose, and were drifting off," said Vera, who had never thought of inquiring after him.

"My father and Griggs think he behaved quite like a hero," was the answer. "He must have managed very well to keep you afloat, and saved you all this time."

"I suppose so," said Vera. "We always did know him, or I should not have let him get me into that boat, when he minded nothing but his verses."

"Those verses, they came all limp and wet out of his pocket, and Francie made him let her dry them and copy them out; and she is so delighted with them. It really is well it is too late to call the baby Cyriac."

"The baby?"

"Oh, yes. We had to leave him behind, though Francie was ready to break her heart over it; but they said that nothing would do for Ivinghoe—after this second influenza—but a sea voyage, so she had to make up her mind to leave him to my mother."

Vera was in a state of bewilderment, caring a great deal more for herself and her own sensations than for any of her surroundings; and her next question was, "When do you think we shall be out of this?"

"We shall put into harbour somewhere as soon as the wind lulls. We cannot venture yet, though we do steam; and then we can telegraph. I am longing to relieve Miss Prescott. We can take you home all the way. We were on our way into Rock Quay to take up Mysie Merrifield if she can go. It really was a wonderful and most merciful thing that we made you out just as it was getting light before running you down. My father saw you first, and old Griggs would hardly believe it, but then we heard Mr. Delrio's hail! But it was a terrible business getting you up the ship's side."

"I did not know anything about it. It was so dreadful in the lightning. And my new hat was blown away. And what is become of all my clothes?"

"Mrs. Griggs has them, and is drying them. We will lend you a hat to land in."

"Oh, when we do! I wish I had never got into that boat, but Hubert Delrio did persuade me so."

"And he is an old friend?"

"Yes, he is come to paint the roof of St. Kenelm's Church, and we want to be attentive to him because my eldest sister would be sure to be cross and keep him at a distance, being only that sort of wall painter, you know, and his father a drawing master."

"My father is very much pleased with him, and thinks him a very superior young man. They have been sitting on deck together, talking as much as they could about architecture and Italy, with their breath all blown away every moment. There! You are really getting better! If you would eat something and come on deck you would be well! I will call the sea gnat, and see what we have."

It was all very wonderful to Vera; and she began to be interested and to forget her troubles. A slice of very salt ham was brought to her and a glass of something, she did not know what, and asked if she could have some tea.

"You could have tea if you like, but there's no milk. You see, we ought to have been in at Rock Quay yesterday evening, and our stores were not adapted to hold out any longer! We shall have another curious experience, though Mrs. Griggs says it won't be so bad as once when they were off the coast of Ireland, and when they put into a bay with a queer name, all Kill and Bally, they could get nothing but potatoes and goat's milk."

"Who is Mrs. Griggs?"

"She is wife to the sailing master; and, like the Norsemen, her home is on the wave, at least in the yacht, for she always lives in it, and her cabin is quite a sight; she is great fun, she cooks when there is anything to cook, and is stewardess and everything. Francie and I knew a maid would be a vain encumbrance, so we are taking care of ourselves, and, if you will let me, I will try and set your hair to rights."

It was in a fearful tangle, after five hours at sea, and many more in the berth in the cabin; but Vera was able to sit up in a dainty dressing-gown, and submit to treatment not quite that of a hairdresser, but made as lively as could be by little jokes and kindly apologies at any extra hard pull at the knots, which really seemed "as if a witch had twined them;" and the two began to feel well acquainted with each other over the operation, though Vera was somewhat impressed when she observed that the brush was ivory handled.

Her bicycling skirt was in tolerable condition, but her once delicate blue blouse was past renovation, so she was invested with a borrowed white one, and led in triumph to the saloon, just as the beautiful "Francie" came to call "Phyllis," and give a helping hand. There were two gentlemen besides Hubert Delrio, and there was a general rejoicing welcome; but Vera did not think Hubert made half enough inquiries or apologies, before she was seated at the table, where everything was secured, and the fare was not very sumptuous or various, being chiefly some concoction of rice and scraps of salt beef, which Francie said was a shame, eating up the poor sailors' fare; also there was potted meat, and cheese, but all the fresh bread was gone, and they praised Mrs. Griggs' construction of ham and rice with all the warmth and drollery each could contribute. Vera began to be puzzled as to who every one was, for no names except Phyl, Fly, Francie and Ivy were heard, and the merry grey-haired head of the family was "Father" or "Papa" to every one, except of course Mr. Delrio, who, however, seemed at his ease, and took a fair share in the talk, and once or twice Vera thought he said, "my lord," but she did not believe it.

"I find you are a friend of a special pet of mine, Mysie Merrifield," said the father.

"I know her a little," stammered Vera, "but Primrose best."

"Nearer your age, eh? But Mysie is our gem! It looks fit for going on deck."

After the apology for a dinner, the young married pair went their way, he to endeavour to add a fish to their provisions, she to look on; the father and Delrio went where the latter could best study the wonderful tints of sunset over the purple retreating clouds, and the still agitated foaming sea,—sights that seemed to be filling him with enchantment, and revealing effects in colour, while his delight was evidently a new pleasure to his companion.

Vera was afraid to move, and sat on a deck chair, with her back to the sunset, while Phyllis, who perhaps would have liked to share in the admiration, sat by her, so that Vera began to accept her as a special friend, and to pour out the explanation of how she came to be tossing in an open boat with this one companion.

"You see, poor fellow," she said, simpering, "he has been always so devoted to me. Everybody observed it, and I could not help just gratifying him a little."

"He does seem to be very full of promise," said Phyllis. "I suppose Miss Prescott is much pleased with him."

"My sister Magdalen, do you mean? Well, we have not introduced him to her yet. You see, he is *only* painting the church, and she is so devoted to swells, and makes such a fuss about our manners."

"Indeed! But surely you could not go out with him without her knowing it."

"She was not at this St. Milburgha's Guild, you know, and Sisters Beata and Mena knew all about it. Oh, yes, she lets us go to them at St. Kenelm's, but they are not swells enough for her."

"Mr. Flight's Sisterhood, are not they?"

"And Primrose Merrifield says that Wilfred declares that they are not ladies; but that's all jealousy, you know, because Will doesn't like my friends, and Magdalen is altogether gone upon grandees."

"Fancy!" was all that Phyllis managed to say.

"She doesn't want us to be friends with anybody who don't belong to some one with a handle to her name. So foolish and stuck up! So we knew she would not be kind to Hubert."

"I think you had better have tried. I thought her one of the kindest people in the world."

"Ah! but, you know, unfortunately she has been a governess, and that teaches toadying."

At that moment "Phyl" was called to see the first star over the sea, and ran up to her father, so as to conceal how nearly she was laughing. Hubert Delrio came towards Vera.

"Can you forgive me, Vera?" he said. "I shall speak to your sister as soon as I am at home, and ask her forgiveness, and—"

"Oh, yes! yes! But do tell me who these people are."

"Did you not know? That most kind of men, is Lord Rotherwood. Those are Lord and Lady Ivinghoe, and—"

"Lady Phyllis! Oh!"

CHAPTER XIII—CHIMERAS DIRE

"Qu'allait-il faire dans cette galère?"

French Comedy.

Vera's first thorough awakening the next morning was to hear outside the door, "Are you up, Fly?"

"I shall be in a minute or two. Do you want me?"

"You are a dab at *parlez-vous*. I want you to come ashore with me and cater for the starving crew."

"What fun! Anon, anon, Sir!"

Vera then perceived that she had been bestowed in Lady Phyllis' cabin, and that the proper owner was dressing herself in haste before the little shelf of a toilette table. So great had been the confusion of last night's discovery that the poor silly child had only thought of hurrying out of sight and tumbling into bed without speaking to any one, and she had not distinctly known, when Lady Phyllis came down a good deal later and disposed of herself on the sofa, that Mrs. Griggs had made ready for her. And now the only thing she could think of was to say, "Oh! Lady Phyllis, I didn't know."

"Take care! Don't knock your head! We ought to have remembered that Boreas, or whichever it was, was hardly a sufficient introduction. Are you all right now? You had better go to sleep again till I bring something to eat. We are lying to off some little Breton fishing village, and I am going with my brother to get some provisions, and telegraph if we can."

It was long before they came back. Vera had another nap, dressed herself, grew very hungry, and came out to find Lord Rotherwood fishing, and his daughter-in-law watching for the boat to put out from the white houses with grey roofs, which, clustered round their church-tower, seemed descending to the water's edge. They were equally famished, though Mrs. Griggs stewed up the poor remnants of last night's banquet; but at last the little boat appeared, gaily dancing over the waves, and Phyllis making signals of success.

"Oh, yes, you may be thankful, you poor starving beings! Here, Mrs. Griggs! Accept, and do all you can! Here are eggs, and some milk and fresh water, four *poulets*, such as they are, and a huge monster of a crab; but all the bread is leavened, and you little guess what Ivy and I had to go through before we were allowed to buy anything. We were had up to the Mayor, and had to *constater* all manner of things about our ship, to prove that we were no smugglers."

"I thought the fat old rogue would have come out to visit the yacht before he would have allowed us a morsel," said Lord Ivinghoe.

"In which case you might have been found a skeleton, father, like Sir Hugh Willoughby! And as to our telegrams, they won't go till the diligence gets to St. Malo, and what they will make of them there is another question. I did not dare to send more than one, for fear they should get mixed up."

Vera heard the joyous chaff as it fluttered round her, not half understanding it any more than if it had been a strange tongue, and not always guessing the cause of the fits of laughter, chiefly at Lord Ivinghoe's misadventures, over which his little sister and his father were well pleased to tease his correctness, and his young wife looked a little hurt at his being tormented. He could not remember that *braconnier* was a poacher by land, not by sea, and very unnecessarily disclaimed to the Maire being such a thing. His father, he said, "was *gentilhomme anglais en*—what's a yacht?—*yac*. (Nonsense! that's a long-haired ox. No!) *Non point contrabandiste, mais galérien dans galère*." "And there I interposed," said Phyllis, "for fear we should be boarded as escaped *galériens*."

"Why, galley was a pleasure-boat sometimes," said Ivinghoe, and his wife supported him with "Cleopatra's galley."

"Well done, Francie! To your oars for Ivy's defence," said Lord Rotherwood. "How did you defend us, Fly, from being towed into harbour at Brest as runaway convicts?"

"She gabbled away most eloquently to the Maire, almost as fluently as a born French-woman," said Ivinghoe, "and persuaded him at last that it was not necessary to come on board to inspect us, nor even to detain us till he had sent for instructions to St. Malo."

"As Ivy managed matters, I thought we might be kept as hostages," said Phyllis.

"But, thanks to her blandishments, the solemn official vouchsafed to send off a messenger for us with a telegram."

"I do not think he sent directions to pursue our suspicious *galère*," added Phyllis; "but I own I shall be glad to be under the lee of old England again."

"What was your telegram?"

"Brevity was safest, nor had we money enough for two; so all I attempted was, 'Delrio to Flight, Rock Quay. Both safe. Picked up by *Kittiwake.*' I thought that would be the quickest means of relieving anxiety, as we were not sure of other addresses; and as to 'home,' Mamma probably hardly was aware of the storm, or, if she were, she knew the capabilities of yachts and of Griggs."

"Right!" returned his father. "Poor Miss Prescott! she must have given you up for lost. Have you been improving your mind with French telegrams?" he added, turning to Delrio.

"No, my lord, I found my way to the church, a wonderful piece of old Norman!—if it may so be called."

"I see you have been sketching."

Griggs here interposed with tidings that eggs and coffee were ready in the saloon, the worthy pair having had respect to the general famine, and prepared what could be made ready in haste. Those who had eaten ashore sat by, making an amusing account of their reception, and difficulties with language and peasants, for, this not being an ordinary place of call, nothing was ready for sale.

Vera, finding herself for the first time in distinguished company, which desired to set her at ease, began to be at ease, and to desire to shine, so she giggled whenever she perceived the slightest excuse, even when Lord Ivinghoe handed her the eggs, and, hoped she had not too British an appetite for French eggs; and Lady Ivinghoe asked if she had seen the fowls, and whether their feathers were ruffled up like a hen's that had been given to Aunt Cherry. Her little sister Joan, she added, had asked whether eating the eggs would make her hair curl.

"Or stand on end," said Phyllis.

"As I am afraid Miss Prescott's is doing till your telegram reaches her. Did you say it was to go from St. Malo?"

"Yes. I thought that the safest place to have a comprehensible message copied."

"To whom did you say?" asked Lady Ivinghoe.

"'Delrio to Flight.' Oh, they will know his name and address fast enough when it gets to Rock Quay."

"He is the clergyman at St. Kenelm's," put in Vera, in explanation; "very very advanced Ritualist, you know."

"Indeed!" was the answer.

"Oh, yes, that he is. My sister Polly is perfectly devoted to him; but we don't go to his church, except now and then, because my eldest sister is just one of those very old-fashioned people, you know, who want everything horrid and dull."

"That is hardly what our cousins think of Miss Prescott," said Phyllis. "I am so sorry for her anxiety! But I was not sure of the name of her place."

"The Goyle! Isn't it frightful?" said Vera.

"You say she was unprepared for your adventure?"

"Oh, yes, quite. Her notions are so dreadfully proper and old fashioned. She hasn't got any sympathy, has she, Hubert?"

"I don't know," he said gravely. "I have always had the greatest respect for her."

"Respect! So you ought. That's just the thing one has for a slow dear old fogey," she said, laughing, "Oh, Hubert!" There was a silence, and Lord Rotherwood made an observation upon the wind.

Vera perceived an awkwardness, and, by way of repairing it, afterwards thought it expedient to communicate to Lady Phyllis that it might be a pity she had said "Hubert." It was so awkward, only he was such an old acquaintance.

"I should have thought the awkwardness was incurred long ago," said Lady Phyllis. "Come, you will have no more concealments from Miss Prescott, will you? You will be ever so much more comfortable, and find out how kind she is."

"Oh, but!—" Vera wanted to talk over all her grievances for the pleasure of talking, saying very much what she had said before, and Phyllis tried to endure and put in as much sense as she could, without lecturing the girl, who struck her as the very silliest she had ever encountered; but she was continually called off to admire the receding French coast, or to look at the creatures brought up by dredging. She always took care to call Vera, and not let her feel herself left out; but Vera, if in solitude for a moment, reflected on the neglect shown of little people by great ones; and when called up to see uncanny slimy creatures, or even transparent balls like watery umbrellas, only was disgusted and horrified.

She began to guess, rather truly, that Lady Phyllis wanted to hinder a *tête-à-tête* between her and Hubert Delrio. In fact, Lord Rotherwood, who was much more of a sympathetic, confidence-inviting personage than his stiffer, much older seeming son, had said to his daughter, "Don't let that poor lad and the girl get together alone, Fly; the boy thinks he is bound to make her an offer."

"Oh, father! Surely not!"

"No more than if they had been two babies in a walnut shell. So I told him, but people don't see what infants they are themselves, and I want to hinder him from putting his foot in it before he has seen her aunt—cousin—sister, or whoever it is that has the charge of her; and she has depicted to him a Gorgon, with Medusa's hair, claws and all—a fancy sketch, isn't it?"

"Of course, sentimental schoolgirl colours! Mysie thinks herdelightful."

"At any rate, let him get a dose of common sense before committing himself. He is a capital fellow, sure to rise; has the soul and head and hands for it, but he ought not to weight himself with a drag."

"Do you think he is really in love with her?"

Lord Rotherwood waved his hands. "He thinks so, but nobody knows with those boys! I had to tell him at last that I would not have any philandering on board *my* ship; and whatever he might think it his duty to say, must be put off for aunt—sister—Gorgon—Medusa or what not. And I don't think he's very bad, Fly, for he modestly asked permission to sketch Francie's head for St. Mildred, or Milburg, or somebody; and was ready to run crazy about the tints on that dogfish. The young fellow is in the queerest state between the artist and the lover! delight and shame! I should like to take him north with us; the colours of the cliffs in the Isles would soon drive out Miss Victoria—what's her name?"

"You don't think him like Stephen in the *Mill on the Floss*, who ought to have married Maggie Tulliver."

"I believe that is his precedent—but it is sheer stuff—pure accident—as a respectable old householder like me is ready to testify to the Gorgons and Chimeras dire—Grundys and all. We must encounter Rock Quay, Fly, if it is only to rescue this unlucky youth."

"What is he doing now? Oh, I see; drawing Francie, who sits as stiff as a Saint of Burne-Jones! Well, I'll have an eye to them! Vera! Have you finished *Rudder Grange*?"

"Not quite. I can't make out who Lord Edward was."

"Why, the big dog! Did you think he was Pomona's hero?"

"I don't know. Wasn't Pomona very silly?"

"If life was to be taken from story-books," said Phyllis, in a very didactic mood; "but you see she imbibed the best side, what they really taught her of good."

"I thought, when you gave me the book, it was to be an adventure like mine, not all standing still in an old river. What do you think Hubert Delrio ought to do after persuading me into such an awful predicament?"

"Tell your sister he is very sorry that you two foolish children got into such a scrape, and very thankful that you were saved."

"We are very thankful to Lord Rotherwood."

"I didn't mean to him. To some One else," said Phyllis, reverently.

"Oh, of course," said Vera. "But what *do* you think, Lady Phyllis?" (Since her discovery of the title she made a liberal use of it.) "What do you think people will say?"

"That a little girl has had a dangerous adventure and a happy escape."

"I am seventeen, Lady Phyllis!"

"One is nothing like grown up at seventeen! I declare there's a big steamer coming into sight. I wonder if it belongs to the Channel Fleet!"

Nothing more sentimental could be extracted for the rest of the voyage.

CHAPTER XIV—PAIRING TIME ANTICIPATED

"I marry without more ado,
My dear Dick Red Cap, what say you?"

COWPER.

THE telegram had been received about mid-day; and Mr. Flight rushed up with it to the Goyle, just in time to prevent poor old Mr. Delrio from starting hopelessly home. It had suffered a good deal in spelling and precision, in spite of Lady Phyllis's precautions; but "both safe" was understood, as it was known in Rock Quay that "Lord Rotherwood and family," as the papers had it, were yachting in the *Kittiwake* and might be expected in the bay.

Agatha and Paula threw their arms round one another and cried; Magdalen, with a choke in her voice, struggled to ask Mr. Flight to lead them in a few words of thanksgiving; and as soon as these were over, Thekla expressed her hopes that they had been cast on a desert island and would bring home Man Friday.

The Goyle ladies walked over to Clipstone with the good news, and the whole party went down afterwards to Rockstone to look out for yachts, and inquire about possibilities. The *Kittiwake* being a steamer, light and swift, might be expected in harbour in the course of the night, and Mr. Delrio meant to wait for her at his son's lodgings. The ladies wished they could do the same; and Paula was allowed to accept Sister Beata's humble entreaty to house her. But they did not know how long before the telegraph from St. Malo the *Kittiwake* from St. Cadoc had spread her wings and hoisted her feather, for, happily, her coals had held out better than her provisions. So, as they were looking their last look from the cliffs of Beechcroft Miss Mohun exclaimed, "A steamer! a yacht! *Kittiwake*!"

Glasses were rushed for, and unaccustomed eyes could trace the graceful course through the gentle evening waves towards the quay.

Every one was on the quay in time to receive the boat, which, rowed by four smart sailors, was seen with the party of six, two sailor hats, and one red cap being at once spied out among the female figures. Then two hats were waved and answered by cheers of welcome; and the figures were recognised, and unnecessarily numerous hands stretched out to assist the landing from the plank extended to the boat.

Vera was put first by her kind rescuers, Lord Rotherwood's hand guiding her to the rail, and, after an insecure step or so, she found herself in the arms of Paulina, sobbing for joy; and the little cluster of sisters seemed to know nothing else, except Thekla, who presently, in the confusion of the greetings, was found by Lord Rotherwood looking about vaguely, and saying, "But where's their man Friday?"

"You must accept me for him," said he. "'Tis Friday, unless we have lost our reckoning! I hope you think me something promising in the way of savages!"

Young Delrio's first proceeding, even while his father was wringing his hand in speechless welcome and thankfulness, was to turn to Captain Henderson. "Sir, your boat is safe, it will be brought in to-morrow. I am much concerned, and beg your forgiveness, but I had no idea that it was yours till Griggs found your name. Only one oar is lost, and a cushion, which I will replace."

"Say no more, pray," said Captain Henderson. "The fault was my servant's, who took it without leave, and left it out. He must repair the very slight damage."

Miss Mohun wanted the whole troop to come up to Beechcroft to drink tea, and her relations consented; but the hearts of the Prescotts were a great deal too full for them not to wish to be alone together; and after Magdalen had given her hand to Lord Rotherwood with a fervent, "You know what I would say, my lord—beyond all words," they turned homewards; but Mr. Flight ran after them to say in a low voice, "Can we meet to-morrow at eight for a service of thanksgiving?" And this was gladly accepted.

Hubert was dragged off by his father.

"Nonsense! they don't want your apologies and explanations. It would only be besetting them. Come home with me, and don't be a fool! But write a few lines to your poor mother, after the intolerable fright you have given her; meddling and presuming where you had no business. A Providence it is that you are not half across the Atlantic, if not at the bottom of it."

Of course this was the reaction of great anxiety; but however meekly Hubert submitted to the queer outpouring of affection, and however thankful they both were, and glad and content over the particulars of the youth's work and progress, still he was not to be withheld from laying hand and heart at Vera Prescott's feet, as he insisted was due to her and her family after the compromising situation in which he had placed her. His father said it was talking novels and folly; but he was a man of three and twenty, and could not well be stopped, as he was earning his own livelihood, and had always been irreproachable. So Mr. Delrio had to leave the matter, only expressing discouragement, and insisting that it must be no more than an engagement.

The thanksgiving took place as arranged, and Lord Rotherwood, his daughter, and Mysie were there. For indeed there had been danger enough during the thunderstorm to make the safety of the *Kittiwake* a matter of thankfulness, though the rescue of the boat had caused it to be almost forgotten in the history of the night.

Lady Flight had begged that all would come to breakfast with her, and this was accepted by the Goyle party; but the Clipstone pony-carriage was waiting for the others, and they could not accede to Lady Flight's impromptu, and rather nervous, invitation. But before they started Lord Rotherwood managed to say a few words aside to Miss Prescott of the impression he had divined from his voyage with Hubert Delrio, whom he thought a young man of great ability and promise, and of excellent principles, but with a chivalry it was quite refreshing to see in youth, perhaps ready to strain honourable scruples almost too far for his own good or that of others.

Magdalen thought she perceived what had been in the marquis's mind when, immediately after her return home, Hubert and Vera came up, hand in hand, and he informed her of their mutual attachment.

"I am afraid, Miss Prescott," he said, "that we may not have acted rightly or squarely by you; and this last adventure was a most unhappy result of my careless awkwardness and preoccupation."

"It was the merest accident. We all quite understand. It is not to be thought of."

"You are very good to say so, but—"

Both he and Magdalen wished that Vera had not been present, blushing and smiling, or rather simpering; and as Hubert hesitated over his "but," Magdalen said:

"Vera, my dear, Hubert and I can talk over this better without you. You had better go and find Paula."

"Only, sister, please do understand that I care for Hubert with all my heart," said Vera, much less childishly than Magdalen had expected.

However, she went, while Magdalen succeeded in saying what she had intended—that Hubert must not consider himself in the smallest degree bound by what had been accident, entirely unintentional and innocent.

"You are generous, Miss Prescott. You understand! But the world! It was public."

"Never mind the world. You see what sensible people think."

"But, indeed, Miss Prescott, I cannot leave you to suppose I am only actuated by the fact of that awkward situation. Of course that would never have been if I did not deeply, entirely love your sister. It has only precipitated matters. I entreat of you to give her to me, as one who is—who is devoted to her! If my station is inferior I will work—"

"That is not the point. Vera is too young for such things. What does your father say?"

"My father sees that I am right."

"I see what that means," said Magdalen, smiling. "But where is he? I should like to talk to him."

Mr. Delrio, pretty well knowing what was going on, was found endeavouring to distract his mind by sketching the Goyle. He and Magdalen walked up and down the drive together, perfectly agreeing that it would be senseless cruelty to permit an early marriage between these two young people, and that it was a pity there should be an engagement; but this could hardly be prevented, since Mr. Delrio could only give advice, and leave a self-supporting worthy son to judge for himself; but the elder sister and the trustee could stipulate for delay till Vera should be of age.

So Hubert was called, and acquiesced, cheerfully observing that he trusted that four years would make him able to render Vera's life an easy and pleasant one; and after heartily thanking both Miss Prescott and his father, he went off to rejoice the heart of the maiden, who was sitting under the pear-tree, watching with anxious eyes.

CHAPTER XV—BROODS ASTRAY

"But ill for him who, bettering not with time,
Corrupts the strength of Heaven-descended will,
And ever weaker grows through acted crime,
Or seeming genial venial fault."

—Tennyson.

"Man Friday hope piccaniny live well—bring her buckra fish from sea!" Such was the greeting from Lord Rotherwood to Thekla when the whole party walked over in time for tea on the lawn, before church at Clipstone, as he presented her with a facsimile oyster which he had hunted up in a sweet shop, making an absurd bow and scrape.

Poor Thekla coloured, and mumbled a shy, "Thank you, my—my—" having had a lecture from Vera on treating a marquis with over familiarity and it was left to Primrose to ask where Friday learnt nigger language. "By nature, Missy buckra," he responded; "all same nigger everywhere." And he repeated his bow so drolly that Primrose's laugh carried Thekla's along with it, as Lady Phyllis walked up with, "Come, father, you are wanted to congratulate."

"Eh! Am I? So they have perpetrated it, have they? More's the pity is what I should say in the Palace of Truth; but the maiden has landed a better fish than she knows—that is, if she have landed him."

"There! take care, don't be tiresome, Papa!" admonished Lady Phyllis, drawing him on, when he met Vera with a courtly manner, and, "I hope I see you recovered, Miss Prescott, and able to rejoice in the pleasant consequences of your adventure."

Vera blushed, and looked very pretty and modest, making not much answer as she retreated among her contemporaries to show them her ring, a hoop of pearls, which Wilfred insisted were Roman pearls, fishes' eyes, most appropriate; but Flapsy felt immeasurably older than Wilfred to-day, and able to despise his teasing, though Hubert Delrio was not present, and indeed Wilfred was not disposed to bestow much of his attention upon her, having much more inclination to beset his cousin, Lady Phyllis, who surely ought to perceive that he had attained at least the same height as his brother Jasper, and could, in his absence, pose as the young man of the household.

Phyllis had not much to say to him, nor after the first to Vera, though she duly admired the ring so exultantly shown, and accepted the assurance that Hubert was the dearest fellow in the world. But there was no getting any condolence out of her upon the misery of having to wait four whole years. She said, "It was a very good thing! There was her cousin Gillian, who had insisted on waiting three years to finish her education."

"Oh, but dear Hubert likes me as I am," simpered Vera.

"You might wish that he should find more in you to like. Gillian," said Phyllis, coming up to her and Agatha, "I want you to assure Vera that four years is not such a great trial in waiting."

"It is what I have been trying to persuade her," said Agatha; "she is hardly seventeen."

"And I would not have been married at seventeen for anything," said Gillian to the pouting Vera. "I want to be more worth having."

Vera did not like it, she had heard the like at home, and she fell back upon Valetta, while the others walked on. "Poor little Flapsy!" said Agatha, "I do hope this engagement may make more of a woman of her."

"My father was very much struck by Mr. Delrio," said Phyllis, "both as artist and personally."

"You must be glad of the time for putting her up to his level," said Gillian.

"Do you think such things are to be done?" asked Agatha.

"Yes," said Phyllis stoutly. "You may not make her able to be a Senior Wrangler—(Oh you are Oxford!)—or capable of it, like this Gillyflower; but you can get the stuff into her that makes a sound sensible wife."

Gillian caught a little hopeless sigh of "*can*," and answered it with, "When all this effervescence is blown off, then will be the time for working at the substance, and she may be all the better wife—especially for the artist temperament, if she is of the homely sort."

"How angry she would be if she heard you say so!" returned Agatha. "Yet certainly I do feel relieved that wifehood is to be my poor Flapsy's portion, for she is not of the sort that can stand alone and make her own way."

"There will always be plenty of such women in the world," said Gillian.

"So much the better for the world," retorted Phyllis, who had never shown any symptoms of exclusive devotion to any one of the other sex, except her father.

One thing Agatha wanted to know, and dared not ask, namely, what impression Vera had made in the *Kittiwake* and what Hubert had said about her; for she and Paula had begun to remark that, lover as he was, not a word about her heroism had escaped him. And it was as well that she did not hear what the extra plain spoken Primrose did not spare the boasting Thekla. “Cousin Rotherwood and Fly both say they can’t think how Mr. Delrio got on with such a silly little hysterical goose upon his hands; and that it is a foolish romantic unlucky notion that he ought to be engaged to her. I think Mamma will tell Miss Prescott so.”

The *Kittiwake*, having arrived three days later than had been expected, there had been an amount of revolution in the general arrangements. The break up of the High School was to be on an early day of the next week. It had become a much more extensive and public matter than in the days of Valetta and Maura, though these were not so very long ago, and there was a great day of exhibitions and speeches to the parents and neighbourhood generally. Two ladies had been secured for the purpose, Elizabeth Merrifield and Miss Arthuret, and the former arrived on the Saturday afternoon, but as the Rotherwood party almost overflowed Clipstone, she was transferred to Miss Mohun.

After the death of their parents, about three years previously, Susan and Elizabeth had gone to live at Coalham, and to be useful to their brother David’s parish; Susan betaking herself to the poor, and Bessie finding herself specially available in the various forms of improvement undertaken by ladies in modern days. To her own surprise, and her sister’s discomfiture, her talent as a public speaker had become developed. With a little assistance from her sister-in-law Agnes’s unwilling stage experience, and entreaties, not easily to be withstood, came from various quarters that she would come and advocate the good cause.

Of course she was ever welcome at Clipstone, and she walked up thither with General Mohun, arriving just after the others from the Goyle; and in the general confusion of greetings, and the Babel of cousinly tongues, there were no introductions nor naming of names. Bessie declared herself delighted with the chance of seeing Lady Ivinghoe, whom she considered more to realise the beauty of women than any one she had hitherto beheld, and the fair face had not lost its simplicity, but rather gained in loveliness by the sweetness of early motherhood, as she and Phyllis sat by Mysie, regaling her with tales of what they regarded as the remarkable precocity of the infant Claude, reluctantly left to his grandmother.

“But where’s Dolores?” asked Bessie. “I miss her among the swarm of mice!”

“Dolores is at Vale Leston,” answered Gillian. “She has been a long time making up her mind to go there, to Gerald's home; and now she is there, they will not let her go till some birthday is over."

"Uncle Felix's!" whispered Franceska to Mysie. "You know it was dear Gerald's place. She had never seen it."

Another voice was now raised, asking, "What had become of Miss Arthuret?"

"She only comes down on Monday," said Bessie. "Just in time for the meeting. She is too valuable to come for more than one meeting."

"But who is she?"

"Arthurine Arthuret? She is a girl, or rather woman, who has some property at Stokesley. In fact, she is one of those magnets that seem to attract inheritance without effort—like the Hapsburgs, though happily she makes a most beneficent, though, sometimes, original use of them."

"Is not that very dangerous?" said Aunt Lily.

"The first came to her early, and coming into it very young, and overflowing with new ideas, she began rather grotesquely; but she has tamed down a good deal since, and really has done an immense deal of good in finding employment for people, making improvements and the like, though she is Sam's pet aversion, a tremendous Liberal, almost a Socialist. They are so like cat and dog that Susan and I were really glad to be away from Stokesley, especially at election times; but altogether she is an admirable person."

Lady Merrifield thought she detected a start of Miss Prescott at the name Stokesley, and that her eyes looked anxiously at the speaker. Bessie was not of the sandy part of the family. Was the unattractive schoolboy, once seen, like his sisters? All that was observable was startling similitudes to her own children, though in them the elements of the handsome dark Mohun generally predominated.

But by and by, in a quiet moment, Bessie suddenly asked, "Did you say her name was Magdalen?"

Lady Merrifield laughed. "Four years *may* do a good deal at that time of life," she said. "I suppose no time ever so changes—changes—what shall I say?—eyes—views—characters. Only constancy in absence is the dangerous thing. There are distinguished examples of—of the mischief of being constant without knowing what one is constant to. Virulent constancy, as Mrs. Malaprop has it."

Magdalen thanked and smiled. Perhaps there was a certain virulent constancy in a remote corner of her heart which had been revived by a certain indescribable look in the eyes and contour of Bessie Merrifield.

And Bessie herself, while sitting under the verandah with Lady Merrifield, while all the others were walking down to embark Lord and Lady Ivinghoe in the yacht, suddenly repeated, "Did you say that her name was Magdalen?"

"Yes; I saw it startled you, my dear."

"It revived an old, old story. I do not know whether there was anything in it. Who or what is she, Aunt Lily? I only know her as the sister of the girl that the Ivinghoes picked up."

"She is the owner of a little property at Arnscombe, and has taken home her four young half-sisters to live with her, after having slaved for them as a governess till she came into this inheritance. She is an excellent person."

"Ah! Was her house at Filsted?"

"I am not sure. Yes, I think the young ones were at school there. You think —"

"I feel certain. May I tell you, Aunt Lily? Some of the others cannot bear to mention my poor Hal; but to me the worst of the sting is gone, since I know he repented."

"My dear, I should be very glad to hear. Your father and mother never mention your brother, and we were away at the time."

"Poor Hal! I am afraid there was a weakness in him. He never had that determination that carried all the others on. He never could get through an examination, and my father put him into a bank at Filsted. By and by, after some years, came a letter telling my father he was gambling very seriously, getting into temptation, and engaging himself to an attorney's daughter. It was while I was living with grandmamma, and he used sometimes to look in on me, and talk to me about this Magdalen. Once he showed me her photograph and I thought I knew her face again. But my father went off, very angry. I have always feared he found poor Hal on the verge of tampering with the bank money, but he never would say a word. He broke everything up, put an end to the engagement if there was one, and sent Hal off to John and George, who had just got their farm in Manitoba, and were getting on by dint of hard work."

"They have done very well, have they not?"

"Yes, by working and living harder than any day labourer at Stokesley. Hal could not stand it, and—and I'm afraid the boys were not very merciful to him, poor fellow, and he got something to do in Winnipeg. There he fell in with a speculator called Golding, they all did in fact; he was a plausible man, whom they all liked, and used to put up at his house when they took waggons in with their produce. He had a daughter, and Johnnie got engaged to her, or thought he was. They all were persuaded to put money into a horrid building speculation,—Henry, what he had brought out, the other two what they had realised. Well, suddenly it all ended. They were all gone, Golding, daughter, Hal and all—yes, all—the money the other boys had put in the thing, off to the States, as we suppose! No trace ever found."

"Really no trace?"

"None! The poor boys lost all they had, and were obliged to begin over again."

"And has really nothing been heard of this unfortunate Hal?"

"There is one thing that does give me a hope. There did come to Stokesley a letter from a Brisbane bank, addressed to J. and G. Merrifield, to the care of Rear-Admiral Merrifield, and in it were bank bills up to the value of what the boys had been robbed of, about two hundred and fifty pounds. Poor Henry must have repented, and wished to make restitution."

"Was there no name, no clue?"

"None at all. We know no more."

"But was there no inquiry made at Brisbane?"

"It was when my father was very ill. The parcel was not opened at first. I have been always sorry he never heard of it; but after all there was no asking of forgiveness, nor anything that could be answered. The boys got it with the tidings of our dear father's death. John came home to see about things, George stayed to look after his Stokesley. They were well over their troubles by that time, and they gave the restored money to David for his churches."

"And no more was done, not even by David?" said Lady Merrifield, thinking over what she had heard from Geraldine Grinstead, and how the Underwoods would have accepted such a token from their lost sheep.

"David did write to Brisbane to the bank, but there never was any answer. There is no knowing how it might have been, if any one had gone out and done his best; but you see we were all much taken up with home duties and cares, and I am afraid we have not dwelt enough upon our poor boy, and he had much against him. The discipline from my dear father, that all the elders responded to with a sort of loyal exultation, only frightened him and made him shifty. They despised him, and I do not think any of us were as kind to him as we ought to have been; though on the whole he liked me the best, for he cared for books and quiet pursuits, such as all laughed at, except David. I wish he could have seen more of David."

"Did your mother hear of this ray of hope?"

"Susan thought it best not to tell her. We used to hear her murmuring his name among all ours in her prayers, Susie, Sam, Hal, Bessie, and so on; but she never was herself enough to understand, and they thought it might only stir her up to expect to see him. Oh, Aunt Lily, I don't think you—any of you—would have gone on so; but you are all much more affectionate and demonstrative than our branch of the family."

"Ah, my dear, I am sure there was a pang in your mother's heart that she never durst mention," said Lady Merrifield, her imagination dwelling in terror on her Wilfred, the one child in whom she could not help detecting the weakness of character of his unhappy cousin. "Depend upon it, Bessie, her prayers were hovering round him all the time, and bringing that act of restitution, though she was not allowed to hear of it."

"I had not thought of that," said Bessie, in a low tone, "though I think David has. I have heard his voice choke over an intercession for the absent."

"Think of it now, my dear, and do not let habitual reserve hinder you from speaking of it to Susan and David, though most likely they have the habit already. Who knows what united prayer may do with Him who deviseth means to bring home His banished?"

Steps returning, Bessie wiped away her tears in haste, actually the first she had shed for the lost Hal, though there was a heartache too deep for tears.

CHAPTER XVI—THE REGIMENT OF WOMEN

"And happier than the merriest games
Is the joy of our new and nobler aims."

F. R. Havergal.

Miss Mohun and Miss Merrifield encountered Miss Prescott and Agatha among a perfect herd of cycles, making Bessie laugh over the recollections of the horror caused at Stokesley by the arrival of Arthurine Arthuret on a tricycle twelve years previously.

The place was the Town Hall, the High School having proved too small for the number of the intended audience, and Lord Rotherwood having been captured, in spite of the *Kittiwake* being pronounced ready to sail, and all the younger passengers being actually on board, entertaining a party from Clipstone. There he sat enthroned on the platform, with portraits of himself, his Elizabethan ancestor, and the Prince of Wales overhead, and, in *propria persona* on either side, the Mayor of Rockstone, Captain Henderson, and a sprinkling of the committee, Jane, of course, being one; while in the space beneath was a sea of hats, more or less beflowered and befeathered.

Lord Rotherwood began by complaining of an act of piracy! After being exposed to a tempest and forced to put in for supplies, here he was captured, and called upon to distribute prizes! He perceived that it was a new act of aggression on the part of the ladies, proving to what lengths they were coming. Tyrants they had always been, but to find them wreckers to boot was a novelty. However, prizes were the natural sequence of a maritime exploit, and he was happy to distribute them to the maidens about to start on the voyage of life, hoping that these dainty logbooks would prove a stimulus and a compass to steer by even into unexplored seas, such as he believed the better-informed ladies were about to describe to them.

Rockstone was used to its Marquis's speeches, and always enjoyed them; and he handed the prize-books to the recipients with a shake of the hand, and a word or two of congratulation appropriate to each, especially when he knew their names; and then he declared that they were about to hear what education was good for, much better than from himself, from such noted examples as Miss Arthuret and Miss Merrifield, better known to them as Mesa. Wherewith he waved forward Miss Arthuret, a slight, youthful-looking lady, fashionably attired, and made his escape with rapid foot and hasty nods, almost furtively, while the audience were clapping her.

She spoke with voice and utterance notably superior to his well-known halting periods, scarcely saved by long training and use from being a stutter. The female population eagerly listened, while she painted in vivid colours the aim of education, in raising the status of women, and extending their spheres not only of influence in the occult manner which had hitherto been their way of working through others, but in an open manner, which compelled attention; and she dwelt on certain brilliant achievements of women, and of others which stood before them, and towards which their education, passing out of the old grooves, was preparing them to take their place among men, and temper their harshness and indifference to suffering with the laws of mercy and humanity, speaking with an authority and equality such as should ensure attention, no longer in home and nursery whispering alone, but with open face asserting and claiming justice for the weakest.

It was a powerful and effective speech; and Agatha's eye lighted with enthusiasm, as did those of several others of the elder scholars and younger teachers, as these high aims were unfolded to them.

Then followed Elizabeth Merrifield, not contradictory, but recognising what wide fields had been opened to womanhood, dwelling on such being the work of Christianity, which had always tended to repress the power of brute animal strength and jealousy, and to give preponderance to the force of character and the just influence of sweet homely affection. Exceptional flashes, even in heathen lands, and still more under the Divine guidance of the Israelites, showed what women were capable of; and ever since a woman had been the chosen instrument of the mystery of the Incarnation, the Church, the chosen emblem of the union of humanity with her Lord, had gradually purified and exalted the sex by training them through the duties of mercy, of wifehood and motherhood, to be capable of undertaking and fulfilling higher and more extensive tasks, always by the appointment and with the help of Him who had increased their outside powers, for the sake of the weaker ones of His flock. What might, by His will, in the government and politics of the country, be put into their hands, no one could tell; but it was right to be prepared for it, by extending their intellectual ability and knowledge of the past, as well as of the laws of physical nature—all, in short, that modern education aimed at opening young minds to pursue with growing faculties. This was what made her rejoice in the studies here followed with good success, as the prizes testified so pleasantly; and she trusted that the cultivation, which here went on so prosperously, was leading—if she might use old well-accustomed words—to the advancement of God's glory, the good of His Church, aye! and to the safety, honour, and welfare of our Sovereign and her dominions.

The words brought tears of feeling into the eyes of some; but Jane Mohun could not help observing, "Ah! I was afraid you were going to hold up to us the example of the ants and bees, where the old maids do all the working and fighting and governing! Don't make Gillian regret that she is falling away from the spinsterhood."

"Come, Aunt Jane, Bessie never did make it the praise of spinsters. I am sure married women can do as much as spinsters, and have more weight," said Gillian, facing round gallantly, and winning the approval of her aunt and of Bessie. There was no doubt but that since her engagement she had been much quieter and less opinionative.

With what different sensations the same occasion may be attended! To Bessie Merrifield, the primary object was, as ever, woman's work, especially her own, for the Church; and the actual business absorbed her. In spite of her evenings' talk to her Aunt Lilias, and the sad and painful recollections it had aroused, still her only look at Magdalen Prescott's face was one half of curiosity half of sorrow, as of the object of the brief calf-love of one of many brothers, and who had been now lost sight of, with the passing wonder whether, if the affection had survived and been encouraged, it might have led him to better things.

While Magdalen felt the poignant renewal of the one romance of a lifetime, as she caught tones, watched little gestures and recognised those indescribable hereditary similarities which more and more bore in upon her the fraternal connection of the bright earnest woman with the lively pleasant young man who had brought the attraction of a higher tone of manners and cultivation into the country town. No more had been heard of him since his promise to write, a promise that had been only once remembered, so that she had tried to take refuge in the supposition, unlikely as it was, that her stepmother had confiscated his letters. All was a blank since that last stolen kiss; and the wonder whether she could by any means discover anything further from Lady Merrifield or Gillian, so occupied her that she hardly heard the tenor of the two speeches, and did not observe Agatha's glowing cheeks and burning eyes, which might have told her that this was one of the moments which direct the current of life.

When Hubert Delrio came up in the evening he was curious to hear about the meeting. His young landlady, who had been a High School girl for a short time, thought Miss Arthuret's speech the most beautiful discourse that ever was spoken; while other reports said that Lady Flight and Miss Mohun were very much shocked, and thought it unwholesome, not to say dangerous; and he wanted to know the meaning of it. Magdalen was quite dismayed to find how entirely her attention had been absent, and how little account she could give of what had passed by her like the wind; but she need not have been at a loss, for Agatha, with sparkling eyes and clasped hands, burst out into a very able and spirited abstract of the speech, and the future it portrayed, showing perhaps more enthusiasm than the practised public speaker thought it prudent to manifest.

"I see," said Hubert with something of a smile, "you ladies are charmed with the great future opened to you."

"I'm sure," said Vera, perhaps a little nettled by attention paid so long to Agatha, "I can't see the sense of it all; I think a woman is made just to love her husband, and be his pet, without all that fuss about societies, and speeches and learning and fuss!" And she gave a little caress to Hubert's hand, which was returned, as he said, "She may well be loved, but, without publicly coming forward, she may become the more valuable to her home."

"Of course she may, at home or abroad. She ought—" began Agatha, but Vera snapped her off. "Well, it only comes to being one of a lot of horrid old maids; and you don't want me to be one of them, do you, darling? Come and look at my doves!"

"What do you think of it all, sister?" asked Paulina.

"So far as I grasp the subject," said Magdalen, to whom, of course, this was not new, "I think that if a larger scope is to be given to women, it is for the sake and under the direction of the Church that it can be rightly and safely used."

She knew she was speaking by rote, and was not surprised that Agatha said, "That is just what one has heard so often, and what Miss Merrifield harped upon! I want to breathe in a fresh atmosphere beyond the old traditions, and know which are Divine and which are only the superstructure of those who have always had the dominion and justified it in their own way!"

"Who gave them that dominion?" said Magdalen.

"Brute strength," began Agatha.

"Nag, Nag!" cried Paula. "Surely you believe—"

"I did not say—I did not mean—I only meant to think it out, and understand what is Divine and what is in the eternal fitness of things."

Here came an interruption, leaving Magdalen conscious of the want of preparation for guiding the thought of these young things, and of self-reproach too, for having let herself be so absorbed in the thought of "her broken reed of earth beneath," as not to have dwelt on what might be the deep impressions of the young sisters under her charge.

A few days later, as Agatha sat reading in the garden, two figures appeared on the drive, wheeling up their bicycles. One was Gillian, the other had a general air of the family, but much darker, and not one of the old acquaintances. Advancing to meet them, she said, "I am the only one at home. My sisters are all at lessons or in the village."

"I'll leave a message," said Gillian. "My mother wants you all to come up to picnic tea to see the foxgloves in the dell, on Monday, and to bring Mr. Delrio —"

"Oh! thank you."

"I forgot, you had not seen my cousin Dolores Mohun before. Mysie calls her a cousin-twin, if you know what that is."

Agatha thought the newcomer's great pensive dark eyes and overhanging brow under very black hair made her look older than Mysie, or indeed than Gillian herself; and when the message had been disposed of, the latter continued, "Dolores wanted to know about Miss Arthuret's lecture, being rather in that line herself. She could not get home in time for it, and I was seeing the *Kittiwake* party on board, and only crept in at the other end of the hall in time for Bessie's faint echoes."

"I was in the very antipodes," said Dolores, "in a haunt of ancient peace, whence they would not let me come away soon enough."

"And, Agatha, Aunt Jane says she saw you devouring Miss Arthuret with your eyes," said Gillian.

"It gave one a sense of new life," said Agatha; and she related again Miss Arthuret's speech, broken only by appreciative questions and comments from Dolores' auditor, to whom, in the true fashion of nineteen, Agatha straightway lost her heart. Dolores, who had seen much more of the outer world than her cousins, and had had besides a deeply felt inward experience which might well render her far more responsive, and able to comprehend the questions working in the girl's mind, and which found expression in, "I went to St. Robert's only wanting to get my education carried on so that I might be a better governess; but I see now there are much farther on, much greater things to aim at, than I ever thought of."

"Alps on Alps arise!" said Dolores. "Yes—till they lose themselves—and where?"

"Miss Merrifield would say in Heaven, by way of the Church."

"The all things in earth or under the earth rising up in circles of praise to the Cherubim and the Great White Throne," said Dolores, her dark eyes raised in a moment's contemplation.

"Ah! One knows. But is that thought the one to be brought home to every one, as if they could bear it always? Are not we to do something—something—for the helping people here in this life, not always going on to the other life—"

"Temporal or spiritual?" said Dolores; "or spiritual through temporal?"

"And our part in helping," said Agatha.

"There is an immense deal to be thought out," said Dolores. "I feel only at the beginning of the questions, and there is study and experience to go to them."

"You mean what one gets at Oxford?"

"Partly. Thorough—at least, as thorough as one can—of the physical and material nature of things, then of the precedent which then results, also of reasoning."

"Metaphysical, do you mean, or logical?"

"That comes in; but I was thinking of mathematical in the indirect training of the mind. It all works into needful equipment, and so does actual life."

"It takes one's breath away."

"Well, we have begun our training," said Dolores, with a sweet sad smile. "At least, I hope so."

"At St. Robert's, you mean?"

"You have, I think. But I believe my aunt will be expecting us."

"Oh! And then they talk about modesty and womanliness and retiring! What do you think about all that?"

"That we never shall do any good without it."

They were interrupted by the hasty rushing up of Paula, who had committed her bicycle to Vera, and came dashing up the steep slope, crying, "O Nag, Nag, they are going away!"

The announcement was interrupted as she perceived the presence of the visitor, and they rose to meet her, but saw that there were tears in her eyes, and she had rushed up so fast that she was panting and could hardly speak, though she gave her hand, as Agatha, after naming the two cousins, asked, "Who are going?"

"The Sisters—Sister Mena—" with another overflow of tears which made

Dolores and Gillian think they had better retreat and leave her to her sister's consolation; so they took leave hastily, Agatha however, coming as far as their machines, and confiding to them, "Poor Polly, it is a great blow to her, but I believe it is very good for her."

"There's stuff in that girl," said Dolores, as soon as they were out of reach. "She has the faculty of hearkening as well as of hearing."

"You would say so if you saw her at a lecture; and she is also gaining power of expressing and reproducing," said Gillian.

"She will be a power by and by, unless some blight comes across her."

"Will me, will me, it seems as if we *had* to do it. Even Mamma, whose ideal was chivalry, Church and home, has to be drawn out to take a certain public part; Aunt Jane, who only wished to live to potter about among neighbours, poor and rich, must needs come out of her traditional conventions, and relate her experiences, and you—"

"Oh, I am only trying to do the work Gerald aimed at!"

"Any way we have our work before us, whether we call it for the Church or mankind."

"Charity or Altruism," said Dolores.

"May not altruism lead to charity?" said Gillian.

"Sometimes, but sometimes disappointment leads only to intolerance of those whose methods differ. Altruism will not stand without a foundation," said Dolores.

"Mysie has been impressing on me, with what she heard from Phyllis Devereux, of the work Sister Angela has been doing at Albertstown—the most utter self-abnegation, through bitter disappointment in her most promising pupils—only the charity that is rooted could endure. It is just the old difference Tennyson points out between Wisdom and Knowledge."

"And with wisdom come those feminine attributes that Agatha began asking about."

"Yes, softening, gentleness, tact. If people have not grown up to them, they must be taught as parts of wisdom."

Gillian sighed. "I wonder what Ernley Armitage will say when he comes home?"

"He won't want you to throw up everything."

"I don't think he will! But if he did—No, I think he will be a staff to guide a silly, priggish heart to the deeper wisdom."

CHAPTER XVII—FOXGLOVES AND FLIRTATIONS

"With her venturous climbings, and tumbles, and childish escapes."

TENNYSON.

HUBERT DELRIO, pleased and gratified, but very shy, joined the ladies from the Goyle in their walk to Clipstone, expecting perhaps a good deal of stiffness and constraint, since every one at St. Kenelm's told him what a severe and formidable person Sir Jasper Merrifield was, and that all Lady Merrifield's surroundings were "so very clever." "They did want *such* books ordered in the library."

Magdalen laughed, and said her only chance of seeing a book she wanted was that Lady Merrifield should have asked for it. At Clipstone, they were directed to the dell where the foxgloves were unusually fine that year, covering one of the banks of the ravine with a perfect cloud of close-grown spikes, nodding with thick clustered bells, spotted withinside, and without, of that indescribable light crimson or purple, enchanting in reality but impossible to reproduce. It was like a dream of fairy land to Hubert to wander thither with his Vera, count the tiers of bells, admire the rings of purple and the crooked stamens, measure the height of the tall ones, some almost equal to himself in stature, and recall the fairy lore and poetry connected with them, while Vera listened and thought she enjoyed, but kept herself entertained by surreptitiously popping the blossoms, and trying to wreath her hat with wild roses.

Thekla meantime admired from the opposite bank, in a state of much elevation at acquiring a dear delicious brother-in-law, and insisted on Primrose sharing her sentiments till her boasting at last provoked the exclamation, "I wouldn't be so cocky! I don't make such a fuss if my sisters do go and fall in love. I have two brothers-in-law out in India, and Gillian has a captain, an Egyptian hero, with a medal, a post captain out at sea in the *Nivelle*. You shall see his photograph coloured in his lovely uniform, with his sword and all! Your Flapsy's man isn't even an officer!"

"He is a poet, and that's better!"

"Better! why, if you *will* have it, Wilfred and Fergus always call him that 'painter cad,'" broke out Primrose, who had not outgrown her childish power of rudeness, especially out of hearing of her elders.

"Then it is very wicked of them," exclaimed Thekla, "when the Marquis of Rotherwood himself said that Hubert Delrio is a very superior young man" (each syllable triumphantly rounded off).

Primrose was equal to the occasion. "Oh, they all laugh at Cousin Rotherwood; and, besides, a superior young man does not mean a gentleman."

Thekla burst into angry tears and sobs, which brought Gillian, and a grave, dark young lady from the other side of a rock to inquire what was the matter —there was a confession on the two tongues of "she did," and "I didn't" of "painter cad, superior young man and no gentleman," but at last it cleared itself into Primrose allowing that, to take down Thekla's conceit, she had declared that a very superior young man did not mean a gentleman.

"I could not have believed that you could have been so abominably ill-mannered," said Gillian gravely; "you ought to apologise to Thekla."

"Oh, never mind," began Thekla ashamed; and at that moment a frantic barking was heard in the depths, and Valetta, Wilfred, Fergus and a dog or two darted headlong past, calling out, "Hedgehogs, hedgehogs! Run! come!" And Primrose, giving a hand to Thekla, joined in the general rush down the glade.

"A situation relieved!" said the newcomer.

"For all ran to see,
For they took him to be
An Egyptian porcupig,"

quoted Gillian. "They have wanted such a beast for some time for their menagerie; but really Primrose is getting much too old to indulge in such babyish incivility to a guest, true though the speech was, 'a superior young man,' not necessarily a gentleman."

"I am colonial enough to like him the better for the absence of a hall mark."

"Should you have missed it? He is very good looking, and has a sensible refined countenance, poor man!"

"He is a little too point device, too obviously got up for the occasion!"

"Too like the best electroplate! No; that is not fair, for it is not pretence, at least, I should think there was sound material below, and that never would brighten instead of dimming it."

"According to Mysie and Fly, there is plenty of good taste; and his principle is vouched for. Mysie is quite furious at any lady-love having gone to sleep to the sound of original verses from a lover!"

"Dear old Mysie! No, she would not. She has a practical vein in her! Would you?"

"I'm not likely to be tried!" said Gillian merrily. "Catch Ernley either practising or not minding his boat! But come! Mamma will want me, I feel only deputy daughter, with Mysie away."

The two girls rose from the mossy bank, and proceeded across the paddock to the opening of the glade.

On the turf Lady Merrifield sat enthroned; making a nucleus to the festivities and delicacies of all sorts, from sandwiches and cakes down to strawberries, cherries and Devonshire cream, were displayed before her; and the others drifted up gradually, Miss Mohun first. "I am later than I meant to be," she said, "but I was delayed by a talk with Sister Beata. I never saw a woman more knocked down than she is by that adventure of Vera's."

"I know," said Magdalen, rousing herself. "It has made her look ten years older, and she could not talk it over or let a word be said to comfort her. She says it was all her fault, and I should have thought it was that silly little Sister Mena's, if that is her name.

"She considers it her fault for objecting to strict discipline in things of which she did not see the use," said Jane Mohun, "and so getting absorbed in her own work, and having no fixed rule by which to train Mena."

"I see," said Lady Merrifield; "it reminds me of a story told in Madame de Chantal's life, how, when, *par mortification*, a Sister quietly ate up a rotten apple without complaint and another made signs of amusement, a rule was made that no one should raise her eyes at meals. It shows that some rules which seem unreasonable may have a foundation."

"It is an unnatural life altogether," said Dolores. "Why should the rotten apple have been swallowed? or, if it was, I should think a joke over it might have been wholesome."

"Hindering priggishness in the mortified Sister," said Gillian.

"The fact is," said Lady Merrifield, "that if you vow yourself to an unnatural life, so to speak, you must submit to the rules that have been found best to work for it."

"And poor Sister Beata did neither the one nor the other, by her own account," said Jane. "She called herself a Sister, but disliked each rule, and chose to go her own way, like any other benevolent woman, doing very admirable work herself, but letting little Mena have the prestige of a Sister, while too busy to look after her, and without rules to restrain her."

"But surely there has been no harm!" exclaimed Lady Merrifield.

"No harm, only a little incipient flirtation with the organist, nothing in any one else, but not quite like a convent maid."

"Ah! I rather suspected," said Agatha.

"I should think the best thing for Sister Mena would be to go to a good school, leave off her veil, in which she looks so pretty, and be treated like an ordinary girl," said Lady Merrifield.

"That is just what Sister Beata intends," said Miss Mohun. "She is to sink down into Miss Marian Jenkins, to wear a straw hat and blue frock, and go to school with the other girls, the pupils, while Sister Beata begins life as a probationer at Dearport."

"Poor Sister Beata!"

"She says she has experienced that it is best to learn to obey before one begins to rule. It is most touching to see how humble she is. Such a real good woman too! I doubt whether she gets a night's rest three days in a week, and she looks quite haggard with this distress," said Jane.

"She will be a great power by and by! But what will Mr. Flight and St. Kenelm's do without her?"

"He is promised relays of Sisters from Dearport, which has stood so many years that they have a supply. You see, he, like Sister Beata, tried a little too much to be original and stand aloof."

“Ah!” said Lady Merrifield, “that is the benefit of institutions. They hinder works from dying away with the original clergyman or the wonderful woman.”

“But, Aunt Lily,” put in Dolores, “institutions get slack?”

“They have their *downs*, but they also have their ups. There is something to fall back upon with public schools.”

“Yes, like croquet,” laughed Aunt Jane. “We saw it rise and saw it fall; and here come all the players, the revival. Well, how went the game?”

So the party collected, and the two Generals came in from some vanity of inspection to grumble a little merrily at the open air banquet, but to take their places in all good humour, and the lively meal began with all the home witticisms, yet not such as to exclude strangers. Indeed, Hubert Delrio was treated with something like distinction, and was evidently very happy, with Vera by his side. Perhaps Magdalen perceived that there was not the perfect ease of absolute equality and familiarity; but his poetical and chivalrous nature was gratified by the notice of a Crimean hero, and he infinitely admired the dignity and courtesy of Lady Merrifield, and the grace and ease of her daughters, finding himself in a new world of exquisite charm for him.

And before they broke up, Magdalen had a quiet time with Lady Merrifield, in which she was able, not without a tell-tale blush even at her years, to ascertain that there were two Henry Merrifields, and that, alas! there was nothing good known of the son of Stokesley, except that anonymous attempt at restitution which gave hopes of repentance.

CHAPTER XVIII—PALACES OR CHURCHES

"And if I leave the thing that lieth next,
To go and do the thing that is afar,
I take the very strength out of my deed."

—MACDONALD.

THOSE were happy days that succeeded Vera's engagement. It had made her more womanly, or at least less childish; and the intercourse with Hubert Delrio became an increasing delight to her sisters, who had never known anything so like a brother.

He was at first shy and not at ease with Magdalen, who, on her side, perceived the lack of public school and university training; but in grain he was so completely a good man, a churchman, and a gentleman, and had so much right sense as well as talent, that she liked him thoroughly and began to rely on him, as a woman with unaccustomed property is glad to do with a male relation.

And to him, the society of the Goyle was a new charm. He had been brought up to the technicalities and the business relations of art, and had a cultivated taste; but to be with a thoughtful, highly educated lady, able to enter into its higher and deeper associations, was an unspeakable delight and improvement to him. Vera was fairly satisfied as long as he sketched her in various attitudes, and held her hand while he talked; though she did grudge having so much time spent on "taste, Shakespeare and the musical glasses." Paula had various ecclesiastical interests in common with him, and began to expand and enter more into realities, while Thekla had in him a dear delightful delicious brother, who petted her, bantered her, mended her rabbit hutch, caught her hedgehog, taught her to guide her bicycle, drew picture games for her, and taught her to sketch.

Agatha had endless discussions with him on his various aspirations, in some of which Magdalen took her share, sometimes thinking with a pang of regret and self-reproach that that brief time of intercourse with Hal Merrifield had been spent in youthful nonsense that could have left no permanent influence for good.

In fact, whether through Hubert or through Agatha, a certain intellectual waft had breathed upon the Goyle. Hubert was eager for assistance in learning German and Italian, and read and discussed books of interest; and even when he had left Rockstone, and his work at St. Kenelm's being finished, the stimulus was kept up by his letters, comments and questions; and the younger girls had entirely ceased to form an opposite camp, or to view "sister" as a taskmistress, even when Agatha had returned to St. Robert's.

Mysie had come home, very brown, fuller of Scott than ever for her mother, and of Hugh Miller for Fergus, for whom she had brought so many specimens that Cousin Rotherwood declared that she would sink the *Kittiwake*. Over the sketches and photographs of Iona, she and Paulina became great friends, and Paula was admitted to hear accounts of the modern missions that had come from the other Harry Merrifield among the Karens in Burmah, or again through Franciska Ivinghoe, of her Aunt Angela Underwood, who was considered to have a peculiar faculty for dealing with those very unpromising natives, the Australian gins. Franciska remembered her tender nursing and bright manner in the days of fever at Vale Leston, and had a longing hope that she would take a holiday and come home; but at present she was bound to the couch of her slowly declining old friend, Sister Constance, the Mother of Dearport. It was another bond of interest with Magdalen, to whom missions to the heathens had always been a dream.

Thus had passed a year uneventful and peaceable, with visits from Hubert whenever he had a day or two to spare. They were looked forward to with delight; but if there were a drawback it was in Vera's viewing him partly as one who held her in a sort of chain, and partly as one whom it was pleasant to tease by allowing little casual civilities from Wilfred Merrifield.

For Wilfred was an embarrassment to his family. He had never been strong, his public school career had been shortened by failure in health, and headaches in the summer, and coughs in the winter made it needful to keep him at home, and trust to cramming at Rockstone, enforced by his father's stern discipline and his mother's authoritative influence.

Thus he was always within reach of the mild social gaieties in which each family indulged, and Vera was not quite so ready as were his sisters to contrast unfavourably his hatred of all self-improvement with Hubert Delrio's eagerness to pick up every crumb of information, thus deservedly getting on well in his profession.

One morning, at breakfast, Hubert opened a letter and made a sudden exclamation; and in answer to Vera's vehement inquiry said, "It seems that the great millionaire swell, Pettifer—is that his name?"

"Oh, yes, he was at Rock Quay."

"Well, he went to see St. Kenelm's, fell in love with the ceiling, and offered Pratt and Pavis any sum they like to decorate a huge new hall he is building in the same style. So they write to propose to me to come and do it, with a promise of future work, at any terms I like to ask."

"Oh! but that's jolly," cried Vera. "Can't you?"

"No," he said; "this is immediate, and I have two churches, reredos and walls, on my hands, enough to last me all the year. Nor could I throw over Eccles and Beamster."

"Is there an agreement with them?" asked Magdalen.

"Not regularly; but Mr. Eccles has been very kind to me, and promised me employment for four years to come; in fact, he has made engagements on that understanding."

"I see," said Magdalen. "You could not break with them."

"Certainly not. Nor do I entirely like the line of this other house. It is a good deal more secular."

"And you have dedicated your talents to the Church!" cried Paulina.

"Not that exactly, Paula," he said, smiling; "but I had rather work for the Church, so I am glad the matter is definitely settled for me."

To that he kept, though he had a very kind letter from Mr. Eccles, who had evidently been applied to, wishing not to stand in his light, especially as he was engaged to be married, and telling him how it might be possible to fairly compensate for the loss to the firm. Between the lines, however, it was plain that it would be a great blow, only possible because the agreement had been neglected; and Hubert was only the more determined, out of gratitude for the generosity, not to break what he felt to be an implied pledge; and all the sisters sympathised with his determination.

He adhered to it even after his return to London, though his father thought it a pity to lose the chance, if it could be accepted without discourtesy to Mr. Eccles; and he had been interviewed by various parties concerned, and there had been an attempt to dazzle him by the prospects held out to him by an enthusiastic young member of the firm. Perhaps he was too shrewd entirely to trust them, but at any rate he felt his good faith to Eccles and Beamster a bond to hold him fast from the temptation; and his heart was really set on the consecration of the higher uses of his art; so that regard to the simple rule of honour was an absolute relief to him.

So he wrote to Vera, who, if there were a secret wish on her part, did not dare to give it shape; while all her sisters, to whom she showed the letters that she scarcely comprehended, were open-mouthed in their admiration. Thekla, who had been seized with a fit of hagiology, went the length of comparing him to

St. Barbara; even Paula pronounced it a far-fetched resemblance.

It was some months later that Sir Ferdinand Travis Underwood had decided on building a magnificent cathedral-like church for the population rising around him in the Rocky Mountains; and meeting Lord Rotherwood in London heard of the work at St. Kenelm's, and resorted to Eccles and Beamster as the employers of young Delrio. There would be plenty of varieties of beautiful material to be found near at hand in the mountains; but Hubert was sent first for a short journey in Italy to study the effect of the old mosaics as well as the frescoes, and then to go out to America to the work that would last a considerable time.

Vera was much excited by the notion of the Italian journey, and thought she ought to have been married at once and have shared it, including as it did a short visit to Rocca Marina. But she was scarcely eighteen, and neither her trustee nor her elder sister thought it advisable to dispense with the decision that her twenty-first birthday must be waited for, at which she pouted. Hubert came for two nights on his return, and was exceedingly full of his tour, talking over Italian scenes and churches with Magdalen, who had never seen them, but had the descriptions and the history at her fingers' ends, and listened with delight to all the impressions of a mind full of feeling and poetry. The time was only too short to discuss or look out everything, and much was left to be copied and sent after him, with many promises on Vera's part of writing everything for him, and translating the books that Magdalen would refer to. He was allowed to take Vera and Paulina to Filsted for a hurried visit to his parents. When they came home again, it soon became plain that it had not been a success. "I am glad to be at home again," said Paula, as the pony carriage turned up the steep drive, and the girls jumped out to walk. "I am quite glad to feel the stones under my feet again!"

Magdalen laughed. "A new sentiment!" she said.

"I don't like the stones," said Vera, "but I did not know Filsted was such a poky place."

"A dead flat!" added Paula. "No sea, no torrs! one wanted something to look at! and *such* a church!"

"Did you see Minnie Maitland?" put in Thekla.

"I saw all the Maitlands in a hurry," said Vera. "I don't remember which was which. They were all dressed alike in horrid colours. Hubert said they set his teeth on edge!"

"How was old Mrs. Delrio?"

"Just the same as ever, lean and pinched."

"But so kind!" added Paula. "She could not make enough of Flapsy."

"I should think not!" ejaculated Vera. "Enough! aye, and too much! just fancy, no dinner napkins! and Edith went away and made the scones herself!"

"Very praiseworthy," said Magdalen. "Don't you know how Hubert always tells us what a dear devoted good girl she is?"

"Well, I only hope Hubert does not expect me to live in that way," said Vera. "His mother looks like a half-starved hare, and Edith is giving lessons as a daily governess!

"Edith is very nice," said Paula; "and I never understood before how excellent old Mr. Delrio's pictures are! Do you remember his 'Country Lane'? What a pity it did not sell!"

"Poor man!" said Magdalen. "He married too soon, and that has kept him down."

"It is beautiful to see how proud they are of Hubert," said Paula, "and his pretty gentle attention and deference to them both. Mr. Delrio is really a gentleman, I am sure; but, Maidie," she said, falling back with her, while Vera and Thekla mounted faster, "it was very odd to see how different things looked to us from what they seemed when we were at Mrs. Best's. Filsted High Street has grown so small, and one could hardly breathe in Mrs. Delrio's stuffy drawing-room. And as to Waring Grange, which we used to think just perfect, it was all so pretentious and in such bad taste. Hubert saw it as much as we did, but I could see he was on thorns to hinder Flapsy from making observations."

Certainly the visit had not done much good, except in making the girls appreciate the refinement of their surroundings at the Goyle.

And when letters arrived from Hubert at the American Vale Leston, asking questions requiring some research in books, either Magdalen's or at the Rock Quay library, Vera dawdled and sighed over them; and when the more zealous Magdalen or Paula took all the trouble, and left nothing for her to do but to copy their notes, and write the letters, she grew cross. "It was for Hubert, and she did not want any one else to meddle! So stupid! If he had only taken Pratt and Pavis's offer, there would not have been all this bother!"

That, of course, she only ventured to utter before Paula and Thekla, and it made them both so furious that she declared she was only in joke, and did not mean it.

She was indulging in reflections on the general dulness of her lot, and the lack of sympathy in her sisters, as she lingered by the confectioner's window, with her eyes fixed on a gorgeous combination of coloured bonbons, when Wilfred Merrifield sauntered out. "Fresh from Paris!" he said. "Going to choose some?"

"Oh no, I haven't got any cash. M. A. keeps us horribly short."

"As usual with governors! But look here! Pocket this. Sweets to the sweet, from an old chum!"

"Oh, Will, how jolly! Such a love of a box."

"Make haste! Some of the girls are lurking about, and if there is any mischief to be made, trust Gill for doing it."

"Mischief!—" but before the words were out of her mouth, Gillian and Mysie appeared from the next shop, a bootmaker's, and Mysie stood aghast with, "What *are* you doing? Buying goodies! How very ridiculous!"

"The proper thing between chums, isn't it, Vera?" said Wilfred, with an indifferent air. "We aren't unlucky Sunday scholars, Mysie, to be jumped upon! Good-bye, Vera, *au revoir*!"

He sauntered away with his hands in his pockets; while Gillian, from her eldership of two years, and her engagement, gravely said, "Vera, perhaps you do not fully know, but I should say this is not quite the thing."

"He told you we are just chums!" exclaimed Vera. "As if there were any harm in it! You've not got a sweet tooth yourself, so you need not grudge me just a few goodies."

Gillian saw that it was of no use to prolong the dispute either for the place or the time, and she hushed Mysie, who was about to expostulate farther, and made her go away with a brief parting, such as she hoped would impress on Vera that the sisters thought very badly of her discretion and loyalty. They could not hear the reflection, "They need not be so particular and so cross. Hubert never thought of giving me anything nice like this. Why should not my chum? Such a sweet little box too, with a dear girl's head on it! Would Polly fuss about it, and set on Sister? I shall put it into my own drawer, and then if they notice it, they may think somebody at Filsted gave it! No one has any business to worry me about Hubert, and Wilfred being civil to me. He *is* a gentleman."

The gentleman had been overtaken by his sisters. He was walking his bicycle up the hill rather breathlessly and slowly. Mysie indignantly began, "Of all the stupid things to do, to give goodies to that girl, like a baby!"

"I have been wishing to speak to you," said Gillian. "You are going the way to get that foolish girl into a scrape."

"Oh, yes, of course. Sisters uniformly object to a little civility to a pretty girl," carelessly answered Wilfred.

"Nonsense!" returned Mysie, hotly. "We don't care! only it is not fair on Mr. Delrio."

"The painter cad! A very good thing too! The sacrifice ought to be prevented. Is not that the general sentiment?"

"Wilfred!" cried the scandalised Mysie, "when it is all the other way, and he is ever so much too good for her."

"Consummate prig! The cheek of him pretending to a lady!"

"But, Wilfred," went on downright Mysie, "is it only mischief, or do you want to marry her yourself?"

"Draw your own conclusions," responded Wilfred, mounting his machine, and spinning down the hill faster than they could follow on foot.

"What is to be done, Gill?" sighed Mysie. "Ought we to get mamma to speak to him?"

"Better not," said Gillian, with more experience. "It would only make it worse to take it seriously. Half of it is play—and half to teaseyou."

"And," said Mysie, with due deference to the engaged sister, "how about Mr. Delrio? Will it make him unhappy?"

"If he finds out in time what a horrid little thing it is, I should say it would be very well for him; but I don't want Will to be the means."

"Oh! when his examination is over, and he gets an appointment, he will go away, and it will be safe."

"I have not much hopes of his getting in!"

"Oh, Gill, none of us ever failed before."

On the side of the Goyle not much was known or cared about Wilfred's little attentions, which were generally out of sight of Magdalen, and did not amount to much; but Paula saw enough of them to consult Agatha on, and to observe that Flapsy was going on just as she used to at Filsted, and she thought Hubert would not like it.

"I believe Flapsy can't live without it," sighed Agatha.

"But would you speak to her? I don't think she ought to let him give her boxes of bonbons—to keep up in her room, and never give a hint to Maidie."

Agatha did speak but the effect was to set Vera into crying out at every one being so intolerably cross about such a trifle, Gillian Merrifield and all!

"Did Gillian speak to you?"

"Yes, as if she had any business to do so!"

"I am sure it is not the way she would treat Captain Armitage."

"I don't believe she cares for Captain Armitage one bit! You said yourself that all the girls at Oxford thought she cared much more for her horrid examination! I wouldn't be a dry, cold-hearted, insensible stick like her for the world."

"Perhaps she is the more quietly in earnest," said Agatha, repenting a little that she had told before Vera the college jokes over what had leaked out of Gillian's reception of Ernley Armitage when he had hastened up to Oxford as soon as his ship was paid off, and she had been called down to him in the Lady Principal's room. Report said that she had only prayed him to keep out of the way, and not to upset her brain, and that he had meekly obeyed—as one who knew what it was to have promotion depending on it.

It was a half truth, exaggerated, but it had not a happy effect on Vera. Nevertheless, the finishing push of preparation brought on such a succession of violent headaches as quite to disable the really delicate boy. Moreover, the tutor declared that there had been little chance of his success, and Dr. Dagger said that he had much better not try again. The best hope for his health, and even for his life, was to keep him at home for a few years, and give him light work.

He had never been the pleasantest element in the household; and if his parents were glad of the avoidance of the risk of a launch into the world, and his mother's love rejoiced in the power of watching over him, there were others who felt his temper a continual trial, while his career was a perplexity.

However, Captain Henderson offered a clerkship at the Marble Works, subject to Mr. White's approval; and this was gratefully accepted. Nor did Agatha come home again at the Long Vacation for more than two days, in which there was no time for consultation with her sisters on matters of uncertain import.

Miss Arthuret and Elizabeth Merrifield had arranged together to take the old roomy farmhouse on Penbeacon for three or four months, and there receive parties of young women in need of rest, fresh air, and, in some cases, of classes, or time for study. It was to be a sort of Holiday House, though not altogether of idleness; and Dolores undertook to be a kind of vice-president, with Agatha to pursue her reading under her superintendence, and to assist in helping others, governesses, students, schoolmistresses from Coalham, in whose behalf indeed the scheme had been first started, and it was extremely delightful to Agatha, among many others.

CHAPTER XIX—TWO WEDDINGS

"How happy by my mother's side
When some dear friend became a bride!
To shine beyond the rest I was
  In gay embroidery drest.
Vain of my drapery's rich brocade,
I held my flowing locks to braid."

Anstice (*from the Greek*).

"Epidemics of marriage set in from time to time," said Jane Mohun. "Gillian has set the fashion."

For the Rock Quay neighbourhood was in a state of excitement over a letter from Mrs. White, of Rocca Marina, announcing the approaching marriage of Mr. White's niece, Maura, with Lord Roger Grey, a nephew of dear Emily's husband, and heir to the Dukedom. The White family were coming home for the wedding, and the interest entirely eclipsed that of Gillian Merrifield's. In fact, though that young lady somewhat justified the Oxford stories, she was in a state of much inward agitation between real love for Ernley, and pain in leaving home, so she put on an absolutely imperturbable demeanour. Her reserve and dread of comments made her so undemonstrative and repressive to her Captain that there were those who doubted whether she cared for him at all, or only looked on her wedding as a mediæval maiden might have done, as coming naturally a few years after she had grown up. Ernley Armytage knew better, and so did her parents. The wedding was hurried on by Captain Armytage's appointment to a frigate on the coast of Southern America, where he had to join at once, in lieu of a captain invalided home; and Gillian accepted the arrangements, which would take her to Rio, "as much a matter of course," said her aunt, "as if she had been a wife for ten years." Her uncle, Mr. Mohun, was anxious that the marriage of his sister Lily's daughter should take place at the family home, Beechcroft. If there had been scruples, chiefly founded on the largeness of the party, and the trouble to Mrs. Mohun, these were forgotten in the convenience of being out of the way of Rockstone gossip, as well as for other reasons.

"I should certainly have escaped," said General Mohun. "I have no notion of meeting that unmitigated scamp."

"Mr. White ought to be warned," said Jane.

"You'll do so, I suppose; and much good it will be."

"I do not imagine that it will. It will be too charming to surpass Franciska and Ivinghoe; but if neither you nor Jasper will speak to old Tom, I shall deliver my conscience to Ada."

"And be advised to mind your own business."

Nevertheless, Jane Mohun did deliver her conscience, when, on the day after the arrival, there had been loud lamentations over the intended absence of the Merrifield family. "It would have looked well to make it a double wedding, all in the family," said Mr. White.

To which Miss Mohun only answered by a silence which Mrs. White was unwilling to break, but Maura exclaimed—

"But I thought Valetta would be sure to be my bridesmaid. Such friends as we were at the High School!"

It did not strike Miss Mohun that the friendship had been very close or very beneficial; but Adeline added, "We thought she would pair so well with Vera Prescott, and then uncle will give all the dresses—white silk with cerise trimmings. We ordered them in Paris."

"Uncle Tom is so generous!" said Maura. "There is no end to his kindness. I'll go and unpack some of the patterns, that Miss Mohun may see them."

She tripped out of the room, and Jane exclaimed, "Poor child! Has Emily written to you, Ada?"

"Yes, rather stiffly. Mr. White thinks it aristocratic pride."

"Ada, you know it is not that."

"Well, I suppose the Greys are hardly gratified by the connection, though Mr. White will make it worth their while. You see the Duke leaves everything in his power to his daughters, so poor Roger will be very badly off."

"But—" There was so much expressed in that "but" that Adeline began to answer one of the sentiments she supposed it to convey. "He can do it easily—for all the rest are provided for by the Marble Works—except the two eldest brothers. Richard has gone away, and Alexis—oh, you know he has notions of his own that Mr. White does not like."

"Does Mr. White know all about Lord Roger, or why the Duke should cut him off as far as possible?"

"My dear Jane, it is not charitable to bring things up against young men's follies."

"It is a pretty considerable folly to have done what compelled him to retire. Reginald was called in at the inquiry, and knows all about it."

"But that was ages ago, and he has been quite distinguished in the Turkish army."

"Yes; and I also know that English gentlemen have associated with him as little as possible. I should call it a fatal thing to let Maura marry him. What does Captain Henderson say?"

"Mr. White thinks that it is all jealousy. And really, Jenny, I do not in the least believe that he will make her unhappy. He is old enough to have quite outgrown all his wild ways, and he has quite gentlemanly manners and ways. Besides, Maura likes him, and is quite bent upon it."

Still there was a dissatisfied look on Jane's face, and Adeline went on answering it, with tears in her eyes. "My dear Jane, I know what you would say, and what Reginald and all the rest feel, that it is not what we should like! But, my dear, don't let the whole family rise up in arms! It would be of no use, only make it painful for me. Maura is quite bent upon it, and she has arrived at turning her uncle round her finger so much that I am sometimes hardly mistress of the house! Oh, I don't tell any one, not Lily nor any one, but it will really be a relief to me when she is gone, with her Greek coaxing ways. Her uncle is wrapped up in her, and so proud of her being a Duchess that he would condone anything. Indeed, I am always afraid of her putting it into his head to suppose that her disappointment about Ivinghoe was in any way owing to my family pride."

Jane was sorry for Adeline, and able to perceive how the wifely feelings, which she had taken on herself, by choosing a man of inferior breeding and nature clashed with her hereditary character and principles.

"You are absolutely relieved that the Beechcroft wedding takes all of us out of the way naturally and without offence," she said so kindly that Ada laid her head on her sisterly shoulder, and allowed herself to shed a few tears.

"Yes, yes," she said; "I am glad to have so good a reason to mention. Only I do hope Jasper will not object to Valetta's coming back to be bridesmaid. That would really be a blow and give offence, and it would make difficulties with others—even James Henderson, who swears by Jasper. I have often wished they would have done as I advised, and have had this wedding at Rocca Marina, out of the way of everybody! I sometimes think it will be the death of me. Do come home to help me through it."

She spoke so like the Ada of old that it went to Jane's heart.

She promised that she would return in time to give the very substantial assistance in which all believed, and the more sentimental support in which nobody believed, though her distaste arose tenfold after seeing the bridegroom, who looked like an old satyr, all the more because Maura was like a Greek nymph. Mrs. Henderson was much grieved, and had tried remonstrance with her sister, but found her quite impervious.

Glad were all the Merrifields to escape to the quiet atmosphere of Beechcroft, where the relations were able to congregate between the Court, the Vicarage, and the more-distant Rotherwood; and the wedding was an ideal one in ecclesiastical beauty, and the festivities of those who had known and loved Lady Merrifield as Miss Lily in early youth, grandmothers who had been her schoolchildren, and were pleased to hear that she was a grandmother herself, and hoped in a year or two to welcome her grandchildren.

Alethea and her little Somervilles she had seen *en route* to Canada, and Phyllis was to come in due time when Bernard Underwood could be spared from the bank in Colombo, and they would bring their little pair.

In the matter of bridesmaids Gillian certainly had the advantage, for she was amply provided with sisters and cousins, Dolores coming for a few days for the wedding; whereas the six whom Maura had provided for beforehand in Paris were only, as Miss Jane said, "scraped up" with difficulty from former schoolfellows. Lord Roger's nieces would not hear of being present. Paulina was unwillingly pressed into the service, as well as the more willing Vera; but Mysie Merrifield was not to be persuaded to give up her visit to Lady Phyllis, and Aunt Jane could only carry home Valetta, who held the whole as "capital fun," and liked the acquisition of the white silk and lace and cerise ribbons. Dolores had negotiated that No. 6 of the Vanderkist girls should spend a year with Miss Mohun for a final polish at the High School at Rock Quay, so as to be with her brother Adrian, who was completing his term at the preparatory school before his launch at Winchester.

Wilfred also returned, father and uncle having decided that he did not merit a game licence, nor to attack the partridges of Beechcroft, and the prospect of the gaieties of Cliffe House consoled him.

Adeline had to endure her husband's mortification at other disappointments. The Ducal family was wholly unrepresented. Even Emily, the connecting link, would not venture on the journey; and the clerical nephew was not sufficiently gratified by Lord Roger's intention to *se ranger* to undertake to officiate; and a Bishop, who had enjoyed the hospitality of Rocca Marina, proved to have other engagements. No clergyman could be imported except Maura's brother Alexis, who had been two years at work at Coalham under Mr. Richard Burnet, and had just been appointed by the newly-chosen Bishop of Onomootka, and both were to go out with him as chaplains. Inthe meantime, while the Bishop was preparing, by tours in England, Alexis undertook the duties of Mr. Flight's curate, rejoicing in the opportunity of seeing his elder sister, and the old friends with whom he had never been since his unlucky troubles with Gillian Merrifield, now no more.

The delight of receiving him compensated to Kalliope Henderson for much that was distressing to both in Maura's choice. The seven years that had passed had made him into a noble-looking man, with a handsome classical countenance, lighted up by earnestness and devotion, a fine voice and much musical skill, together with a bright attractive manner that, all unconsciously on his part, had turned the heads of half the young womanhood of Coalham, and soon had the same effect at Rock Quay.

Vera and Paulina were in a state of much excitement over their white silks, in which the three other sisters took great pleasure in arraying them, and Thekla only wished that Hubert could see them. She should send him out a photograph, buying it herself with her own money.

She was, of course, to see the wedding, in her Sunday white and broad pink sash, of the appropriateness of which she was satisfied when, at Beechcroft, they met Miss Mohun's young friend, Miss Vanderkist, in the same garb. She and her brother had been put under Magdalen's protection, as Miss Mohun was too much wanted at Cliffe House to look after them; but Sir Adrian, a big boy of twelve, wanted to go his own way, and only handed her over with "Hallo, Miss Prescott! you'll look after this pussy-cat of ours while Aunt Jane is dosing Aunt Ada with salts and sal volatile. She—I'll introduce you! Miss Prescott, Miss Felicia Vanderkist! She wants to be looked after, she is a little kitten that has never seen anything! I'm off to Martin's."

The stranger did look very shy. She was a slight creature, not yet seventeen, with an abundant mass of long golden silk hair tied loosely, and a very lovely face and complexion, so small that she was a miniature edition of Lady Ivinghoe.

Her name was Wilmet Felicia, but the latter half had been always used in the family, and there was something in the kitten grace that suited the arbitrary contractions well. In fact, Jane Mohun had been rather startled to find that she had the charge of such a little beauty, when she saw how people turned around at the station to look, certainly not at Valetta, who was a dark bright damsel of no special mark.

At church, however, every one was in much too anxious a state to gaze at the coming procession to have any eyes to spare for a childish girl in a quiet white frock. St. Andrew's had never seen such a crowded congregation, for it was a wedding after Mr. White's own heart, in which nobody dared to interfere, not even his wife, whatever her good taste might think. So the church was filled, and more than filled, by all who considered a wedding as legitimate gape seed, and themselves as not bound to fit behaviour in church. On such an occasion Magdalen, being a regular attendant, and connected with the bridesmaids, was marshalled by a churchwarden into a reserved seat; but there they were dismayed by the voices and the scrambling behind them, which, in the long waiting, the Vicar from the vestry vainly tried to subdue by severe looks; and Felicia, whose notions of wedding behaviour were moulded on Vale Lecton and Beechcroft, looked as if she thought she had got into the house of Duessa, amid all Pride's procession, as in the prints in the large-volumed "Faërie Queene."

And when, on the sounds of an arrival, the bridegroom stood forth, the resemblance to Sans Foy was only too striking, while the party swept up the church, the bride in the glories of cobweb veil, white satin, &c., becomingly drooping on her uncle's arm, while he beamed forth, expansive in figure and countenance, with delight. Little Jasper Henderson, anxious and patronising to his tiny brother Alexis, both in white pages' dresses picked out with cerise, did his best to support the endless glistening train.

The bridesmaids' costumes taxed the descriptive powers of the milliners in splendour and were scarcely eclipsed by the rich brocade and lace of Mrs. White, as she sailed in on Captain Henderson's arm; but her elaborate veil and feathery bonnet hardly concealed the weary tedium of her face, though to the shame, well nigh horror, of her sister, she was rouged. "I must, I must," she said; "he would be vexed if I looked pale."

It was true that "he" loved her heartily, and that he put all the world at her service; but she had learnt where he must not be offended, and was on her guard. Hers had been the last wedding that Jane had attended in St. Andrew's. "Did she repent?" was Jane's thought. No, probably not. She had the outward luxuries she had craved for, and her husband was essentially a good man, though not of the caste to which her instincts belonged—very superior in nature and conscience to him to whom his blinded vanity was now giving his beautiful niece, a willing sacrifice.

It was over! More indecorous whispering and thronging; and the procession came down the aisle, to be greeted outside by a hail of confetti and rice; the schoolboys, profiting by the dinner interval, and headed by Adrian, had jostled themselves into the foreground, and they ran headlong to the portico of Cliffe House to renew the shower.

And there, unluckily, Mr. White recognised the boy, and, pleased to have anything with a title to show, turned him round to the bridegroom, with, "Here, Lord Roger, let me introduce a guest, Sir Adrian Vanderkist."

"Ha, I didn't know poor Van had left a son. I knew your father, my boy. Where was it I saw him last? Poor old chap!"

"You must come in to taste the cake, my boy," began Mr. White.

"Thank you, Mr. White, I must get back to Edgar's. Late already. The others are off."

"Not a holiday! For shame! He'll excuse you. I'll send a note down to say you must stay to drink the health of your father's old friend."

Those words settled the matter with Adrian. The holiday was enticing, and might have overpowered the chances of a scholarship, for which he was working; but he had begun to know that there were perplexities from which it was safer to retreat; and that he had never transgressed his Uncle Clement's warning might be read in the clear open face that showed already the benefits, not only of discipline, but of self-control. So obedience answered the question; though, as he again thanked and refused, he looked so dogged as he turned and walked off, that Ethel Varney whispered to Vera that at school he was called, "the Dutchman, if not the Boer."

Nor did he ever mention the temptation or his own resistance. Only Mr. White asked Miss Mohun to bring him to the dance which was to be given in the evening, telling her of his refusal of the invitation to wedding cake and champagne and she—mindful of her duty to her charge as hinted by Clement Underwood—had not granted the honour of his presence on the score of his school obligations.

The afternoon was spent in desultory wanderings about the gardens, Magdalen and her sisters being invited guests, and Vera in a continual state of agitated expectation. Had not Wilfred Merrifield always been a cavalier of her own? And here he was, paying no attention to her, with all the embellishment of her bridesmaid's adornments, and squiring instead that little insignificant Felicia, in a simple hat, and hair still on her shoulders; whilst she had to put up with nothing better than a young Varney, who was very shy, and had never probably mastered croquet.

She was an ill-used mortal; and why had she not Hubert to show how superior she was to them all, in having a piece of property of her own to show off?

There was Paula, too, playing animated tennis with that clerical brother of the bride, who had been talking to Magdalen about the frescoes of St. Kenelm's (as if she, Vera, had not the greatest right to know all about those frescoes!). Even little Thekla was better off, for she was reigning over a merry party of the little ones, which had been got up for the benefit of the small Hendersons, and of which Theodore White had constituted himself the leader, being a young man passionately devoted to little children.

So when the guests dispersed to eat their dinner at their homes and dress for the dance, Vera was extremely cross. Each of the other three had some delightful experiences to talk over; but whether it was Mr. Theodore's fun in acting ogre behind the great aloe, or Mr. Alexis's achievements with the croquet ball, or his information about the Red Indians and Onomootka, she was equally ungracious to all; she scolded Thekla for crumpling her skirt, and was quite sure that Paula had on the wrong *fichu* that was meant for her. Each bridesmaid had been presented with a bracelet, like a snake with ruby eyes; but Vera, fingering hers with fidgeting petulance, seemed to have managed to loosen the clasp, and when arranging her dress for the evening thought that her snake had escaped.

Upstairs and downstairs she rushed in hopes of finding it. The cab in which they had returned was gone home to come again, and there was the chance that it might be there or in the Cliffe House gardens; and then the others tried to console her, but they were not able to hinder a violent burst of crying, which scandalised Thekla.

"I am sure you couldn't cry more if you had lost Hubert's, and that would be something worth crying about."

Hubert's was an ingeniously worked circle of scales of Californian gold, the first ornament that Vera had ever possessed, and that all the sisters had set great store by. But with an outcry of joy Vera exclaimed, "Here's the snake all safe! I pushed the other up my arm because it looked so plain and dull, and it was that which came off."

"That is a great deal worse than losing the snake," said Thekla. "He has a nasty face, and I don't like him, with his red eyes."

"Don't be silly," returned Vera; "this is a great deal more valuable."

"Surely the value is in the giver," said Paula; to which Vera returned in the same vein, "Don't be silly and sentimental, Polly."

She was so much cheered by the recovery of the snake that they brought her off to the evening dance without a fresh fit of ill-humour, and she sprang out under the portico of Cliffe House, with her spirits raised to expectation pitch.

But disappointment was in store for her. It was not disappointment in other eyes. Paula had all the attention she expected or desired, she danced almost every time and did not reckon greatly on who might be her partner. What pleased and honoured her most was being asked to dance by Captain Henderson himself.

What was it to Vera, however, that partners came to her, young men of Rock Quay whom she knew already and did not care about? And she never once had the pleasure of saying that she was keeping the next dance for Wilfred Merrifield! To her perceptions, he was always figuring away with Felicia Vanderkist, her golden hair seemed always gleaming with him; and though this was not always the case, as the nephew of the house was one of those who had duties to guests and was not allowed by his aunts to be remiss, yet whenever he was not ordered about by them, he was sure to be found by Felicia's side.

Vera's one consolation was that Alexis White took her to supper. To be sure he was a clergyman, and had stood talking to Lady Flight half the time, and his conversation turned at once to Hubert Delrio's frescoes; but then he was very handsome, and graceful in manner, and he sympathised with her on the loss of her bracelet, and promised to have a search for it by daylight in the gardens.

CHAPTER XX—FLEETING

"And variable as the shade
By the light quivering aspen made."

—Scott.

The bracelet came to light in the gardens of Cliffe House the next morning, and Alexis White walked over to the Goyle to return it safely, little guessing, when he set forth to enjoy the sight of the purple moors, and to renew old recollections, what a flutter of gratified vanity would be excited in one silly little breast, though he only stayed ten minutes, and casually asked whether the sisters were coming to Lady Flight's garden party. Everybody was going there. Miss Mohun even took Felicia, as it was on a Saturday's holiday; and, unwittingly, she renewed all the agitation caused by Wilfred's admiration, and that of others, to the all-unconscious girl. Vera could no longer think herself the reigning belle of Rock Quay, though she talked of Felicia as a schoolgirl or a baby, or a horrid little forward chit! Her excitement was, however, divided between Wilfred and Mr. Alexis White, who could not look in her direction without putting her in a state of eagerness.

In this, however, she was not alone. Half the ladies were interested about him; his manners were charming, his voice in church beautiful, and his destination as chaplain to a missionary bishop made him doubly interesting; while he himself, even though his mind was set on higher things, was really enjoying his brief holiday, and his sister, Mrs. Henderson, was delighted to promote his pleasure, and garden parties and the like flourished as long as weather permitted; and as Vera was a champion player, she was sure to be asked to the tournaments, and to have to practise for them.

Inopportunely there arrived a letter from Hubert, requiring an answer about the form of ornament in the moulding of the fourteenth century! Paula dutifully went to the library, looked out and traced two or three examples, French and English. Nothing remained but for Vera to write the letter after the early dinner. However, she went to sleep in a hammock, and only roused herself to recollect that there was to be tea and lawn tennis at Carrara.

"Won't you just write to Hubert first?"

"Oh, bother, how can I now? Don't worry so!" "But,

Flapsy, he really needs it without loss of time."

"I'm sure he has no right to make me his clerk in that horrid peremptory way, as if one had nothing else to do but wait on his fads."

"Flapsy, how can you?" broke out even Thekla.

"Surely it is the greatest honour," said Paula.

"Well, do it yourself then, I'm not going to be bothered for ever."

Thekla went off, in great indignation, to beg "sister" to speak to Flapsy, and beg her not to use dear Hubert so very very badly, which of course Magdalen refused to do, and Thekla had her first lesson on the futility of interfering with engaged folk; Paula meanwhile sent off the despatch, with one line to say that Vera was too busy to write that day.

There had been two or three letters from Hubert, over which Vera had looked cross, but had said nothing; and at last she came down from her own room, and announced passionately, "There! I have done with Mr. Hubert Delrio, and have written to tell him so!"

"Vera, what have you done?"

"Written to tell him I have no notion of a man being so tiresome and dictatorial! I don't want a schoolmaster to lecture me, and expect me to drudge over his work as if I was his clerk."

"My dear," said Magdalen, "have you had a letter that vexed you? Had you not better wait a little to think it over?"

"No! Nonsense, Maidie! He has been provoking ever so long, and I won't bear it any longer!" and she flounced into a chair.

"Provoking! Hubert!" was all Paulina could utter, in her amazement and horror.

"Oh, I daresay you would like it well enough! Always at me to slave for him with stupid architectural drawings and stuff, as if I was only a sort of clerk or fag! And boring me to read great dull books, and preaching to me about them, expecting to know what I think! Dear me!"

"Those nice letters!" sighed Paula.

"Nice! As if any one that was one bit in love would write such as that! No, I don't want to marry a schoolmaster or a tyrant!"

"How can you, Flapsy?" went on Paula, so vehemently that Magdalen left the defence thus far to her; "when he only wishes for your sympathy and improvement."

The worst plea she could have used, thought the elder sister, as Vera broke out with, “Improvement, indeed! If he cared for me, he would not think I wanted any *improving*! But he never did! Or he would have taken Pratt and Povis’ offer, and I should have been living in London and keeping my carriage! Or he would have taken me to Italy! But that horrid home of his, and his mother just like a half-starved hare! I might have seen then it was not fit for me; but I was a child, and over-persuaded among you all! But I know better now, and I know my own mind, as I didn’t then. So you need not talk! I have done with him.”

“Oh, Flapsy, Flapsy, how can you grieve him so? You don’t know what you are throwing away!” incoherently cried Paula, collapsing in a burst of tears. “Maidie, Maidie, why don’t you speak to her, and tell her how wicked it is—and—and—and—”

The rest was cut short by sobs.

“No, Paula, authority or reasoning of mine would not touch such a mood as this. We must leave it to Hubert himself. If she really cares for him, she will have recovered from her fit of temper by the time his letter can come, and it may have an effect upon her, if our tongues have not increased her spirit of opposition. I strongly advise you to say nothing.”

Paula tried to take her sister’s advice, and would have adhered to it, but that Vera would talk and try to make her declare the rupture to have been justified; and this produced an amount of wrangling which did good to no one. Magdalen really rejoiced when the frequent golf and tennis parties carried Vera on her bicycle out of reach of arguing, even if it took her into the alternative of flirtation.

Thekla cried bitterly, and declared that she should never speak to Flapsy again; but in half an hour’s time was heard chattering about the hedgehog’s meal of cockroaches. In another week the excitement was over. The Bishop of Onomootka had come and gone, after holding meetings and preaching sermons at Rock Quay and all the villages round, and had carried off Alexis White with him.

Nothing had come of the intercourse of the latter with his rich uncle, nor of the varieties of encounters with the damsels of Rock Quay, except that society was declared by more than one to have become horridly flat and slow.

Vera was one of these, and the letters received from Hubert Delrio did not stir up a fresh excitement. There were no persuasions to revoke her decision, no urgent entreaties, no declaration of being heart-broken. He acquiesced in her assurance that the engagement had been a mistake; and he wrote at more length to Magdalen, avowing that he had for some time past traced discontent in Vera’s letters, and fearing that he had been too didactic and peremptory in writing to her. He relinquished the engagement with much regret, and should always regard it as having been a fair summer dream—but, though undeserving, he hoped still to retain Miss Prescott's kindness and friendship, which had been of untold value to him.

A little more zeal and distress would have been much more pleasing to Vera; and she began to be what Agatha and Thekla called cross, and Paula called drooping, and even excited alarm in her, lest Flapsy should be going into a decline. But a note came to the Goyle which Magdalen read alone, and likewise she cycled alone to Rockstone.

"Miss Mohun, can you give me a few minutes?" said she, as the trim little figure emerged from beneath the copper beeches, basket in hand.

"By all means; I shall not be due at the cutting-out meeting till three o'clock."

"I wanted to consult you about an invitation that Mrs. White has been so very kind as to give my little sister, Vera."

"Oh!" quoth Jane Mohun, in a dry sort of tone.

"I know that she had wished to take out one of her own nieces to Rocca Marina, but that Sir Jasper did not wish it, and I thought perhaps it would be easier for you than for Lady Merrifield to tell me whether there is any objection that would apply to Vera."

"I suppose Vera wishes to go?"

"She is so wild with delight that it would be a serious thing to disappoint her. Mrs. White is very kind and good, and has thought that she has flagged of late, and has supposed it might be due to poor Hubert Delrio, but, indeed, it was no fault of his."

"None at all, except for out-growing her."

"The offer was hinted at to go with Valetta even before we knew it was declined at Clipstone, and that made me anxious to know whether it would be well for me to send Vera. I suppose she would pick up pronunciation of languages, which would be a great advantage, as she will have to earn her own living, and Mrs. White is so good as to promise lessons in arts and music. I hear, too, it is quite an English colony, with a church and schools."

"Oh, yes, Mr. White is a very good and careful man about his workmen. I have been there at the Henderson's wedding, and it is a charming place, a castle fit for Mrs. Radclyffe, with English comforts, and an Italian garden and an English village on the mountain side. My sister would do all that she promises, and would look after any young girl very well; you may quite trust her."

“Then is there any fear of Italian society?—not that poor Vera has any attraction *of that kind*,” hesitated Magdalen.

“None at all. All the society they have is of English travellers coming with introductions. I fancy it is very dull at times, and that Adeline wants a young person about her. You need have no fears. Ah! I see you still want to know why the Merrifields don’t consent. It is not their way. They would not let the Rotherwoods have Mysie to bring up with Phyllis, and—and Val is just the being that needs a mother’s eye over her. But I really and honestly think that your Vera may quite safely be put under Adeline’s care, and that she is likely to be all the better for it.”

“One thing more,” added Magdalen, with a little hesitation; “is your nephew, Wilfred, likely to be one of the party?”

“None at all. His father wants to keep him under his own eye, and his mother is anxious about his health; nor do I think Mr. White wants him, having his own two nephews, who are useful, so he will remain under Captain Henderson here.”

“Thank you! That settles it in my mind. I am sure the change to a fresh home will be an excellent thing for my poor Vera, and that the training of imitation of one to whom she looks up is what she most needs.”

“Very true,” said Miss Mohun.

And as she afterwards said to Lady Merrifield, “It was in all sincerity and honesty that I gave the advice to Magdalen, who is very sensible in the matter. In plain English, Ada can’t do without a lady in waiting, and Vera probably fancies that Lords, young or old, start from every wave like the spirits of our fathers, at Rocca Marina, in which she will probably be disappointed; but Ada will be a very dragon as to her manners and discretion, and not being his own niece, old Tom White will not be deluded by his ambition and any blandishments of hers. As people go, they are very safe guardians, and Vera—Flapsy as they call her—is just of the composition to be improved, and not disimproved, by living with Ada.”

“Probably, though I do not like the foolish little puss to be rewarded for throwing over young Delrio.”

“He was so much too good for her that I am more inclined to reward her for doing so!”

Agatha, however, came home somewhat annoyed by the whole arrangement. She supposed the rupture with Hubert might have been inevitable; but she was very sorry for it, thinking that Vera might have grown up to him, and regretting the losing him as a brother. Nor did she like the atmosphere of the

Whites and Rocca Marina for her feather-brained young sister. "Dolores had no great opinion of her Aunt Adeline," she said.

"My dear," said Magdalen, as they sat over their early fire, "I have talked it over with Lady Merrifield and Miss Mohun, and they both tell me that Mrs. White is very sensible, and sure to be discreet for any girl in her charge—probably better for Flapsy than a more intellectual woman."

"But—! Such a marriage as this one!" said Agatha.

"It was Mr. White's own niece, and taken out of Mrs. White's hands," said Magdalen. "Besides," as Agatha still looked unconvinced, "one thing that made me think the invitation desirable was that it would break off any foolishness with Wilfred Merrifield—I think it was in their minds too."

"Wilfred! Oh, there was a little nonsense."

"Less on his side, since Felicia Vanderkist has been here; but I think Vera has been all the more disposed to—to—"

"Run after him," said Agatha. "I could fancy it in Flapsy; but he is such a boy, and not half so nice-looking as the rest of them either."

"My dear Agatha, I must tell you he reminds me strangely of a young Mr. Merrifield whom I knew at Filsted when I was younger than you."

"A brother of Bessie?"

"Even so. He got into some kind of trouble at Filsted, his father came and broke it off, and sent him out to Canada, where I fear he did not do well, and nothing has been heard of him since, except—"

She spoke with a catch in her voice which made Agatha look up at her, and detect a rising colour.

"Nothing!" she repeated.

"Except an anonymous parcel, returning to the brothers in Canada the sum he had taken with him. Strangely, the clue was not followed up, and he is lost sight of! But Wilfred's air, and still more his manner, is always recalling his cousin to me, and, Nag, dear, I could not bear to see Vera go through the same trial by my exposing her to the intercourse. Not that I know any harm of Wilfred, but his parents could not like anything of the kind."

"Certainly not! Yes, I suppose you are right, dear old Maidie." But Agatha pondered over those words that had slipped out, "the same trial."

CHAPTER XXI—THE ELECTRICIANS

"Thou shalt have the air
Of freedom. Follow and do me service."

—"THE TEMPEST."

"Is Agatha in?" asked Dolores Mohun, jumping off her bicycle as she saw Magdalen, on a frosty day the next Christmas vacation, in her garden.

"She is doing scientific arithmetic with Thekla; giving me a holiday, in fact! You University maidens quite take the shine out of us poor old teachers."

"Ah! if we can give shine we can't give substance. But I want to borrow Nag, if you have no objection."

"Borrow her! I am sure it is something she will like."

"It is in the way of business, but she will like it all the same. They want me to give a course of lectures on electricity at Bexley to the Institute and the two High Schools, and I particularly want a skilled assistant, whom I can depend upon; not masters, nor boys! Now Nag is just what I should like. We should stay at Lancelot Underwood's, a very charming place to be at."

"Isn't he some connection?"

"Connection all round. Phyllis Merrifield married his brother, banking in Ceylon, and may come home any day on a visit; and Ivinghoe's pretty wife is Lancelot's niece. He edits what is really the crack newspaper of the county, in spite of its being true blue Conservative, Church and all."

"The *Pursuivant*? It has such good literary articles."

"Oh, yes! Mrs. Grinstead and Canon Harewood write them. His wife is a daughter of old Dr. May—rather a peculiar person, but very jolly in her way."

"But would they like to have Agatha imposed upon them?"

"Certainly; they are just the people to like nothing better, and it will only be for a fortnight. I have settled it all with them."

At which Magdalen looked a little doubtful, but Dolores reiterated that there need be no scruple, she might ask Aunt Lily if she liked; but Lance Underwood was Mayor, and member of all the committees, and the most open-hearted man in the world besides, and it was all right.

To the further demur as to safety, Dolores answered that to light a candle or sit by the fire might be dangerous, but as long as people were careful, it was all right, and Agatha had already assisted in some experiments at Rock Quay, which had shown her to be thoroughly understanding and trustworthy, and capable of keeping off the amateur—the great bugbear.

So Magdalen consented, after rapturous desires on the part of Agatha, and assurances from General Mohun that Dolores had it in her by inheritance and by training to meddle with the lightning as safely as human being might; and Lady Merrifield owned with a sigh that she must accept as a fact that what even the heathens owned as a Divine mystery and awful attribute, had come to be treated as a commonplace business messenger and scientific toy, though (as Mrs. Gatty puts it) the mystery had only gone deeper. So much for the peril; and for the other scruple, it was set at rest by a hospitable letter from Mrs. Underwood, heartily inviting Miss Agatha Prescott, as an Oxford friend of Gillian.

So off the two electricians set, and after two days of business and sight-seeing in London, went down to Bexley. In the third-class carriage in which they travelled they were struck by the sight of a tall lady in mourning—a sort of compromise between a conventual and a secular bonnet over short fair hair, and holding on her lap a tiny little girl of about six years old, with a small, pinched, delicate face and slightly red hair, to whom she pointed out by name each spot they passed, herself wearing an earnest absorbed look of recognition as she pointed out familiar landmark after landmark till the darkness came down. Also there were two cages—one with a small pink cockatoo, and another with two budgerigars.

As the train began slackening Dolores exclaimed:

"There he is! Lance—!"

"Lance! Oh, Lance!" was echoed; and setting the child down, her companion almost fell across Agatha, and was at the window as the train stopped.

What happened in the next moment no one could quite tell; but as the door was torn open there was a mingled cry of "Angel!" and of "Lance!" and the traveller was in his arms, turning the next moment to lift out the frightened little girl, who clung tight round her neck; while Lance held out his hand with, "Dolores! Yes. This is Dolores, Angel, whom you have never seen."

Each knew who the other was in a moment, and clasped hands in greeting, as well as they could with the one, and the other receiving bird-cages, handbags, umbrellas, and rugs from Agatha, whom, however, Lance relieved of them with a courteous, "Miss Prescott! You have come in for the arrival of my Australian sister! What luggage have you?" Wherewith all was absorbed in the recognition of boxes, and therewith a word or two to an old railway official, "My sister Angela."

"Miss Angela! this is an unexpected pleasure!"

"Tom Lightfoot! is it you? You are not much altered. Mr. Dane, I should have known you anywhere!" with corresponding shakes of the hand.

"Yes, that's ours. Oh, the birds! There they are! All right! Oh! not the omnibus, Lance! Let the traps go in that! Then Lena will like to stretch her legs, and I must revel in the old street."

Dolores and Agatha felt it advisable to squeeze themselves with the bird-cages into the omnibus, and leave the brother and sister to walk down together, though the little girl still adhered closely to her protector's hand.

"Poor Field's little one? Yes, of course."

"But tell me! tell me of them all!"

"All well! all right! But how—"

"The *Mozambique* was out of coal and had to put in at Falmouth. You know, I came by her because they said the long sea voyage would be best for this child, and it was so long since I had heard of any one that I durst not send anywhere till I knew—and I knew Froggatt's would be in its own place. Oh! there's the new hotel! the gas looks just the same! There's the tower of St. Oswald's, all shadowy against the sky. Look, Lena! Oh! this is home! I know the lamps. I've dreamt of them! Tired, Lena, dear? cold? Shall I carry you?"

"No, no; let me!" and he lifted her up, not unwillingly on her part, though she did not speak. "You are a light weight," he said.

"I am afraid so," answered Angel. "Oh! there's the bus stopping at Mr. Pratt's door."

"Mine, now. We have annexed it."

"But let me go in by the dear old shop. The window is as of old, I see. Ernest Lamb! don't you know me?" as a respectable tradesman came forward. "And Achille, is it? You are as much changed as this old shop is transmogrified! And they are all well? Do you mean Bernard?"

"Bernard and Phyllis may come home any day to deposit a child. They lost their boy, and hope to save the elder one. But come, Angel! if you have taken in enough we must go up to those electrical girls. Dolores is come to give a lecture, with the other girl to assist, Miss Prescott."

"Dolores! Yes, poor Gerald's love! They are almost myths to me. Ah!" as

Lancelot opened his office-door, “now I know where I am! And there’s the old staircase! This is the real thing, and no mistake.”

“Angel, Angel, come to tea!” And Gertrude, comfortable and substantial, in loving greeting threw arms round the new comers, Lance still carrying the child, who clung round his neck as he brought her into the room, full of his late fellow travellers, and also of a group of children.

“It is as if we had gone back thirty years or more,” was Angela’s cry, as she looked forth on what had been as little altered as possible from the old family centre; and Lance, setting down the child, spoke as the pretty little blue-eyed girls advanced to exchange kisses with their new aunt.

“Margaret, or Pearl, whom you knew as a baby; Etheldred, or Awdrey, and Dickie! Fely is at Marlborough. There, take little Lena—is that her name—to your table, and give her some tea.”

“Her name is Magdalen,” said Angela, removing the little black hat and smoothing the hair; but Lena backed against her, and let her hand hang limp in Pearl’s patronising clasp. Nor would she amalgamate with the children, nor even eat or drink except still beside “Sister,” as she called Angela. In fact, she was so thoroughly worn out and tired, as well as shy and frightened, that Angela’s attention was wholly given to her and she could only be put to bed, but not in the nursery, which, as Angel said, seemed to her like a den of little wild beasts. So she was deposited in the chamber and bed hastily prepared for the unexpected guest; and even there, being wakeful and feverish from over-fatigue, there was no leaving her alone, and Gertrude, after seeing her safely installed, could only go down with the hope that she would be able to spare her slave or nurse, which was it? by dinner-time.

“Who is that child so like?” said Dolores, in their own room.

“Very like somebody, but I can’t tell whom,” said Agatha. “Who did you say she is?”

“I cannot say I exactly know,” said Dolores. “I believe she is the daughter of Fulbert Underwood’s mate, on a sheep-farm in Queensland, and that as her mother died when she was born, she has been always under the care of this Angela, living in the Sisterhood there.”

“Not a Sister?”

“Not under vows, certainly. I never saw her before, but I believe she is rather a funny flighty person, and that Fulbert was afraid at one time that she would marry this child’s father.”

“Is he alive?”

"Which? Fulbert died four or five years ago, and I think the little girl's father must be dead, for she is in mourning."

"There's something very charming about her—Miss Underwood."

"Yes there is. They all seem to be very fond of her, and yet to laugh about her, and never to be quite sure what she will do next."

"Did I not hear of her being so useful among the Australian black women?"

"No one has ever managed those very queer gins so well; and she is an admirable nurse too, they say. I am very glad to have come in her way."

They did not, however, see much of her that evening. The head master of the Grammar School and his wife, the head mistress of the High School, and a few others had been invited to meet them; and Angela could only just appear at dinner, trusting to a slumber of her charge, but, on coming out of the dining-room, a wail summoned her upstairs at once, and she was seen no more that night.

However, with morning freshness, Lena showed herself much less *farouche*, and willing to accept the attentions of Mr. Underwood first, and, later, of his little daughter Pearl—a gentle, elder sisterly person, who knew how to avert the too rough advances of Dick—and made warm friends over the pink cockatoo; while Awdrey was entranced by the beauties of the budgerigars.

Robina had been informed by telegram, and came up from Minsterham with her husband, looking just like his own father, and grown very broad. He was greatly interested in the lecture, and went off to it, to consider whether it would be desirable for the Choristers' School. Lancelot had, of course, to go, and Angela declared that she must be brought up to date, and rejoiced that Lena was able to submit to be left with the other children under the protection of Mrs. Underwood, who averred that she abhorred electricity in all its forms, and that if Lance were induced to light the town, or even the shop by that means, he must begin by disposing of her by a shock.

It was an excellent lecture, only the two sisters hardly heard it. They could think of nothing but that they were once more sitting side by side in the old hall, where they had heard and shared in so many concerts, on the gala days of their home life.

The two lecturers, as well as the rest of the party, were urgently entreated to stay to tea at the High School; but when the interest of the new arrival was explained, the sisters and brother were released to go home, Canon Harewood remaining to content their hostesses.

CHAPTER XXII—ANGEL AND BEAR

"Enough of science and of art!
  Close up those barren leaves,
Come forth, and bring with you a heart
  That watches and receives."

—WORDSWORTH.

A TELEGRAM had been handed to Mr. Mayor, which he kept to himself, smiling over it, and he—at least—was not taken utterly by surprise at the sight of a tall handsome man, who stepped forward with something like a shout.

"Angel! Lance! Why, is it Robin, too?"

"Bear, Bear, old Bear, how did you come?"

"I couldn't stop when I heard at Clipstone that Angel was here, so I left Phyllis and the kid with her mother. Oh, Angel, Angel, to meet at Bexley after all!"

They clung together almost as they had done when they were the riotous elements of the household, while Lance opened the front door, and Robina, mindful of appearances, impelled them into the hall, Bernard exclaiming, "Pratt's room! Whose teeth is it?"

"Don't you want Wilmet to hold your hands and make you open your mouth?" said Lance, laughing.

Gertrude, who had already received the Indian arrival, met Angela, who was bounding up to see to her charge, with, "Not come in yet! She is gone out with the children quite happily, with Awdrey's doll in her arms. Come and enjoy each other in peace."

"In the office, please," said Angela. "That is home. We shall be our four old selves."

Lance opened the office door, and gave a hint to Mr. Lamb, while they looked at each other by the fire.

Bernard was by far the most altered. The others were slightly changed, but still their "old selves," while he was a grave responsible man, looking older than Lancelot, partly from the effects of climate; but Angela saw enough to make her exclaim, "Here we are! Don't you feel as if we were had down to

Felix to be blown up?"

"Not a bit altered," said Bernard, looking at the desks and shelves of ledgers, with the photographs over the mantelpiece—Felix, Mr. Froggatt, the old foreman, and a print of Garofalo's Vision of St. Augustine, hung up long ago by Felix, as Lance explained, as a token of the faith to which all human science and learning should be subordinated.

"A declaration of the *Pursuivant*," said Angela. "How Fulbert did look out for *Pur*! I believe it was his only literature."

"Phyllis declares," said Bernard, "that nothing so upsets me as a failure in *Pur's* arrival."

"And this is *Pur's* heart and centre!" said Robina.

"Only," added Angela, "I miss the smell of burnt clay that used to pervade the place, and that Alda so hated."

"Happily the clay is used up," said Lance. "I could not have brought Gertrude and the children here if the ceramic art, as they call it, had not departed. Cherry was so delighted at our coming to live here. She loved the old struggling days."

"Fulbert said he never felt as if he had been at home till he came here. He never *took* to Vale Leston."

"Clement and Cherry have settled in very happily," said Robina, "with convalescent clergy in the Vicarage."

"I say, Angel, let us have a run over there," cried Bernard, "you and I together, for a bit of mischief."

"Do, *do* let us! Though this is real home, our first waking to perception and naughtiness, it is more than Vale Leston. We seem to have been up in a balloon all those five happy years."

"A balloon?" said Bernard. "Nay, it seems to me that till they were over, I never thought at all except how to get the most rollicking and the finest rowing out of life. It seems to me that I had about as much sense as a green monkey."

"Something sank in, though," said Lance; "you did not drift off like poor Edgar."

"Some one must have done so," said Angela. "I wanted to ask you, Lancey, about advertising for my little Lena's people; the Bishop said I ought."

"I say," exclaimed Bernard, "was it her father that was Fulbert's mate? I thought he was afraid of your taking up with him. You didn't?"

"No, no. Let me tell you, I want you to know. Field and a little wife came over from Melbourne prospecting for a place to sit down in. They had capital, but the poor wife was worn out and ill, and after taking them in for a night, Fulbert liked them. Field was an educated man and a gentleman, and Ful offered them to stay there in partnership. So they stayed, and by and by this child was born, and the poor mother died. The two great bearded men came galloping over to Albertstown from Carrigaboola, with this new born baby, smaller than even Theodore was, and I had the care of her from the very first, and Field used to ride over and see the little thing."

"And—?" said Bernard, in a rather teasing voice, as his eyes actually looked at Angela's left hand.

"I'll own it *did* tempt me. I had had some great disappointments with my native women, running wild again, and I could not bear my child having a horrid stepmother; and there was the glorious free bush life, and the horses and the sheep! But then I thought of you all saying Angel had broken out again; and by and by Fulbert came and told me that he was sure there was some ugly mystery, and spoke to Mother Constance, and they made me promise not to take him unless it was cleared up. Then, as you know, dear Ful's horse fell with him; Field came and fetched me to their hut, and I was there to the last. Ful told each of us again that all must be plain and explained before we thought of anything in the future. He, Henry Field, said he had great hopes that he should be able to set it right. Then, as you know, there was no saving dear Fulbert, and after that Mother Constance's illness began. Oh! Bear, do you recollect her coming in and mothering us in the little sitting-room? I could not stir from her, of course, while she was with us. And after that, Harry Field came and said he had written a letter to England, and when the answer came, he would tell me all, and I should judge! But I don't think the answer ever did come, and he went to Brisbane to see if it was at the bank; and there he caught a delirious fever, and there was an end of it!"

At that moment something between a whine or a call of "sister" was heard. Up leapt Angela and hurried away, while Lance observed, "Well! That's averted, but I am sorry for her."

"It was not love," said Robina.

"Or only for the child," said Bernard; "and that would have been a dangerous speculation."

"The child or something else has been very good for her," said Lance; "I never saw her so gentle and quiet."

"And with the same charm about her as ever," said Bernard. "I don't wonder that all the fellows fall in love with her. I hope she won't make havoc among

Clement's sick clergy."

"I suppose we ought to go up and fulfil the duties of society," said Robina, rising. "But first, Bear, tell me how is Phyllis?"

"Pretty fair," he answered. "Resting with her mother, but she has never been quite the thing of late. I almost hope Sir Ferdinand will see his way to keeping us at home, or we shall have to leave our little Lily."

Interruption occurred as a necessary summons to "Mr. Mayor," and the paternal conclave was broken up, and had to adjourn to Gertrude's tea in the old sitting-room.

"I see!" exclaimed Agatha, as she looked at the party of children at their supplementary table. "I see what the likeness is in that child. Don't you, Dolores? Is it not to Wilfred Merrifield?"

"There is very apt to be a likeness between sandy people, begging your pardon, Angel," said Gertrude.

"Yes, the carroty strain is apt to crop up in families," said Lance, "like golden tabbies, as you ladies call your stable cats."

"All the Mohuns are dark," said Dolores, "and all Aunt Lily's children, except Wilfred; and is not your Phyllis of that colour?"

"Phyllis's hair is not red, but dark auburn," said Bernard, in a tone like offence.

"I never saw Phyllis," said dark-browed Dolores, "but I have heard the aunts talk over the source of the—the fair variety, and trace it to the Merrifields. Uncle Jasper is brown, and so is Bessie; but Susan is, to put it politely, just a golden tabby, and David's baby promises to be, to her great delight, as she says he will be a real Merrifield. So much for family feeling!"

"Sister, Sister!" came in a bright tone, "may I go with Pearl and get a stick for Ben? He wants something to play with! He is eating his perch."

Ben, it appeared, was the pink cockatoo, who was biting his perch with his hooked beak. The children had finished their meal, and consent was given. "Only, Lena, come here," said Angela, fastening a silk handkerchief round her neck, and adding, "Don't let Lena go on the dew, Pearl; she is not used to early English autumn, I must get her a pair of thicker boots."

"What is her name?" asked Agatha, catching the sound.

"Magdalen Susanna. Her father made a point of it, instead of his wife's name, which, I think, was Caroline."

"I don't think I ever knew a Magdalen except my own elder sister," said

Agatha, “and Susanna! Did you say Miss Merrifield had a sister Susan?”

“An excellent, sober-sided, dear old Susan! Yes, Susanna was their mother’s name,” said Dolores “and now that you have put it into my head, little Lena, when she is animated, puts me more in mind of Bessie than even of Wilfred, though the colouring is different. Why?”

“Did you never hear,” said Agatha, “that there was one of the brothers who was a bad lot, and ran away. My sister says Wilfred is like him. I believe,” she added, “that he was her romance!”

“Ha!” exclaimed Bernard, “that’s queer! We had a clerk in the bank who gave his name as Meriton, and who cut and ran the very day he heard that Sir Jasper Merrifield was coming out as Commandant. Yes, he was carroty. I rarely saw Wilfred at Clipstone, but this might very well have been the fellow, afraid to face his uncle.”

Angela did not look delighted. “She is not destitute, you know,” she said, “I am her guardian, and she will have about two hundred a year.”

“Is there a will?” asked Lance.

“Oh, yes, I have it upstairs! It is all right. It was at the bank at Brisbane, and they kept a copy. I brought her because the Bishop said it was my duty to find out whether there were any relations.”

“Certainly,” said Bernard. “In our own case, remember what joy Travis’s letter was!”

Angela was silent, and presently said, “You shall see the will when I have unpacked it, but there is no doubt about my being guardian.”

“Probably not,” said Bernard, rather drily.

“If it be a valid will, signed by his proper name,” said Lance.

Whereupon the two brothers fell into a discussion on points of law, not unlike the editor of the *Pursuivant*, as he had become known to his family, but most unlike the Bernard they had known before his departure for the East. At any rate it dissipated the emotional tone of the party; and by and by, when Bernard and Angela had agreed to make a bicycle rush to Minsterham the next day, “that is,” said Angela “if Lena is happy enough to spare me,” the Harewoods took leave.

When the children had gone to bed, and Angela had stayed upstairs so long that Gertrude augured that she was waiting till her charge had gone to sleep, and that they should have no more of her henceforth but “Lena’s baulked stepmother,” she came down, bringing a document with her, which she displayed before her brothers.

There was no question but that it was a will drawn up in due form, and very short, bequeathing his property at Carrigaboola, Queensland, to his daughter, Magdalen Susanna, and appointing Fulbert Underwood and Angela Margaret Underwood and "my brother Samuel" her guardian. It was dated the year after his daughter's birth, and was signed Henry Field, with a word interposed, which, as Lance said, might be anything, but was certainly the right length for the first syllables of Merrifield. Bernard looked at it, and declared it was, to the best of his belief, the same signature as his former clerk used to write.

"And this," he said, looking at the seal, "is the crest of the Merrifield's—the demi lion. I know it well on Sir Jasper's seal ring."

"Have you nothing else, Angel?" asked Lance.

"Here is the certificate of her baptism, but that will tell you nothing."

No more it did, it only called the child the daughter of Henry and Caroline Field, and the surname was omitted in the bequest.

"Who was the mother?" asked Lance.

"I never exactly knew. Fulbert thought she had been a person whom Field had met in America or somewhere, and married in a hurry. Fulbert said she was rather pretty, but she was a poor helpless, bewildered thing, and very poorly. He wanted to bring her to Albertstown for fit help and nursing; but she cried so much at the idea of either horse or wagon over the-no-roads, that it was put off and off and she had only his shepherd's housekeeper, so it was no wonder she did not live! Field was dreadfully cut up, and blamed himself extremely for having given way to her; but it is as likely as not the journey would have been just as fatal."

"Poor thing!"

"You never heard her surname?"

"No, it did not signify."

"He did not name his child after her?"

"No. I remember Fulbert saying he supposed she should be called Caroline; and he exclaimed, 'No, no, I always said it should be Magdalen and Susanna.'"

"My sister's name," repeated Agatha.

"And Susan Merrifield," addedDolores.

"But she is mine, mine!" cried Angela, with a tone like herself, of a sort of triumphant jealousy. "They can't take her away from me!"

"Gently, Angela, my dear," said Lance, in a tone so like Felix of old, that it almost startled her. "Tell me what arrangement is this about the property. Your share of Fulbert's has never been taken out, I think?"

"No, Macpherson, the purchaser, you know, of Fulbert's share, pays me my amount out of it, and agreed to do the same by Lena. I don't think the value is quite what it used to be. It rather went down under Field; but Macpherson is all there, and it has been a better season. I could sell it all to him, hers and mine both; but I have thought how it would be, as it is her native country, and I have not parted with my own to go out again to Carrigaboola, and bring her up there. I assure you I am up to it," she added, meeting an amused look. "I know a good deal more about sheep farming than either of you gentlemen. I can ride anything but a buckjumper, and boss the shepherds, and I do love the life, no stifling in fields and copses! I only wish you would come too, Bear; it would do you ever so much good to get a little red paint on those white banker's hands of yours."

"Well done, sister Angel!" And the brothers both burst out laughing.

"But really," proceeded Angela, "it is by far the best hope of keeping up Christianity among those hands. Fulbert had a sort of little hut for a chapel, and once a month one of the clergy from Albertstown came over there; I used to ride with him when I could, and if I were there, I could keep a good deal going till the place is more peopled, and we can get a cleric. It is a great opportunity, not to be thrown away. I can catch those cockatoos better than a parson. And there are the blacks."

The brothers had not the least doubt of it. Angela was Angela still, for better or for worse. Or was it for worse? Yet she went up to bed chanting—

> "His sister she went beyond the seas,
> And died an old maid among black savagees."

CHAPTER XXIII—WILLOW WIDOWS

"Set your heart at rest.
The fairyland buys not that child of me."

—"Midsummer Night's Dream."

An expedition to Minsterham finished the visit of Dolores and her faithful "Nag," whose abilities as an assistant were highly appreciated, and who came home brilliantly happy to keep her remaining holiday with Magdalen; while Dolores repaired to Clipstone. Bernard had been obliged to go to London, to report himself to Sir Ferdinand Travis Underwood, but his wife and little girl were the reigning joy at Clipstone. Phyllis looked very white, much changed from the buxom girl who had gone out with her father two years ago. She had never recovered the loss of the little boy, and suffered the more from her husband's inability to bear expression, and it was an immense comfort to her to speak freely of her little one to her mother.

The little Lilias looked frail, but was healthy, happy, and as advanced as a well-trained companion child of six could well be, and the darling of the young aunts, who expected Dolores to echo their raptures, and declare the infinite superiority of the Ceylonese to "that little cornstalk," as Valetta said.

"There's no difficulty as to that," said Dolores, laughing. "The poor little cornstalk looks as if she had grown up under a blight."

"It is a grand romance though," said Mysie; "only I wish that Cousin Harry had had any constancy in him."

"I wonder if Magdalen will adopt her!" was Valetta's bold suggestion.

"Poor Magdalen has had quite adopting enough to do," said Mysie.

"Besides," said Dolores, "Sister Angela will never let her go. And certainly I never saw any one more *taking* than Sister Angela. She is so full of life, and of a certain unexpectedness, and one knows she has done such noble work. I want to see more of her."

"You will," said Mysie. "Mamma is going to ask her to come, for Phyllis says there is no one that Bernard cares for so much. She was his own companion sister."

"Magdalen might have the little cornstalk," said Valetta.

"Well," said Mysie, "it is rather funny to have two—what shall I say?—willow widows, and a child that is neither of theirs! How will they settle it?"

Magdalen had heard from Agatha on the first evening of the arrival of the sister, and the probability of the identification of little Lena's father with the Henry Merrifield of her former years, and she was deeply touched by the bestowal of her name—so much that Nag avoided saying more, but only kissed her and went to bed.

The Merrifields discussed the subject dispassionately.

Sir Jasper recollected what his brother had written to him of his anxieties and disappointment in his son Henry, and of his absconding from Manitoba, since which time all trace of him had been lost, except in the restoration to the two brothers in Canada. To the surprise and indignation of Sir Jasper, there had been no attempt to follow it up.

"If my poor brother Edgar had done anything of the kind," said Bernard, "none of us would have rested."

So far as they could put recollections together this act of restitution must have been made soon after the connection with Fulbert Underwood began, perhaps at the time of the wife's death. If there had been another letter, as Sister Angela thought, it was more recent, certainly within the last two years.

Captain Samuel Merrifield, of Stokesley, had been on a voyage for four years, and had not long been at home. His wife had been charged with the forwarding of the letters that she thought of immediate interest, and there was an accumulation of those that had been left for his return, as yet not looked over.

Of course, Sir Jasper impelled him to plunge into these, and by and by one came to light, which Mrs. Merrifield had taken "for only some Australian gold mines," and left to wait, especially as it was directed to his father instead of himself.

It was a letter full of repentance, and entreaties for forgiveness, describing in part poor Henry's past life, and adding that the best thing that had ever befallen him was his association with "such a fellow as Underwood."

It was to be gathered that Fulbert's uprightness of mind had led him to the first impulse of restitution, and he went on to mention his first hasty marriage and the loss of his wife, with the kindness of the Carrigaboola Sisterhood; above all, of Sister Angela, and declaring his love and admiration for her, and his sense that she was the one person who could keep him straight now that her brother was gone.

He had more than once offered to her, but he found that her brother had solemnly charged her not to accept him till he had made all his past clear before her, and could show her that he was acknowledged by his family, and had his father's forgiveness, and for this he humbly craved, as one deeply sensible of his own demerits.

It was piteous to think of the poor fellow waiting and hoping for an answer to such a letter as this, and dying without one, while all the time it was lying unread in the Captain's desk, and no one even knew of the changed life and fresh hopes. Sir Jasper was much moved by it; but Sam said, "Ay, ay! poor Harry always was a plausible fellow!" and his wife was chiefly concerned to show that the suppression was not by her fault. Sir Jasper had brought the will with him, and the certificate of the child's baptism.

Both were met with a little hesitation. So little had been said in the letter about the marriage that the Captain wanted to know more, and also whether the will had been properly proved in Australia, and whether it had force in England. In that case he was surely the right person to have the custody of his brother's child. His wife, who had been bred up in a different school, was not by any means satisfied that she should be consigned to a member of a Sisterhood.

David came to Stokesley, saw the letter, and agreed with his brother on the expediency of obtaining full proof of the validity of the will in both Queensland and England, and put in hand the writing of inquiries for the purpose, from the legal authorities at Brisbane, for which purpose Angela had to be consulted.

She had been (having left the budgerigars to the delight of Pearl and Awdrey), in the meantime, at Vale Leston, enjoying the atmosphere of peace that prevailed wherever were Clement and Geraldine, and hailed with delight by all her old village friends, as well as Lady Vanderkist and her somewhat thinned flock.

She won Adrian's heart by skating or golfing with him, and even, on one or two hunting days, joining in his pursuit of the chase, being altogether, as he said, ever so much better a fellow than even his youngest sister Joan, and entrancing them all with tales of kangaroos. Lena had really a tame kangaroo at Carrigaboola. Oh, why did they not bring it home as well as Ben, the polly? She quite pined for it, and had tears in her eyes when it was spoken of.

Indeed the joyous young Vanderkists were too much for the delicate little girl, and sorry as Angela was to leave Vale Leston, she was not ungrateful for an invitation to the Goyle, where there was more room for them than at Clipstone in the holidays, and with the Bernard Underwoods making it their headquarters.

Lena and she were much better and happier with "Sister" always at her service, and Paula and Thekla were delighted to amuse her. Paula was in a state of delight with Sister Angela, only a little puzzled by the irregularity of her course, though it was carefully explained that she had never been under any vows. To hear of her doings among the Australian women was a romance, often as there had been disappointment. "Paula is a born Sister," said Angela, "a much truer one than I have ever been, for there does not seem to be any demon of waywardness to drive her wild."

These talks with Magdalen, often prolonged hours after the young people had gone to bed, were a great solace to both the elders. Girls like Mysie Merrifield and Phyllis Devereux thought sitting up to converse a propensity peculiar to themselves, and to their own age, of new experiences and speculations; but the two "old girls," whose experiences were not new, and whose speculations had a certain material foundation, they were equally fascinating.

There were no small jealousies in either of them—"willow widows"—though Mysie's name stuck. There was nothing but comfort to Magdalen in the certainty of the ultimate "coming home" of one who had finished a delusive dream of her younger days, and been yearned after with a heartache now quenched; and Angela, who had never been the least in love with Henry Merrifield, could quite afford her interest in the scanty records of his younger days, and fill up all she knew of the measure of the latter and better days. There was another bond, for Mrs. Best's daughter was, "as distances go," a neighbour to Carrigaboola, and resorted thither on great occasions.

Angela's vision began to be, to take Magdalen and her sisters out to Carrigaboola, where a superior school for colonists' daughters was much needed, and where Paula might enter the Sisterhood. She longed all the more when she saw how much better Magdalen could deal with Lena as to teaching and restraint than she could. The child was very backward, and could hardly read words of one syllable, though she knew any amount of Scripture history and legends of Saints, and was very fairly intelligent; but though she was devoted to "Sister," always hanging on her, and never quite happy when out of sight of her, she had hardly any notion of prompt obedience or of giving up her own way.

Angela's visit to Vale Leston had been partly spoilt by the little girl's fretful worry at the elder children, and by the somewhat uncalled for fears that all the Vanderkists were hard on the poor little colonial damsel; but whether it was the air of Rock Quay, or the quiet influence of Miss Prescott, Lena certainly improved in health at the Goyle, and was much more amenable, and less rudely shy. But her guardian trembled at hearing that, pending Captain Merrifield's correspondence with Brisbane, the sisters, Susan and Elizabeth, were coming to Miss Mohun's to see their niece, there being no room for them at Clipstone.

They came—Susan, plump, comfortable and good-natured looking, as like an apricot as ever, with an air many years more than three above her sister Bessie, who as ever was brisk and bright, scarcely middle aged in face, dress or demeanour. They arrived too late for visiting, and only dined at Clipstone to be introduced to Bernard Underwood, and see their cousin Phyllis, whom they had once met when all were small children. Dolores was much amused, as she told her Aunt Jane, to see how gratified they were at the "sanguine" colouring of Phyllis and Wilfred, quite Merrifields, they said, though Phyllis with auburn eyes and hair was far handsomer than any other of the clan had ever been; and Wilfred had simply commonplace carrots and freckles.

"The fun is," said Jane, "to remember how some of us Mohuns have sighed at Lily's having any yellow children, and, till we saw Stokesley specimens, wondering where the strain came from! As if it signified!"

"It does in some degree," said Dolores; "something hereditary goes with the complexion."

"I don't know," said Jane. "I believe too much is made in these days of heredity, and by those who believe least in the Bible indications on the effect, forgetting the counteracting grace."

"Well," said Dolores, "Wilfred was always a *bête noire* to me—no, not *noire* —in my younger days, and I can't help being glad he is not of our strain! Though you know the likeness was the first step to identifying that poor little girl."

"Poor child! I am afraid she will be a bone of contention."

The two aunts were at Clipstone early; and might be satisfied with the true Merrifield tints of Magdalen Susanna, but perhaps she had been over much warned to be gracious, for the very contrary was the effect. She had been very civil to her great-aunt Lilias, and had allowed both her uncles to take her up in their arms; but she retreated upon Angela, planted an elbow on the well-known lap, turned her back, and put a skinny little finger in her mouth by way of answer to Susan's advances, advances which had hardly ever before been repelled even by the most untamable of infants.

Angela tried to coax, lift her up and turn her round; but this only led to the shoulder being the hiding-place, and it might be suspected that there was a lurking perception that these strangers asserted a closer claim than the beloved "Sister." She would not even respond to Susan's doll or Bessie's picture book; and Bessie advised leaving her alone, and turned to the window with Agatha, who was nothing loth to tell of her Bexley and Minsterham experiences.

Angela tried to talk about the voyage, or any thing that might save the child from being discussed or courted; but Susan's heart was in the subject, and she had not enough tact or knowledge of the world to turn away from it. Regret for the past was strong within her, and she could not keep from asking how much "little Magdalen" (at full length) remembered of her father, how much she had been with him, whether he had much altered, whether there were a photograph of him, and a great deal more, with tears in her eyes and a trembling in her voice which made Angela feel much for her, even while vexed at her pertinacity, for the child was by no means the baby she looked like, but perfectly well able to listen and understand, and this consciousness made her own communications much briefer and more reserved than otherwise they would have been.

Bessie, with more perception, saw the embarrassment, turned round from Agatha, went up to the cockatoo in his cage, and asked in a pleasant voice if Magdalen would show him to her, and tell her his name. Angela was glad enough to break off poor Susan's questioning, and come forward, with the child still clinging, to incite the bird to display the rose colour under his crest, put up a grey claw to shake hands, and show off his vocabulary, laughing herself and acting merriment as she did so, in hopes to inspire Lena.

"Come, Ben, tell how you were picked up under a gum tree, quite a baby, a little grey ball, and brought over in the shepherd's pocket for a present to the little Boss, and how we fed you and nursed you till you turned all rose-colour and lovely! There! put up your crest and make red revelations. Can't you speak? Fetch him a banana, Lena. That will open his mouth."

At sight of the banana, the bird put his head on one side and croaked in a hoarse whisper, "Yo ho!"

"No, you need not be afraid of any more sailors' language," said Angela. "They were as careful as possible on board. I overheard once, 'Hold hard, Tom, Polly Pink is up there, and she's a regular lady born!"

Whereupon Polly indulged in a ridiculous chuckle, holding the banana cleverly in one foot, while Angela laughed and chattered more and more nervously, but only succeeded in disgusting the visitors by what Susan at least took for unbecoming flippancy.

"*That* Sister," said Susan, as they drove away, "does not seem to me at all the person to have the charge of Henry's poor little girl!"

"I wish she had not thrust herself in," said Bessie, "to prevent me from getting on with the child over the cockatoo."

"She calls herself a Sister! I don't understand it, for she seems to have been bent on marrying poor Henry."

"She never took any vows."

"Then why does she wear a ridiculous cap over all that hair?"

By and by they were met by Bernard Underwood striding along. "Holloa! have you seen Angel and her darling? She is a perfect slave to the little thing, and one only gets fragments of her."

"She seems very fond of her," said Bessie.

"Just kept her alive, you see. Poor old Angel! She is all for one thing at a time! Are you going up to Clipstone?"

"I think we shall find Phyllis at Beechcroft."

"Yes, she is driving there to lunch, and Angel is to bring the little cornstalk over to make friends with our Lily! I trust the creature goes to sleep now, and I may get a word out of Angel!" Wherewith he dashed on, and the two ladies agreed that "those Underwoods seemed to be curiously impulsive."

They were, however, much better satisfied with the Ceylonese Lily, who was a very well trained civilised specimen, conversing very prettily over one of Aunt Jane's picture books, which Bessie looked at with her, and showing herself fully able to read the titles beneath, a feat of which Lena was quite incapable, though she was less on the defensive than she had shown herself at the Goyle, and Angela was far more at her ease than when she was conscious that "Field's" original love was watching the introduction to his sisters. Besides, Bernard's presence was sunshine to her, and the two expanded into bright reminiscences and merry comparisons of their two lives, absolutely delightful to themselves, and to Phyllis and her Aunt Jane, and which would have been the same to Elizabeth, if she had not been worried at Susan's evident misunderstanding of—and displeasure at—the quips and cranks of the happy brother and sister; also she was bent on promoting an intercourse between Lily and Lena, over the doll she had brought for the former. She was a little hurt that Lena had not been accompanied by the blue-eyed article with preposterously long eyelashes that had been bestowed on her at the Goyle; but the little Australian had no opinion of dolls, and had let the one bought for her at Sydney be thrown overboard by the ship's monkey.

"That was cruel!" said Lily, fondling her black-eyed specimen.

"She could not feel," reasoned Lena, with contempt.

“I don’t know,” said Lily, knitting her brows. “It’s not *all* make believe! I do love my Rosamunda Rowena, and she loves me, and I shall tell her not to be jealous of this dear Betsinda. For, do you know, when Rosamunda was ill in the Red Sea, father carried her up and down on deck, and made her a dear little deck chair.”

“But she is not alive. She *couldn’t* be,” sighed Lena. “I like my Ben and my kangaroo! Oh, I do want to go back to my kangaroo!”

“And does Lily want to go back to her riki-tiki?” asked Lily’s father, lifting a little girl on each knee, so that they might be *vis-à-vis*, when certainly his own had the advantage in beauty, as she answered, leaning against him, “Granny’s better than riki-tiki!”

For which pretty speech some of the ladies gave her much credit; but her father, with a tender arm round her, said, “Ah! you are a sentimental little pussy-cat! Is anything here as good as Carrigaboola? Eh, Lena?”

But Lena resolutely shook her carrots; but kept silence, while Bernard turned over the leaves of a great book of natural history, till as a page was displayed with a large kangaroo under a blue-gum tree, with a yellow wattle tree beside him, her lips quivered, her face puckered, and she burst into an uncontrollable fit of crying; “Oh! I want to go home, home! Sister, Sister, take me home!”

Angela was in a minute beside her, took her within loving arms, and carried her off.

CHAPTER XXIV—CRUEL LAWYERS

"Tender companions of our serious days,
  Who colour with your kisses, smiles and tears,
Life's worn web woven over wasted ways."

—Lowell.

There was a good deal of worry and anxiety for some little time, while correspondence was going on about Henry Merrifield's will, and in the meantime Angela decided to board with Miss Prescott, since her charge was certainly much better in health there; and besides, as Mrs. Bernard Merrifield was naturally at Clipstone, it became the head quarters of her husband, though he made many excursions to his own people, and on business affairs to Sir Ferdinand Travis Underwood in London.

And Clipstone suited him well for his holiday. Sir Jasper had, of course, a certain amount of intercourse with the garrison at Avoncester, and the officers stationed there at present had already some acquaintance with Bernard Underwood, who was known to be a champion in Ceylon in all athletic sports, especially polo and cricket. Tall and well made, he had been devoted to all such games in his youth, and they had kept up his health in his sedentary occupation. Now, in his leisure time, his prowess did much to efface the fame of the much younger and slighter Alexis White, and, so far as might be, Angela enjoyed the games with him, keeping well within bounds, but always feeling activity a wholesome outlet for her superfluous strength, and, above all, delighting in an interval of being a child again with her Bear of old times; and her superabundant life, energy, and fun amazed all, especially by the contrast with her poor little languid charge, who seemed, as Jane Mohun said, centuries older.

The Merrifield lads were also devoted to him. Even Fergus was somewhat distracted from his allegiance to Dolores and her experiments, and in the very few days that Christmas afforded for skating, could think of nothing else.

And as to Wilfred, his whole mind seemed to be set on sports, and marble works to be only an incident thrown in. Bernard, whom he followed assiduously, and who took him to Avoncester, and introduced him to young officers, began to have doubts whether he had done wisely. Bernard had, in his time, vexed Felix's soul by idleness and amusement, but he had been one betted upon, not himself given to betting. He loved football and cricket for their bodily excitement, not the fictitious one of a looker on, or reader of papers, and it struck him that Wilfred knew a good deal too much about this more dangerous side of races and athletics.

He said so to Angela, and she answered, "Oh, nonsense! Young men are out of it if they don't know the winning horse. Even *Pur* had to be up to the Derby."

And Angela had her own bitter trial in the decision of the lawyers. Not only was the signature of the will unsatisfactory, from the confusion between Field and Merrifield, but the two witnesses failed to be traced, John Shepherd and George Jones were not to be identified, and though Brisbane might accept wills easily, an English court of law required more certainty. The little daughter being the only child and natural heiress, this was not felt to be doing her any injury; but the decision deprived her of the guardian her father had chosen, and Angela was in despair. She was ready to write to the *Pursuivant*, to the Bishop of Albertstown, to the Lord Chancellor, with an exposition of the wicked injustice and hardness of heart of lawyers, and the inexpedience of taking the poor child from her earliest motherly friend, expressly chosen by her father. All Bernard's common sense and Magdalen's soothing were needed to make her hold her peace, when correspondence made it plain that the guardianship being assumed by the uncles, Captain Merrifield would not hear for a moment of the scheme of taking the child out to Carrigaboola. In his opinion, and his sister Susan's, the only fit thing to be done with her was to place her with the two aunts at Coalham to be educated. He came down to Rock Quay to inspect her. It was a cold, raw day, with the moors wrapped in mist, and the poor little maid looked small, peaky and pinched. He was sure that the dry winds of the north were what she needed, wanted to carry her off immediately, and looked regardless of Angela's opinion, though backed by Miss Prescott, that it would be highly dangerous to take the delicate child of a semi-tropical climate off in the depth of winter to a northerly town. Angela walked off to ask Dr. Dagger to inspect the child and give his opinion, while Captain Sam repaired to Clipstone to visit his relations and lunch with them.

He did not meet with all the sympathy he expected. Lady Merrifield said that Coalham had not agreed with her own son Harry, and that little Lena ought not to be taken there till after the cold winds of spring were over; and her daughters all chimed in with a declaration that Angela Underwood was perfectly devoted to the little one, and that no one else could make her happy.

"Petting her! spoiling her!" scoffed the Captain. "Why, Susan and Bessie were full of the contrast with your little girl."

"Health," began Phyllis.

"An Indian child too!" he went on. "Just showing what a little good sense in the training can do! No, indeed! Since I am to be her guardian, I have no notion of swerving from my duty, and letting poor Hal's child be bred up to Sisterhoods and all that flummery."

"It will just break Angela's heart," cried Valetta, with tears in her eyes, at which the Captain looked contemptuous.

"I must say," added Bernard, "that I should think it little short of murderous to take that unlucky child from the one woman who understands her up into the bleak north at this time of year."

"Decidedly!" added Sir Jasper. "Miss Underwood deserves every consideration in dealing with the child who has been always her sole charge."

Wherewith he changed the conversation by a question about Stokesley; but he held to his dictum when alone with his nephew, and as he was the only person for whose opinion Captain Sam had any respect, it had its effect, though there was a sense that he might be biassed by his son-in-law and his herd of womanfolk, and that he did not partake Mrs. Samuel Merrifield's dislike to the very name of Sister or of anything not commonplace.

Angela obtained Dr. Dagger's opinion to reinforce her own and Lady Merrifield's, and the Captain was obliged to give way so far as to consent to Magdalen, as he insisted on calling her, being allowed to remain at Arnscombe till after Easter, when her aunts were to fetch her to Coalham, there to send her to the kindergarten.

After Angela's period of raging against law and lawyers and all the Stokesley family, and being on the verge of impertinence to Captain Merrifield, she submitted to the prospect more quietly than her friends had dared to hope. Lance had almost expected her to deport her charge, parrot and all, suddenly and secretly by an Australian liner, and had advised Bernard, on a fleeting meeting at Bexley, to be on his guard if she hinted at anything so preposterous; but Bernard shook his head, and said Angel was more to be trusted than her elders thought. "Waves and storms don't go over us for nothing, I hope," he said.

And he found himself right on his return. Angela had bowed her head to the inevitable, and was quietly trying to prepare her little charge for the change, accustoming her to more discipline and less petting. When Angela proposed to walk over to Clipstone with her brother on his return, and the whine was set up, "Let me go, Sister," it was answered, "No, my dear, it is too far for you. You must stay and walk with Paula."

"I want to go with Sister."

"You must be a good child, and do as Sister tells you. No, I can't have any fretting. Paula will show you how to drive your hoop. Keep her moving fast, Paula, don't let her fret and get cold."

And Angela actually detached the clinging hand, and put it into Paulina's, and, holding up her finger, silenced the burst of weeping, though tears sprang to her own eyes as she resolutely turned away, and, after running out and shutting the back gate after her, put her arm with a clinging gesture into Bernard's.

"That's right!" he said, pressing her hand.

"Cruel," she said, "but better by and by for her. Oh, Bear, if one could but learn to lie still and say, 'Thou didst it,' when it is human agency that takes away the desire of one's eyes with a stroke."

"The desire of thine eyes!" repeated Bernard. "How often I thought of that last February."

It was the only time he had referred to the loss of his little boy. His wife had told her mother that he could not bear to mention it, and had poured out all her own feelings of sorrow and her struggle for cheerfulness and resignation alone with her or with Mysie; but he had shrunk from the least allusion to the little two year old Felix, who slept beneath a palm tree at Colombo.

Now, however, still holding his sister's hand, he drifted into all the particulars of the little ways, the baby language, the dawning understanding, and the very sudden sharp illness carrying the beautiful boy away almost before they were aware of danger; and he took out the photograph from his breast, and showed her the little face, so recalling old fond remembrances. "Forbear to cry, make no mourning for the dead," he repeated. "Yes, the boy is saved the wear and tear and heat and burthen of the day, but it is very hard to bethankful."

"Ah, and it is all the harder if you have to leave your Lily."

"If—yes; but Travis *may* so arrange that we can stay, or I make only one voyage out to settle matters and then come home for good. If you are still bent on Carrigaboola you might come as far as Frisco with me. I may have to go there about the Californian affairs."

"That would be jolly. Yes, I think it will clench the matter, for I believe I am of more good at Carriga than anywhere else, though the heart of it is taken out of it for me; but one lives on and gets on somehow without a heart, or a heart set where I suppose it ought not to be entirely at least! And, indeed, I think that little one taught me better than ever before how to love."

"That's what the creatures are sent us for," said Bernard, in a low voice.

"And here are, looming in the distance, all the posse of girls to meet us."

"Ah-h!" breathed Angela, withdrawing her arm. "Well, Bear, you have given me something to look forward to, whether it comes to anything or not. It will help me to be thankful. I know they are good people, and the child will do well when once the pining and bracing are over. They are her own people, and it is right."

"Right you are, Angel!" said Bernard, with a fresh squeeze of the hand, as he resumed his own cheerful, resolute voice ere joining his sisters-in-law.

"What! Angela without her satellite!" cried Primrose.

"Too far," murmured Angela; but Mysie tried to hush her sister, perceiving the weaning process, and respecting Angela for it.

And the next moment Angela was challenging Bernard to a game at golf.

CHAPTER XXV—BEAR AS ADVISER

"Weary soul and burthened sore
Labouring with thy secret load."

—Keble.

The early spring brought a new development. Thekla, who attended classes at the High School, came home with unmistakable tokens of measles, and Primrose did the same, in common with most of their contemporaries at Rockstone. Nor was there any chance that either Lily Underwood at Clipstone or Lena Merrifield at the Goyle would escape; indeed, they both showed an amount of discomfort that made it safer to keep them where they were, than to try to escape in the sharp east wind and frost.

No one was much dismayed at what all regarded as a trifling ailment, even if dignified as German. Angela owned that she regarded it as a relief, since infection might last till the summer, and the only person who was—as he owned—trying to laugh at himself with Angela, was Bernard, who could not keep out of his mind's eye a little grave at Colombo. As he walked home, at the turning he saw a figure wearily toiling upwards, which proved to be Wilfred. "Holloa! you are at home early!"

"I had an intolerable headache!"

"Measles, eh?"

"No such thing! Once when I was a kid in Malta. But I say, Bear," he added, coming up with quickened pace, "you could do me no end of a favour if you would advance me twenty pounds."

"Whew!" Bernard whistled.

"There is Lady Day coming, and I can pay you then—most assuredly." And an asseveration or two was beginning.

"Twenty pounds don't fly promiscuously about the country," muttered Bernard, chiefly for the sake of giving himself time.

"But I tell you I shall have a quarter from the works, and a quarter from my father (with his hand to his head). That's—that's—. Awful skinflints both of them! How is a man to do, so cramped up as that?"

"Oh! and how is a man to do if he spends it all beforehand?"

"I tell you, Bernard, I must have it, or—or it will break my mother's heart! And as to my father, I'd—I'd cut my throat—I'd go to sea before he knew! Advance it to me, Bear! You know what it is to be in an awful scrape. Get me through this once and I'll never—"

Bernard did not observe that the scrape of his boyhood over the drowned Stingo had hardly been of the magnitude that besought for twenty pounds. He waived the personal appeal, and asked, "What is the scrape?"

"Why, that intolerable swindler and ruffian, Hart, deceived me about Racket, and—"

"A horse at Avoncester?" said Bernard, light beginning to dawn on him.

"I made sure it was the only way out of it all, and they said Racket was as sure as death, and now the brute has come in third. Hart swears there was foul play, but what's that to me? I'm done for unless you will help me over."

"If it is a betting debt, the only safe way is to have it out with your father, and have done with it."

"You don't know what my father is! Just made of iron. You might as well put your hand under a Nasmyth's hammer." And as he saw that his hearer was unconvinced, "Besides, it is ever so much more than what I put upon Racket! That was only the way out of it! It is all up with me if he hears of it. You might as well pitch me over the cliff at once!"

"Well, what is it then?"

Incoherently, Wilfred stammered out what Bernard understood at last to mean that he had got into the habit of betting at the billiard table, surreptitiously kept up in Ivinghoe Terrace in a house of Richard White's, not for any excessive sums, and with luck at first on his side than otherwise; but at last he had become involved for a sum not in itself very terrible to elder years, and his creditor was in great dread of pressure from his employers, and insisted on payment. Wilfred, who seemed to have a mortal terror of his father, beyond what Bernard could understand, had been unable to believe that the offence for so slight a sum might be forgiven if voluntarily confessed, had done the worst thing he could, he had paid the debt with a cheque which had, unfortunately, passed through his hands at the office, trusting in a few days to recover the amount by a bet upon the horse, in full security of success! And now!

Before the predicament was made clear, Wilfred reeled, and would have fallen if Bernard had not supported him, and he mumbled something about giddiness and dazzling, insisting at the same time that it was nothing but the miserable pickle, and that if Bernard would not see him out of it, he might as well let him lie there and have done with it.

Happily they were in the immediate neighbourhood of the house, and it was possible to get him into the hall before he entirely collapsed upon a chair; but seeming to recover fresh vigour from alarm at the sound of voices, he rushed at the stairs and dashed up rapidly the two flights to his own room, only throwing back the words, "Dead secret, mind!"

Bernard was glad to have made no promise, and, indeed, Wilfred's physical condition chiefly occupied him at the moment, for one or two of the girls were hurrying in, asking what was the matter, and at the answer, "He is gone up to his room with a bad headache," Valetta declared with satisfaction, "Then he has got it! We told him so! But he would go to the office! and, Bernard, so has Lily."

"Pleasing information!" said Bernard, nettled and amused at the tone of triumph, while Mysie, throwing behind her the words, "It may be nothing," went off to call Mrs. Halfpenny, who was in a state of importance and something very like pleasure. Bernard strode up to his wife's room, leaving Valetta half-way in her exposition that when all the family had been laid low by measles at Malta, Wilfred had been a very young infant, and it had always been doubtful whether he had been franked or not; and how he had been reproached with looking ill in the morning, but had fiercely insisted on going down to the office, which he was usually glad to avoid on any excuse.

By the time the household met at dinner, it was plain that they had to resign themselves to being an infected family, though there were not many probable victims, and they were likely only to have the disorder favourably, with the exception of Wilfred, who had evidently got a severe chill, and could only be reported as very ill, though still he vehemently resented any suspicion of being subject to such a babyish complaint. But when the break up for the night was just over, Lady Merrifield came in search of Bernard, entreating him to come to speak to Wilfred, who was more and more feverish, almost light-headed, and insisting that he must speak to Bear, "Bear had not promised," reiterating the summons, so that there was no choice but to comply with it.

He found Wilfred flushed with fever, and violently restless, starting up in bed as he entered, and crying out, "Bear, Bear, will you? will you? You did not promise!"

"I will see about it! Lie down now! There's nothing to be done to-night."

"But promise! promise! And not a word!"

All this was reiterated till Wilfred at last was exhausted for the time, and to a certain degree pacified by the reassuring voice in which Bernard soothed him and undertook to take the matter in hand, hardly knowing what he undertook, and only feeling the necessity of quieting the perilous excitement, and of helping the mother to bring a certain amount of tranquillity.

His own little girl was going on well, and quite capable of being amused in the morning by being compared to a lobster or a tiger lily; and Primrose was reported in an equally satisfactory state, ready either for sleep or continuous reading by her sisters. Only Wilfred was in the same, or a more anxious, state of fever; and as soon as Bernard had satisfied himself that there was no special use in his remaining in the house, he set out for the marble works office, having made up his mind as to one part of what he had expressed as "seeing about it."

He had hardly turned into the Cliffe road before he met Captain Henderson walking up, and they exchanged distant inquiries and answers as to whether each might be thought dangerous to the other's home; after which they forgathered, and compared notes as to invalids. The Captain had heard of Wilfred's going home ill, and was coming, he said, to inquire.

"He seems very seriously ill," was the answer. "I imagine there has been a chill, and a check. I was coming to speak to you about him."

"He has spoken to you?"

Both could now consult freely. "It is a very anxious matter—not so much for the actual amount as for the habits that it shows."

"The amount? Oh, I have made up that as regards the firm. I could not let it come before Sir Jasper, especially in the present state of things! I meant to give the young chap a desperate fright and rowing, but that will have to be deferred."

"You must let me take it!"

"No, no. Remember, Sir Jasper was my commanding officer, and I and my wife owe everything to him. I could supply the amount, so that no one would guess from the accounts that anything had been amiss."

Bernard could hardly allow himself to be thus relieved, but there was the comfort of knowing that Wilfred's name was safe, and that the unstained family honour would not have to suffer shame. Still the other debts remained, of which Captain Henderson had been only vaguely suspicious, till the two took counsel on them. Wilfred had not given up the name of the person for whom he had meant to borrow from the office; but Captain Henderson had very little doubt who it was, and it was agreed that he should receive the amount through a cheque of Bernard on Brown and Travis Underwood, from

Captain Henderson's hands, with a scathing rebuke and peremptory assurance of exposure to Mr. White, and consequent dismissal, if anything more of the same kind among the younger men were detected. The man was a clever artist in his first youth, and had always been something of a favourite with the authorities, and had a highly respectable father; so Captain Henderson meant to spare him as much as possible, and endeavour to ascertain how far the mischief had gone among the young men connected with the marble works, also to consult Mr. White on the amount of stringency in the measures used to put a stop to it. All this, of course, passed out of Bernard Underwood's hands and knowledge, but a sad and anxious day was before him. All the young girls were going on well, but Wilfred was increasingly ill all day, and continually calling for Bernard. Being told, "I have settled the matter" did not satisfy him. He looked eagerly about the room to find whether his mother were present, and fancying she was absent demanded, "Does he know? Do they know?" reiterating again and again. It was necessary to tell Lady Merrifield that there was an entanglement about money matters on his mind, which had been settled; but towards evening he grew worse and more light-headed, apparently under the impression that only Bernard could guard him from something unknown, or conceal, whenever he was conscious of the presence of his mother; and on his father's entrance he hid his face in the pillows and trembled, of course to their exceeding distress and perplexity; and when he believed no one present but Bernard and Mrs. Halfpenny, he became more and more rambling, sometimes insisting that his father must not know, sometimes abusing all connected with the racing bet, and more often fancying that he was going to be arrested for robbing the firm, the enormity of the sum and of the danger increasing with the fever, and therewith his horror of his father's knowing. It was of no use for his mother to hang over him, hold his hands, and assure him that she knew (as, in fact, she did, for Bernard had been obliged to make a cursory explanation), and that nothing could hinder her loving him still; he forgot it in the next interruption, and turned from her with terror and dismay, and once he nearly flung himself out of bed, fancying that the policeman was coming.

Bernard held him on this occasion, and told him, "Nothing will do you good, Willie, but to tell your father, and he will keep all from you. Let him know, and it will be all right."

It only seemed to add to his misery and terror. Something that passed in his hearing, gave him the impression that he was in great danger, if not actually dying; but his cry was still for Bernard, who had not ventured to go to bed; but it was still, "Oh, Bear, save me! Don't let me die with this upon my name! I can't go to God!"

"There's nothing for it, Wilfred, but to tell your father. He will pardon you. Your mother has, you see. Tell him, and when he forgives, you will know that God does. It will come right. Let me call him!"

"Let me bring him, my boy, my dear boy!" entreated his mother. "You know he will."

Wilfred seemed as if he did not know, but still held fast by Bernard's strong hands, as though there were support in them; and when in a few moments Sir Jasper entered the room, there was the same clinging gesture and endeavour to hide, in spite of the gentle sweetness of the tone of, "Well, my poor boy."

It was Bernard who was obliged to say, turning the poor flushed face towards him, "Wilfred wishes to say—"

"Father," it came with a gasp at last, "I've done it. I've disgraced us all. Forgive!"

He was repeating his own exaggerated ideas of what his crime had been, and what Sir Jasper would have said to him if all had been discovered in any other way.

"Do not think of it now, my boy. I forgive you, whatever it is."

Thereupon Dr. Dagger entered. He turned every one out except Mrs. Halfpenny, and gave a draught, which silenced the patient and put him to sleep in a few minutes. While Bernard hastily satisfied the parents that a good deal was exaggerated feeling, and that an old soldier must have known of a good many worse things in his time, though not so near home.

There was a general sense of relief in the morning, for Wilfred's attack had become an ordinary, though severe one, and the other cases were going on well. But Sir Jasper, who had not been able to grasp the extent of Wilfred's delinquency, and had been persuaded by his despair that it was much more serious than it really was, called his son-in-law into council, and demanded whether the whole could have been told.

Bernard was certain that it was so, and related his transactions with Captain Henderson, much of course to the father's relief, so far as the outer world was concerned; but what principally grieved him, besides the habits thus discovered, was his son's abject terror of him, not only in the exaggeration of illness, but in his mode of speaking of him.

It had never been thus with any of his sons before.

Claude, the soldier, had always been satisfactory, so had Harry the clergyman, though often widely separated from the parents in their wandering life; but the bond of confidence had never been broken. Jasper had never teased any one but his sisters. Fergus, too, the youngest of all the sons, and of an individual, rather peculiar nature, was growing up in straight grooves of his own; but Wilfred, who from delicate health, had been the most at home, had never seemed to open to his father. The family discipline of the General seemed only to oppress and terrify him, and the irregularities and subterfuges that had from time to time been detected had been met with just anger, never received in such a manner as to call forth the tenderness of forgiveness. Each discovery of a misdemeanour had only been the prelude to fresh and worse concealments and hardening.

And experience of mankind did not give any decided hope that even the last day's agony of repentance would be the turning over of a new leaf, when convalescence should bring the same surroundings and temptations, and perhaps the like disproportionate indignation and impatience in dealing with errors and constitutional weakness. "And the example of my brother's poor son is not encouraging," he added. "He who seems to have owed everything to your brother and sister."

"Yet poor Fulbert and I were to our homes, perhaps not the black sheep, but at any rate the vagrant ones."

"And what made a difference to you, may I ask?"

"Strong infusion by character and example of principle," said Bernard thoughtfully; "then, real life, and having to be one's own safeguard, with nothing to fall back on. As my brother told me at his last, I should swim when my plank was gone."

"Yes, but, plainly, you were never weak," and as Bernard did not answer at once, "Old-fashioned severity used to be the rule with lads, but it seems only to alienate them now and make them think themselves unjustly treated. What is one to do with these boys?"

A question which Bernard could not answer, though it carried him back with a strange yearning, yet resignation, to the little figure that had curled round on his knee, and the hopes connected with the hands that had caressed his cheek.

He thought over it the more the next week, when he was called to sit by Wilfred, who was getting better and anxious to talk.

"My father is very kind," he said. "Oh, yes, very kind now; but it will be all the same when I get well. You see, Bear, how can a man be always dawdling about with a lot of girls? There's Dolores bothering with her science, and Fergus every bit as bad; and Mysie after her disgusting schoolchildren; and Val and Prim horrid little empty chatterboxes; and if one does turn to a jolly girl for a bit of fun, their tongues all go to work, so that you would think the skies were going to fall; and if one goes in for a bit of a spree, down comes the General like a sledge-hammer! I wish you would take me out with you, Bear."

The same idea had already been undeveloped in Bernard's mind, and ever on his tongue when alone with his wife; but he kept it to himself, and only committed himself to, "You would not find an office in Colombo much more enlivening."

"There would be something to see—something to do. It would not be all as dull as ditch-water—just driving one to do something to get away from the girls and their fads."

This was nearly a fortnight from the night of crisis, when Wilfred, very weak, was still in bed; when Primrose and Lily were up and about, but threatened with whooping cough. Thekla much in the same case, and very cross; and little Lena weak, caressing and dependant, but angelically good and patient, so much so that Magdalen and Angela were quite anxious about her.

CHAPTER XXVI—NEW PATHS

"I'll put a girdle round the earth
In forty minutes."

—SHAKESPEARE.

THE visitation had not been confined to the High School. The little cheaply-built rows for workmen and fishermen had suffered much more severely, owing chiefly to the parents' callous indifference to infection. "Kismet," as they think it, said Jane Mohun, and still more to their want of care. Chills were caught, fevers and diphtheria ensued, and there was an actual mortality among the children at the works and at Arnscombe. Mr. Flight begged for help from the Nursing Sisterhood at Dearport, and, to her great joy, Sister Beata was sent down to him, with another who was of the same standing as Angela, and delighted to have a glimpse of her; though Angela thought it due to her delicate charge, and the Merrifields, not to plunge into actual nursing while Lena needed her hourly attention, and was not yet in a state for the training to do without it to continue. Paulina, however, being regarded as infection proof, was permitted to be an attendant and messenger of her dear Sister Beata, to her own great joy. She was now nineteen, and her desire to devote herself to a Sisterhood had never wavered, and intercourse with Sister Angela had only strengthened it.

"Oh, Maidie!" she said, "I do not think there can be any life so good or so happy as being really given up to our Lord and His work among the sick and poor."

"My dear, He can be served if you are in the world, provided you are not *of* the world, and if you keep yourself from the evil."

"Yes; but why should I run into the world? It is not evil, I know, so far as you and all your friends can manage; but it stirs up the evil in one's self."

"And so would a Sisterhood. That is a world, too."

"I suppose it is, and that there would be temptation; but there is a great deal to help one to keep right. And, oh! to have one's work in real good to Christ's poor, or in missions, instead of in all these outside silly nonsensical diversions that one doubts about all the time. If you would only let me go back with dear Sister Beata and Sister Elfleda as a probationer!"

"You could not be any more yet," said Magdalen; "but I will think about it, and talk it over with Sister Angela. You know your friend Sister Mena, as she called herself, does not mean to be a Sister, but a governess."

"Yes; she wrote to me. She has never seen or known anything outside the Convent, and it is all new and turns her head," said Paulina, wisely. "I know she helped me to be all the more silly about Vera and poor Hubert Delrio."

Magdalen promised to talk the matter over with Sister Angela.

"I should call it a vocation," said Angela. "I have watched her ever since I have been here, and I am sure her soul is set on these best things, in a steady, earnest way."

"She has always been an exceedingly good girl ever since I have had to do with her," said Magdalen. "I have hardly had a fault to find with her, except a little exaggeration in the direction of St. Kenelm's."

"A steady, not a fitful flame," said Angela.

"But she is so young."

"If you will believe me, Magdalen, such a home as that Dearport Sisterhood is a precious thing—I have not been worthy of it. I have been a wild colt, carried about by all manner of passing excitements. Oh, dear! love of sheer fun and daring enterprise, and amusement, in shocking every one, even my very dearest, whom I loved best. I have done things too dreadful to think of, and been utterly unreasonable and unmanageable, and proud of it; but always that Sisterhood has been like a cord drawing me! I never quite got free of it, even when I sent back my medal, and fancied it had been playing at superstition. I was there for a month as almost a baby, and the atmosphere has brought peace ever since. That, and my brother, and Sister Constance, and Bishop Fulmort, have been the saving of me, if anything has. I mean, if they will have me, to spend a little time at Dearport after all this perplexity is over, and I know how it is with Lena, and I could see how it is with Paula if you liked."

Magdalen accepted the suggestion, perhaps the more readily because of a fleeting visit from Hubert Delrio, who had finished his frescoes at the American Vale Leston, and came for a day or two to Mr. Flight's. She had sometimes doubted whether the supposed love of Vera had not been a good deal diffused among the young ladies, and might not so far awaken in Paulina as to render her vocation doubtful; but there were no such symptoms. Paula was quiet and cheerful, with a friendly welcome, but no excitement; but it was Thekla, now fifteen, who was all blushes whenever Hubert looked or spoke to her, all her forwardness gone; and shyness, or decidedly awkwardness, set in, resulting chiefly in giggle.

Hubert looked more manly and substantial, and he had just had an order for an important London church, which pleased him much, and involved another journey to Italy to study some of the designs in the Lombardic churches.

Not that there was any chance of meeting Vera. Mr. and Mrs. White had spent the last summer at Baden; and Vera, who had many pretty little drawing-room talents, and was always obliging, had been very acceptable there. This winter an attack of rheumatism had made them decide on trying Algiers, with a view to the Atlas marbles, and then German baths again might claim them for the summer.

In fact, the fear of infection had rendered Rock Quay a deserted place during the Easter vacation. Fergus Merrifield might not come near Primrose and Lily, and was charmed to accept an invitation from his friend and admirer, Adrian Vanderkist, to Vale Leston, where he would be able to explore the geology of Penbeacon, to say nothing of the coast; while his sister Felicia, who had been one of the victims, remained to be disinfected with Miss Mohun. Dolores was at Vale Leston Priory, and Agatha Prescott with her, so as to have a clean bill of health for her return to Oxford for her last term.

The Holy Week was calm and grave; and the two girls, with Anna Vanderkist and her little sisters, were very happy over their primroses and anemones on Easter Eve, with the beautiful Altar Cross that no one could manage like Aunt Cherry, whose work was confined to that, and to the two crosses on the graves.

Another notion soon occupied them. There was a vague idea that a sort of convalescent or children's hospital might be established for the training of women intending to study medicine or nursing, chiefly at Miss Arthuret's expense, and Dolores was anxious to consider the possibility of placing it in the sweet mountain air, tempered by the sea breezes of Penbeacon.

It was an idea to make Mrs. Grinstead shudder; but neither she nor her niece, Anna Vanderkist, could forget Gerald's view that Penbeacon was not only to be the playground of Vale Leston, and they always felt as if Dolores had a certain widow's right to influence any decision. So she cheerfully acquiesced in what, in her secret heart, seemed only a feeble echo of the past, though, to the young generations it was a very happy hopeful present when all the youthful party, under the steerage of Mary and Anna, and the escort of Sir Adrian and Fergus, started off with ponies, donkeys, cycles and sturdy feet to picnic on Penbeacon, if possible in the March winds—well out of the way of the clay works.

How Fergus divided his cares between the strata and Dolores' kodak, how even his photography could not spoil Aunt Alda; how charming a group of sisters Dolores contrived to produce; how Adrian was the proud pioneer into a coach adorned with stalactites and antediluvian bones; how Anna collected milkwort and violets for Aunt Cherry; how a sly push sent little Joan in a headlong career down a slope that might have resulted in a terrible fall, but did only cause a tumble and great fright, and a severe reprimand from the elder sisters; how Agatha was entranced by the glorious view in the clearness of spring, how they ate their sandwiches and tried to think it was not cold; how grey east wind mist came over the distance and warned them it was time to trot down,—all this must belong to the annals of later Vale Leston; and of those years of youth which in each generation leave impressions as of sunbeams for life. And on their return, Dolores found a letter which filled her with a fresh idea. It was from her father in New Zealand, telling her that there was an opening for her to come and give a course of lectures on electricity at Canterbury, Auckland and the other towns, and proposing to her to come out with her lady assistant, when she might very probably extend her tour to Australia.

"Would you come, Naggie?" asked Dolores.

"Oh! I should like nothing half so well. If you could only wait till my turn is over, and the exam!"

"Of course! Why, we shall not have finished the correspondence till after the examination! How capital it will be! My father will like your bright face, and you will think him like Fergus grown older. Will your sister consent?"

"Oh! Magdalen will be glad enough to have me off on a career. We will write and prepare her mind. I believe I am not to go home, so as to bring a clean bill of health to St. Robert's."

"I really think," added Dolores, "that Magdalen would make an admirable head matron, or whatever you call it!"

"Dear old thing! She is very fond of her Goyle."

"True, but Sophy's engineer husband tells us that a new line is projected to Rock Quay, through the very heart of the Goyle, Act of Parliament, compulsory sale and all."

"Well! work might console her for being uprooted, and she is quite youthful enough to take to it with spirit."

"Besides that she would greatly console Clement and Cherry for the profanation of their Penbeacon. I declare I will suggest it to Arthurine!"

So the two young people resolved, not without a consciousness that what was to them a fresh and inspiring gale, to the elder generation was "winds have rent thy sheltering bowers."

CHAPTER XXVII—A SENTENCE

"What should we give for our beloved?"

—E. B. Browning.

No sooner had the visitors departed than the others now out of quarantine appeared at Vale Leston. Angela was anxious to spend a little time there, and likewise to have Lena overhauled by Tom May. The child had never really recovered, and was always weakly; and whereas on the journey, Lily, now in high health, was delighted with all she saw, though she could not compare Penbeacon to Adam's Peak, Lena lay back in Sister Angela's arms, almost a dead weight, hardly enduring the bustle of the train, though she tried not to whine, as long as she saw her pink Ben looking happy in his cage.

Angela was an experienced nurse, and was alarmed at some of the symptoms that others made light of. Mrs. Grinstead had thought things might be made easier to her if the Miss Merrifields came to meet her and hear the doctor's opinion; and Elizabeth accepted her invitation, arriving to see the lovely peaceful world in the sweet blossoming of an early May, the hedges spangled with primroses, and the hawthorns showing sheets of snow; while the pear trees lifted their snowy pyramids, and Lily in her white frock darted about the lawn in joyous play with her father under the tree, and the grey cloister was gay with wisteria.

Angela was sitting in the boat, safely moored, with a book in her hand, the pink cockatoo on the gunwale, nibbling at a stick, and the girl lying on a rug, partly on her lap. Phyllis and Anna, who had come out on the lawn, made Elizabeth pause.

"That's the way they go on!" said Phyllis. "All day long Angela is reading to the child either the 'Water Babies' or the history of Joseph."

"Or crooning to her the story of the Cross," said Anna; "and as soon as one is ended she begins it again, and Lena will not let her miss or alter a single word."

"They go on more than half the night," added Phyllis. "Bear sat up long over his letters and accounts, and as he went up he heard the crooning, and looked in; and the very moment Angela paused, there came the little plaintive voice, 'Go on, please.' 'Women are following'—"

"But is not that spoiling her?" asked Bessie.

A look of sad meaning passed between her two companions. Phyllis shook her head slightly, and, instead of answering, conducted Bessie on to the bank, when Angela looked up and made a sign that she could not move or speak, for the child was asleep. The yellow head was shaded by Angela's parasol, the thin hair lying ruffled on the black dress, and the small face looked more pinched than when the aunt had last seen it, nearly a year previously. She had watched the decay of aged folks, but she was unused to the illnesses of children; and she recoiled with a little shock, as she looked down at the little wasted face, with a slight flush of sleep. "Recovery from measles," she said.

Phyllis smiled a little pitifully as her own little girl, all radiant with health and joy, came skipping up, performing antics over her father's hand. "Take care, Lily, don't wake poor little Lena," was murmured quietly.

"Northern breezes—" began Bessie, but the voices had broken the light slumber; and as Angela began, "See, Lena, here is Aunt Bessie," the effect was to make her throw herself over Angela's shoulder and hide her face; and when her protector tried to turn her round and reason her into courtesy, she began to cry in a feeble manner.

"She has had a bad night," said motherly Phyllis; "let her alone."

"May not I get down into the boat?" asked Lily. "I'll be very good."

There would have been a little hesitation, but at the voice Lena looked up and called "Lily, Lily!" Bernard lifted his small daughter down, Elizabeth was not sorry to be led away for the present, and when, after a turn in the rose garden, she came back, the two children were sitting with arms round one another, holding a conversation with Ben, the cockatoo, and making him dance on one of the benches of the boat, under Angela's supervision, lest he should end by dancing overboard. The rich fair hair, shining dark blue eyes, and plump glowing cheeks of Lily were a contrast to the wan wasted colouring of her little cousin; but Lena was more herself now than when just awake, and let Lily lead her up and introduce her, as it might be called, to Cousin Bessie as Lily called her, a less formidable sound than "Aunt Elizabeth." They were both kissed, and she endured it. Angela was, as her brothers and sisters said, "very good," and scrupulously abstained from absorbing the child all the evening, letting Elizabeth show her pictures and tell her stories, to which, by Lily's example, she listened quietly enough and with interest.

When the two children went off, hand in hand, to their beds, Elizabeth said, "Really, Magdalen is improved. If you leave Lily with her, Phyllis, I think we should get on beautifully. The bracing air will do wonders for themboth."

"Thank you," said poor Phyllis forbearingly; "we have not made our plans about Lily yet."

But Elizabeth thought out a beautiful scheme of discipline and study in the long light hours of the morning, and began to feel herself drawn towards her delicate little niece, feeling sure that the little thing would soon be Susan's darling, if Susan could be brought to endure the cockatoo walking loose about the house.

Early in the day Professor May appeared, and was hailed as an old friend by all the Underwoods. He rejoiced to see Clement looking well and active; and "as to this fellow," he said, looking at Bernard, "it shows what development will do."

"Not quite the young Bear of Stoneborough," said Clement, leaning affectionately on his broad shoulder; "our skittish pair are grown very sober-minded. But you have not told us of your father."

"My father is very well. He walks down every day to sit with my wife, and visits a selection of his old patients, who are getting few enough now. This is not my patient, I suppose?"

"Unless you are ready to prescribe only laughing and good Jersey cows' milk," said Bernard, pulling the long silky brown hair. "Where's mother, little one?"

"Mother sent me to say Aunt Angel is ready, if Dr. May will come up to Aunt Cherry's room. Lena is frightened, and they did not like to leave her."

It was a long visit, after Phyllis had come down; and, walking up and down the cloister with Bessie Merrifield, listened to her schemes of education for the little maidens. Lily she liked and admired, and she was convinced that Magdalen's weak health and spirits were the result of the spoiling system. Phyllis trembled a little as she heard of the knocking about, out-of-doors ways that had certainly produced fine strong healthy frames and upright characters, but she forbore to say that if her little girl had to be left, it would be to her mother and Mysie.

By and by Tom came down, and finding Geraldine alone in the drawing-room, he answered her inquiry with a very grave look. "Poor little thing! You do not think well of her! Is it as Angel feared?"

"Confirmed disease, from original want of development of heart. Measles accelerated it. I doubt her lasting six months, though it may be longer or less."

"Have you told Angel?"

"She knew it, more or less. She is ready to bear it, though one can see how her soul is wrapped up in the child, and the child in her."

"One thing, Tom, will you tell Miss Merrifield yourself, and alone, and make her feel that it is an independent opinion? It may save both the poor child and Angel a great deal."

"Are you prepared to keep her here?"

"Of course we are. It is Angel's natural home. Clement and I could think of nothing else."

"I knew you would say so. If I understand rightly there is something like a jealousy of her case in the Merrifields, prompted greatly by their wish to expiate any neglect of her father."

"That is what I gather from what Phyllis tells me."

"What a lovely countenance hers is in expression! No wonder Bernard has softened down. There is strength and solidity as well as sweetness in her face. Ah, there they are!"

"I will call Phyllis in. Bessie Merrifield has almost walked her to death by this time."

So Phyllis was called and told. What she said was, "I only hope he will make her understand that it could not be helped, and it was not Angela's fault."

Tom May had wisdom enough to make this clear in what was a greater shock to Elizabeth than it was to Angela, who had suspected enough to be prepared for the sentence, and had besides a good deal of hospital experience, which enabled her thoroughly to understand the Professor's explanations. So, indeed, did it seem to Elizabeth at the time he was speaking; but she had lived a good deal in London, and had a great idea that a London physician must be superior to a man who had lived in the country, and, moreover, whom all the household called Tom, and she asked Mrs. Grinstead if he were really so clever.

"Indeed, I think he is; and I have seen a great deal of his treatment. You may quite trust him. He lives down here at Stoneborough for his father's sake, or he would be quite at the head of his profession."

"Superior to the two Doctors Brownlow?"

"I should not say superior, but quite equal."

"The Brownlows," said Clement, looking up from his paper, "helped me through an ordinary malarial fever. John Lucas is a brilliant specialist in such cases, but certifying an affection of the heart. Tom May latterly has treated me better. As far as I understand the case of your little niece, I should say both that it was more in the line of Tom May, and likewise that it would be very hurtful to her to take her about and subject her to more examinations."

"Poor little thing! no doubt it would be a terrible distress," acquiesced Bessie; "but still, if it is bracing that she needs—northern air might make all the difference."

Clement sighed a little hopelessly over making a woman understand or give way, and returned to his newspaper; while Geraldine tried to argue that air could not make much difference, speaking in the interest of the child herself and of her sister. Elizabeth listened and agreed; but there was in the Merrifield family a fervour of almost jealous expiation of their neglect of Henry, inattention to his daughter, and desire to appropriate her, and to restore her to health, strength, and wisdom, in spite of her would-bestepmother.

"They hate me as much as if I were her stepmother!" cried Angela. "I wish I was, to have a right to protect her! No, Clem; I'll not break out, if I can help it, as long as they don't worry her; and I think Bessie does see the rights of it."

Yes; the peaceful, thoughtful atmosphere of Vale Leston, unlike the active bustle of Coalham, had an insensible influence on Elizabeth's mind; and she saw that Angela's treatment of the child, always cheerful though tender, was right, and that it would be sheer cruelty to separate them. She promised to use all her power to prevent any such step, and finally left Vale Leston, perfectly satisfied that it was impossible to take Lena with her.

But her family did not see it thus, especially Mrs. Samuel Merrifield, the child's guardian. She insisted that it was her husband's duty to bring the little one to London for advice, and to remove her from all the weakening, morbid influences of Vale Leston.

CHAPTER XXVIII—SUMMONED

"What would we give to our beloved?"

—E. B. Browning.

"I wish they all would not go so very fast," said little Lena, hiding her face against him from the whirl of cabs and omnibuses.

"They bewilder us savages," said Angela, smiling. "Remember we are from the wilds."

"She shall have her tea, and a good rest," said Marilda; "and then I have asked her uncle and aunts to meet you at dinner, and Fernan hopes to bring home another old friend. Whom do you think, Angel?"

"Oh! Not our Bishop?"

"Yes, the Bishop of Albertstown! He is actually in town; Fernan saw him yesterday at the Church House."

"Oh! that is joy!" cried Angela; and Lena raised her head, with, "Is it mine—mine own Bishop?"

"Mine own, mine own Bishop and godfather, my sweet!" said Angela; "more to us in our own way than any one else. Oh! it is joy! How happy Clement will be!"

It was with much feeling, almost akin to shame, that Bessie wrote to Angela this decision of her brother, that a London authority must be consulted—not Dr. Brownlow, but one whom Mrs. Sam had heard highly spoken of.

"That man!" cried Angela. "I have heard of him! He is a regular mealy-mouthed old woman of a doctor! And she is so well just now! How horrid to shake her up again! Oh, Bear! if I could only sail away with her to Queensland!"

"You would if it was ten years ago," said Bernard.

"Yes! Is it the way of the world, or learning resignation, that makes one know one must submit? Giving up an idol is a worse thing when the idol is made of flesh and blood."

Bernard wanted to see Sir Ferdinand, so made it an excuse for helping his sister on the way; and he did so effectively, for his knee and broad breast were Lena's great resting-place; and his stories of monkeys and elephants were almost as good as kangaroos. Was there not a kangaroo to be seen in London, which she apparently thought would be a place of about the size of Albertstown?

Lady Underwood had insisted on receiving the travellers from Vale Leston in her house in Kensington; and there was her broad, kindly face looking out for them at the station, and her likewise broad and kindly carriage ready to carry them from it. How natural all looked to Angela, with all her associations of being a naughty, wild, mischievous schoolgirl, the general plague and problem!

"But always a dear," said Marilda, with her habit of forgetting everybody's faults. "Why didn't you bring your wife, Bernard, and your little girl for this darling's playfellow?"

"She is her best playfellow," said Angela; "Adela's Joan is too rough, and fitter for Adrian's companion."

"She is my playfellow," said Bernard, holding her up. "Look out, Lena. Here's Father Thames to go over."

"And Fernan is so glad," added Marilda.

For Bishop Robert Fulmort had, when Vicar of St. Wulstan's, been the guide and helper of Ferdinand Travis's time of trial and disappointment, as well as the spiritual father of Clement Underwood; he had known and dealt with Angela in her wayward girlhood, and aided her bitter repentance; and in these later days in Australia had been her true fatherly friend, counsellor and comforter in the trials and perplexities that had befallen her. Bernard read, in her lifted head and brightened eye, that she felt the meeting him almost a compensation for the distress and perplexity of this journey to London.

Bernard carried the little girl up to the room and laid her down to sleep off her fatigue, while Marilda waited on her and Angela with her wonted bustling affection, extremely happy to have two of her best beloved cousins under her roof.

Bernard went off to find Sir Ferdinand at his office, and quiet prevailed till nearly dinner time, when Lena awoke and would not be denied one sight of her godfather. So Angela dressed her in her white frock, and smoothed her thin yellow hair, and took her down to the great stiff handsome room that all Emilia's efforts had never made to look liveable. Emilia Brown was there, very fashionably attired, but eager for news of Vale Leston, and the Merrifields soon arrived with, "Oh! here she is!" from the Captain, "Well! she looks better than I expected!"

"Poor little dear!" observed his wife, dressed in a low dress and thin fringe on her forehead in honour of what, to the country mind, was a grand dinner party, at which Angela's plain black dress and tight white cap were an unbecoming sight. Elizabeth was there, kissing Angela with real sympathy; and Lena, who had grown a good deal more accustomed to strange relations, endured the various embraces without discourtesy.

But when the door opened and the grey-headed Bishop came in there was a low half scream of "Oh! oh!" and with one leap she was in his arms, as he knelt on one knee, and clasped her, holding out a hand to Angela, whose eyes were full of tears of relief and trust. Marilda gave a glad welcome, but they were startled by perceiving that the joy of meeting had brought on a spasm of choking on Lena, who was gasping in a strange sort of agony. Angela took her in her arms and carried her out of the room. Marilda presently following, came back reporting that the little girl had been relieved by a shower of tears, but was still faint and agitated, and that Angela could not leave her, but begged that they would not wait dinner.

"Such sensitiveness needs anxious care," said Elizabeth.

"If it be not the effect of spoiling. Just affectation!" replied the sister-in-law in a decided voice, which made Bessie glad that the poor child's home was not to be among the rough boys at Stokesley, who were not credited with any particular feelings.

Angela's absence gave the Bishop the opportunity of telling what she had been during her years at Albertstown, what a wonderful power among the natives, though not without disappointment, and she had been still more effective among the settlers and their daughters. Carrigaboola, Fulbert's farm, had been an oasis of hope and rest to the few clergy of his scanty staff, and Fulbert himself had been a tower of strength for influence over the settlers who had fallen in his way, by his unswerving uprightness and honour, with the deeper principles of religion, little talked of but never belied. Even after his death, the power he had been told over all with whom he had come in contact.

Bernard heard it with immense pleasure, as did the faithful Ferdinand and Marilda; while Elizabeth felt more and more that Sister Angela was not to be treated, as she feared Sam and his wife were inclined to do, as a mere interloper in their family affairs, but as one to be not merely considered with gratitude, but even reverenced.

Indeed, Sam began to feel it, as he saw how the other men, both practical business men, listened, and were impressed; but it was not quite the case with his wife, who did not particularly esteem colonial Bishops, and still less Sisterhoods or devotion to missionary efforts, especially among the

Australian blacks, whom her old geography book had told her were the most degraded and hopeless of natives, scarcely removed from mere animals.

When Angela appeared half through dinner time and said that Lena was safely asleep, and Marilda sat her down to be happy in exchange of Carrigaboola tidings with her Bishop, Fernando greeted her with a reverence not undeserved, though perhaps all the more from the contrast to the mischievous little sprite who used to disturb the days of his philandering with Alda.

How much shocked Mrs. Samuel was, when the magnificent Sir Ferdinand, whom she regarded with awe as a millionaire, was flippantly answered by this extraordinary Sister, "Thank you, Fernan, I should like to have a sight of the old office. I hope you have a descendant of the old cat, Betty. Didn't she come from your grandmother, Marilda? Do you remember her being found playing tricks with the nugget, just come from Victoria?"

"That was in her kitten days," said Ferdinand.

"Is that personal, Fernan?"

"A compliment, Angel," said the Bishop. "Kittens alter a good deal."

"Not much for the better," said Angela. "If you only could see Mrs. Lamb, who used to be the very moral of a kitten, scratchiness and all!"

"I thought her very much improved," said Lady Underwood gravely.

"Oh, yes; grown into a sleek and personable tabby, able to wave her tail at the tip and tuck her paws—her velvet paws—well under her; and lick her lips over the—oh, dear!—what do you call it?—your *menu* is quite too much for us poor savages, Marilda. A bit of damper is quite enough for us, isn't it, Bishop?"

"Varied with opossum and fern root," he said smiling; "but that's only when we have lost our way."

The talk drifted off to the history of a shepherd's child, who had strayed into the bush, and after much searching, in which the Bishop and Fulbert had been half starved, had finally been found and carried home by Angela's "crack gin," as she told it to Bernard; and as Marilda thought the poor child was in a trap, it had to be translated into "favourite pupil," though Bernard carried on the joke by asking Marilda if she thought the natives cannibals given to the snaring of mankind.

Altogether it was a thoroughly merry evening, such as comes to pass in the meeting of old friends and comrades in too large numbers for grave discourse, but with habits of close intercourse and associations of all kinds. Emilia and her husband tried in all courtesy not to let the Merrifields feel themselves neglected; and indeed Bessie was only too glad to listen and join at times in the talk; but it all went outside Mrs. Sam, who was on the whole scandalised at the laughter of a Bishop, and a Sister. Indeed, it was true that Bishop Fulmort, naturally a grave man, very much so in his early days, comported himself on this occasion as if he realised Southey's wish—

"That in mine age as cheerful I mightbe,
Like the green winter of the holly tree."

At any rate, that evening was long a bright remembrance. Lena slept all night, and was so fresh and well in the morning that Angela foreboded that the examination might not detect her delicacy. They met Mrs. Merrifield, and took her with them to the doctor's, Lady Underwood Travis having placed her carriages at their disposal.

It was very much as Angela had expected, knowing by hospital reputation what the doctor was supposed to be to old ladies and fanciful mothers, while perhaps he had also heard of her *fracas* long ago at the hospital. For he was not more courteous to her than could be helped, treating her much as if she were only the nursery maid, and hardly looking at the opinion which she had made Professor May write out for him.

To her mind, it was a very cursory examination that he made; and the upshot of his opinion, triumphantly accepted by Mrs. Merrifield, was that there was nothing seriously amiss with the child, that she only needed care, regularity and bracing, and that the stifling, gasping spasms were simply the effect of hysteria.

Hysteria! Angela felt as if she should run wild as she heard Mrs. Merrifield's complacent remarks on having always thought so, and being sure that a few weeks of good air and good management would make an immense difference. The need of not alarming or prejudicing the poor little victim was all that kept Angela in any restraint; and Mrs. Merrifield went on to say that she had promised her youngest boy, who was with her in London, to take him to the Zoological Gardens, and it would be a good opportunity for Magdalen to see them.

"Is that where there is a kangaroo?" asked Lena, so eagerly that Angela, though thinking that morning's work enough for the feeble strength, could not withstand her. Besides, if the Merrifields were to have her wholly in another day, what was the use of standing out for one afternoon? One comfort was that Elizabeth, who would really have the charge of the child, had much more good sense and knowledge of the world than her sister-in-law.

Still Angela felt the only way of bearing it was that after setting Mrs. Merrifield down, she stopped the carriage at a church she knew to have a noon-tide Litany, knelt there, with the little girl beside her, and tried to say, "Thy will be done! To Thy keeping I commit her." Her "hours" came to help her.

"Quench Thou the fires of hate and strife,
  The wasting fever of the heart,
From perils guard her feeble life,
  And to our souls Thy help impart."

She was able to be calm, and to utter none of her rage when they came back to luncheon; and Marilda, declaring she liked nothing so well as seeing children at the Zoo, wished to go with the party. All, save Mrs. Merrifield and her boy, had gone different ways in London, so there was plenty of room in the barouche.

The boy's mind was set on riding on the elephant, and they walked on that way, turning aside, however, to the yard where towered the kangaroo, tall, gentle, graceful and gracious. Lena sprang forward with a cry of joy, and clasped her hands; but in one moment the same spasm, at first of ecstasy then of overpowering feeling, becoming agony, came over her, and gasping and choking, Angela held her in her arms and carried her to a seat, holding her up, loosening her clothes; but still she did not come round. Her aunt tried to say, "hysteric." Some one brought water, but it was of no use—there were still the labouring gasps, and the convulsive motion. "Let us take her home," Marilda said.

"Nothing but hysterics!" repeated the aunt. "I will stay with Jackie."

Marilda found her servant and the carriage, and in the long drive, a few drops of strong stimulant at a chemist's brought a little relief though scarcely consciousness; and when Angela had carried her up to her room, there was a blueness about the lips, a coldness about the fingers, that told much. Marilda had at once sent for Dr. Brownlow as the nearest, and he was at home; but he could only look and do nothing, but attempt to revive circulation, all in vain; and with Marilda standing by, with one convulsive clutch of Angela's hand, the true mother of her orphaned life, little Lena sank to a peaceful rest from the tribulations that awaited her here.

CHAPTER XXIX—SAFE

> "Rest beyond all grief and pain,
> Death to thee is truest gain."
>
> KEBLE.

ANGELA's nearest and best friends had anticipated that the peaceful climax of all her cares would be a relief to her; and so indeed in the long run it would be to her higher sense, and she would be thankful. But even those who knew her most thoroughly had not estimated the pangs of personal affection and deprivation of the child she had fostered with a mother's tenderness for seven years, and the absolute suffering of the sudden parting, even though it was to security of bliss, instead of doubt and uneasiness.

She was quite broken and really ill with neuralgia and exhaustion, unable to attend the funeral, which the Merrifields wished to have at Stokesley, and unfit for anything but lying still with the pink parrot on the rail below, kindly watched over by good Marilda. The strain of many disturbed nights, the perplexities, the struggle for resignation, all coming after a succession of trying events in Australia, had told heavily upon her. Indeed, no one guessed how much she had undergone, physically as well as spiritually, till Marilda would not be denied the consulting Dr. Brownlow, who questioned her closely, and extorted confessions of the long continued strain of exertion. Rest was all she needed; and Marilda took care that she had it, bringing Robina up from Minsterham to make it more effectual, and letting her have visits from her Bishop and from Bernard as they could afford the time, both being very and variously busy.

Angela had made up her mind to go out to Australia again, and to make Carrigaboola an endowment for the Sisterhood; but the means of doing this could best be arranged there, and she intended to go out when her Bishop should return in the autumn, feeling that her vocation was there, though there was a blank in all she had most cared for on earth in that home.

As soon as she had recovered, she wished to spend a fortnight at Dearport, beginning with a retreat that was held there. Remembering her old career there, and the abrupt close of her novitiate, she felt and spoke as if she was to be received as in penitence, but to the Sisters who surrounded her it was more as if they were receiving a saint.

When she came back to Vale Leston, she had recovered cheerfulness, more equable than it had ever been, and Cherry and Alda found her a charming companion. There was much going on at Vale Leston just then. Miss Arthuret and Dolores were at Penbeacon, seriously considering of the scheme of converting the old farm house into a kind of place of study for girls who wanted to work at various technicalities, and to fit themselves for usefulness or for self-maintenance. There was to be more or less of the Convalescent Home or House of Rest in combination, and it had occurred to Dolores that there could hardly be a better head of such an establishment than Magdalen Prescott.

Magdalen had been asked to the Priory to meet Angela, to whom it was now a comfort and pleasure to talk of her treasure, so much less lost to her than in the uncongenial surroundings threatened at Coalham. And the invitation, followed by the proposal, came at a not unpropitious moment. A railway company, after much surveying, much disputing, and many heartburnings, were actually obtaining an Act of Parliament, empowering it to lay its cruel hands upon the Goyle, running its viaducts down the ravine of Arnscombe, and destroy all the peace and privacy! It did much, as Agatha had said, to make the new scheme of Penbeacon acceptable though.

"That comes of making one's nest," she sighed, "and thinking one's self secure in it for life! Oh! it is worse and more changeable in this latter century than in any other! Does the world go round faster?"

"Of course it does," said Geraldine. "Think how many fashions, how many styles, how many ways of thinking, have passed away, even in our own time."

"And what have they left behind them?"

"Something good, I trust. Coral cells, stones for the next generation of zoophytes to stand upon to reach up higher."

"Is it higher?"

"In one sense, I hope. The same foundation, remember, and each cell forms a rock for the future—a white and beautiful cell, remember, as it grows unconsciously, beneath this creature."

Magdalen smiled, delighted with the illustration.

"It forms into the rocks, the strong foundations of the earth," she said.

"When it has undergone its baptism beneath the sea," added Geraldine. "But practically and unpoetically, perhaps—how the young folk mount upon all our little achievements in Church matters, and think them nearly as old-fashioned and despicable as we did pews and black gowns! Or how attempts like the schools that brought up Robina and Angela have shot out into High Schools, colleges, professions, and I know not what besides."

"Ah! we come to my old notions for my sisters. I thought they would have been governesses like myself, but they married; and now tell me, what do you think of this scheme of Miss Mohun and Agatha?"

"You know Dolores is going to her father first. I never saw him, but Lady Merrifield and Jane tell me he is a very wise, highly-principled person, perfectly to be trusted; and they like all that they have heard of his young wife. I should think if Agatha is to become a scientific lecturer, she could not begin her career under better training."

"Career, exactly! People used not to talk of careers."

"Life and career! Tortoise and hare, eh? But the hare may and ought still to reach the goal, and have her cell built, even if she does have her *wander yahr*, like the young barnacles, before becoming attached! No! she need not become the barnacle goose. That is fabulous," said Mrs. Grinstead, laughing off a little of her seriousness, and adding, "Tell me of the other girls. I think Vera did not come home last year."

"No; nor the year before. She has a good many pretty little talents, and is very obliging. Mrs. White seems to be very fond of her, and did not want to spare her when they went to Gastein for the summer. And this year, when there was so much infection about, I could not press it."

"Is it true that there is anything between her and Petros White?"

"I know Miss Mohun—Jane—infers it, but I don't like to build upon it."

"I should build on most inferences that Jane Mohun ventured to make known," said Geraldine, smiling; "and Paulina's fate is pretty well fixed, I suppose!"

"Dear child, she has never had any other purpose since I first knew her thoroughly, and I do not think her present stay at Dearport will disenchant her. I think she is really devoted, not to the theoretical romance of a Sisterhood, but to the deeper full purpose of self-devotion."

"I can fully believe it of her. Hers have not been the ups and downs of my Angela, though indeed, after all she has gone through, there is something in her face that brings to my mind, 'After that ye have suffered awhile, stablish, strengthen, settle you.'"

"It is a lovely countenance—so patient, and yet so bright."

"I do not think anything in all her life has tried her so much as the distress about little Lena; and after knowing her wildness—to use a weak word for it—under other troubles, I see what grace and self-control have done for her.

You still keep your Thekla!" she added, as the girl flashed by, in company with a coeval Vanderkist.

"For a few years to come, though I am beginning to feel like the old hens who do but bring their children up to launch them on the waters."

"Well, it is happy if the launch can be made with hope present as well as faith; and to see what Angel has become after many vicissitudes, not confined to her first years of youth, is an immense encouragement."

To Angela's great delight, the affairs of Brown and Underwood were found to require inspection at San Francisco, as well as at Colombo, where Bernard was to put the firm into the hands of one of the Browns, who was to meet him there, and he would then be able to come home to the central office in England.

It was not expedient for Phyllis to make the voyage for so brief a stay, so it was decided that she should remain with her mother, and she declared that she should be happy about Bernard being taken care of if Angela, before settling in at Carrigaboola, would go and stay with him at Ceylon. "No one can tell the pleasure it is," she said to Magdalen, "to borrow one's own especial brother from his wife for a little while. Oh, yes, I know it goes against the grain with him, and it is right it should; but the poor old sister enjoys her treat nevertheless and notwithstanding."

There was a great family gathering at Vale Leston, including both the Harewoods; and the Bishop of Albertstown came to spend that last fortnight in England with Clement, the boy who had been committed to him as a chorister, then trained as a young deacon, and almost driven out in his inexperience to the critical charge of the neglected parish and the old squire, only to be recalled after seven years to the more important charge in London on the Bishop's appointment, there to serve till strength gave way, and he must perforce return to his former home. There was a farewell picnic of the elders at Penbeacon, merry and yet wistful in its hopeful auguries that the loved play place would be a glad and beneficial home.

It was a strange retrospect, talked over by the two old friends in deep thankfulness, yet humility over their own shortcomings and failures, and no less strange were the recollections of the wild noisy insubordinate schoolgirl whom the Bishop's sister had failed to tame, and who had to both seemed to live only on sensation, whether religious or secular, and who had been one continual care and perplexity to each. By turns they had thought that the full Church system acted as a hotbed on her peculiar temperament, and at others they had thought it only an alternative to the amusements of vanity and flirtation. Each had felt himself a failure with regard to her, and had hoped for a fresh start from each crisis of repentance, notably, from the death of Felix, only to be disappointed by some fresh aberration.

However, in Queensland, her work had been noble, and thoroughly effective in many cases; it had involved much self-denial and even danger, and though these might agree with her native spirit of adventure, there had likewise been not fitful, but steadily earnest devotion in her convent life, as well as the tenderest reverent care of Mother Constance in a long and painful decline, and therewith a steady cheerful influence which had immensely assisted the growth of Fulbert's character. For some years past, Sister Angela had been not a care, but a trusty helper to the Bishop; and the later trials and difficulties, especially the sore rending of the tie with the being she had come to love with all the force of her strong nature, had been borne in a manner that bore witness to the subduing of that over-rebellious and vehement spirit.

And, as she said to Geraldine on the last evening as they bade good-night, "This has been the very happiest time I ever spent here—yes, happier than in those exultant days of new possession and liberty. Oh, yes, all experiments, as it were, bold ventures, self-reproach and failure, defiance and fun, and then —oh, the ache I would not confess, the glory of being provoking, and, oh, the final anguish I brought on myself and on you all; and I went on, when it began to wear away, still stifling the sting which revived whenever I came home, and all was renewed! Really, whenever I shammed it was only remorse. I don't think that real repentance, and the peace after it, began till those quiet days with dear Mother Constance."

"And is it peace now?"

"Yes, I think so. Even the parting with my child has not torn me up. I can say it is well—far better than leaving her, far better, indeed! And Felix is what he meant to be, my treasure, not my accuser. Oh, I am glad to have been at home, and made it all up, to bear away—and leave with you the sense of Peace."

All who had loved and feared for her were very happy over her when all joined in that farewell service on her own birthday, St. Michael and All Angels' Day.

The party were joined by Dolores and Wilfred at Liverpool; Bernard having undertaken to establish the latter at Colombo in hands as safe as might be.

CHAPTER XXX—THE MAIDEN ROCKS

"What need we more if hearts be true,
Our voyage safe, our port in view."

—Keble.

A telegram that a steamer had been wrecked on the Maiden Rocks filled three homes with dismay. The rocks were sought out in maps, and found to be specks lying between County Antrim and Scotland—no doubt terrible in their reality.

Another day brought something more definite. It *was* the *Afra*,—"wrecked in the fog of October 11th. Boats got off."

That was all; but a day's post brought letters, of which the fullest was from Dolores:

"Corncastle, Larne, co. Antrim, Ireland,
October 12.

"Dearest Aunt Lily,—

"I trust Phyllis has by this time heard from Bernard, as I heard him called on, as a good oarsman, to go in the first boat, and we saw Angela's bonnet. We—that is Wilfred, Nag, and the Bishop—are all safe here, with eight or nine others. Will will do well, I trust. He quite owes his life to Nag. This is how it was: We had not long been out of the Mersey before an impenetrable fog came down upon us, and we could not see across the deck; but on we went, on what proved to be our blind way, till, after a night and day, just as we were getting up from dinner, there came a hideous shock and concussion, throwing us all about the room; and in less than a minute it was repeated, with horrible crackings, tearings, yells and shouts. No one needed to tell us what it meant, and down came the call, 'Don't wait to save your things, only wraps, ladies! Up on deck! Life-belts if you can!' I remember Bernard standing at the top of the ladder, helping us up, and somehow, I understand from him, that we were on a reef, and might either remain there, and sink, or be washed off. The fog was clearing, and there was a dim light up high, somewhere, one of the lighthouses, I believe. I don't quite know how it all went; I think we kept in the background, round the Bishop, and that a boat full of emigrant women was put off. I know there were only about half a dozen women left, who had been crying and refusing to leave their husbands; and about thirty altogether, men and women, were somehow got into our boat with the chief mate; the Bishop all consolation and prayer; poor Wilfred limp, cold and trembling, for he had been very seasick till the last moment, when Bernard pulled him out of his berth, and put him into a lifebelt. The sea was not very rough, with an east wind; but the mate said the current was so strong he could make no way against it. It would bring us on to the Irish cliffs, and then, God help us! Knowing what that coast is, I thought there was no hope; and as it was beginning to grow light there rose an awful wall, all black and white, ready to close upon us; but just as I set my teeth and tried to recollect prayers, or follow the Bishop's, but I could only squeeze Agatha harder and harder, there was a fresh shouting among the men, and the boat was heaved up in a fearful way, then down. It was tide, and we were near upon breakers; but there were answering shouts, or so they said—I believe a line was thrown, and a light shown. But as the boat rose again, Nag and I expected to be hurled on the rocks the next moment, and clung together. But instead—though the waves had almost torn us asunder—we were lying on a stony beach, and human hands were dragging at us—voices calling and shouting about our not being dead. God had helped us! We had been carried into a clift where there is a coastguard station; and the good men had come down and were helping us on shore. But before I well knew anything, Agatha was on her feet; I heard her cry 'Wilfred, Wilfred!' and then I saw her dragging him, quite like a dead thing, out of the surf, just in time before another great wave rushed in which would have washed them both back, if a man had not grappled her at the very moment, calling out, 'Let go, let go, he's a dead man!' She did not let go; when the wave broke, happily, just short of them, and another came to help, and saved them from being sucked back. Then the Bishop came and assured us that he was alive, and got the men to carry him up to the coastguard cottages; indeed, it was an awful escape; for of our boatload most were lost altogether, three lie dead, dashed against the rock, and two more, the mate one of them, have broken limbs. Wilfred was unconscious for a long time, at least an hour; but by the help of spoonfuls of whiskey he came round to a dreamy kind of state, and he does not seem to suffer much; and the Bishop, the Preventive man and Nag all are sure no limbs are broken, but he seems incapable of movement except his hands. It may be only jar upon the spine, and go off in another day or two; but we do not dare to send for a doctor, or anything else, indeed, till we have some money; for we all of us have lost everything except five shillings in my pocket and two in Nag's. Even our wraps were washed off—I believe Agatha gave hers to a shivering woman in the boat. The Bishop, too, gave away his coat, forgetting to secure his purse. But the people are very kind to us—North, or Scotch Irish Presbyterians, I think—for they don't seem to know what to make of his being a Bishop when they found he was not R.C., though they call him His Reverence. Please send us an order to get cashed, at Larne, six miles off, where this is posted. Wilfred lies on the good Preventive woman's bed, clean and fairly comfortable, and they have made a shake-down in their parlour for Nag and me. The Bishop *says* he is well off, but I believe he is always looking after the mate and the other man in the other house, and sleeps, if at all, in a chair. Nag is *the* nurse. She had ambulance lessons, you know, when at the High School, and profited by them more than I ever did, and Wilfred likes to have her about him, and when he is dazed, as he always is at first waking, he calls her Vera. But don't be uneasy about him, dear Aunt Lily. Deadly sea-sickness, a night of tossing and cold, and then this terrible landing may well upset him, and probably he will be on his legs by the time you get this letter.

"I find our disaster was on the Maiden Rocks, a horrible group, I only wonder that any one gets past them. There are five of them, the wicked Sirens, and three have lighthouses, but not very efficient ones, and apt to disappear in the fog, and there are reefs beneath on one of which we came to grief. The folk here think a wreck on these Maidens absolutely fatal, so we cannot be but most thankful for being alive, though it is a worse experience than the Rotuma earthquake.

"Fergus would think the place worth all we have undergone. The crags are wonderful, chalk at the bottom, basalt above, and of course all round to the Giant's Causeway it is finer still. Well may we, as the Bishop is always doing, give thanks that we were taken, by the Divine Hand guiding tide and current, to this milder and less inhospitable opening.

"We can afford to dispense with less majesty, for one of those finer cliffs would have been our destruction.

"This is going to Larne, where there is a railway station and something of a town, and the Bishop has written to the doctor of the place. I will write again when he has been here. I hope to send you another and more cheery account to-morrow, or whenever post goes.

"Nag is writing to her sister. I trust you will have heard of Bernard and Angela. Their boat was a better one than ours, and certainly got off safely. Let us know as soon you can.

"Your most loving niece,

"D. M. Mohun."

Agatha had also written to Magdalen, very briefly, to assure her of her safety and thankfulness, and to say she could not leave Wilfred till more efficient care arrived, or till she had means to come back with. She was evidently too busy over her patient to have much possibility of writing, even if she had paper, which seemed to be scarce at Corncastle.

The Bishop also wrote to Clement, and to Sir Jasper and others; but he also could say little, only that he trusted that Angela and Bernard were safe elsewhere, having heard them called, and, as he believed, seen them off in the first boat, so that probably they had been already heard of before these letters arrived. Their own party had been spared from being dashed against the rocks almost by a miracle; and Agatha Prescott's courage and readiness, as now her nursing faculties, were beyond all praise, as indeed was the brave patience of Miss Mohun. He could only look on and be thankful, and hope for tidings of those who were as his own children. The next day's letters spoke of the doctor as so much perplexed about Wilfred, and nothing had been heard at Larne of the other boats.

But no tidings came; there was too much cause to fear that the first boat had been borne away by the currents and swamped. Lady Merrifield could not leave Phyllis in such a crisis of suspense, and Sir Jasper was hardly fit for such a journey, so that his wife was much relieved when her brother, General Mohun, came to Clipstone, and undertook to hasten out to Corncastle, with money and appliances, including a nurse.

"Oh, Reggie, always good at need! I hardly dare to send my good old Halfpenny—!"

"No, Mamma, send me. You know I had the ambulance lessons with Nag," said Mysie, "and we could get a real nurse from Belfast or Dublin, if it was wanted."

So it was arranged, and uncle and niece started, but hope faded more and more! Were those two precious young lives so early quenched?

CHAPTER XXXI—THE WRECK

"How purer were earth, if all its martyrdoms,
If all its struggling sighs of sacrifice
Were swept away!"

E. HAMILTON KING.

NO tidings of Bernard and Angela. The suspense began to diminish into "wanhope" or despair; and the brothers and sisters continued to say that they were sorry above all for Phyllis, whose gentle sweetness had made her one with them.

But at last, one forenoon, a telegram was put into Clement's hand, dated from Ewmouth:

Muriel Ellen, Ewmouth Harbour, October 14th. Blaine to Rev. Underwood. Brother here. Come to infirmary.

Clement and Geraldine lost no time in driving to the infirmary, too anxious to speak to one another. Blaine's name was known to them as a Gwenworth lad, who had gone to sea, and risen to be sailing master of the *Muriel Ellen*, a trader plying between Londonderry and Bristol. He, with another, who proved to be the American captain of the *Afra*, were at the gate of the hospital, where an ambulance had just entered.

"Oh! Sir," as Clement held out his hand, "I could not save her. I'd have given my life!"

"My brother?" as Clement returned his grasp fervently.

"We've just got him in here, Sir. I hope! I hope! And here's the doctor."

The house surgeon, who, of course, knew the Rector of Vale Leston, met him with, "Best see him before we touch him, it will set his mind at rest—You must be prepared, Sir—No, better not you, Mrs. Grinstead."

Clement followed in silence, leaving Geraldine to the care of the matron. All he was allowed to see was a ghastly, death-like face and form, covered with rugs, lying prostrate on a mattress; but as he came in, at the sound of his step, there was a quiver of recognition, the eyes opened and looked up, the lips moved, and as Clement bent down with a kiss, there was a faint sound gasped out, "Telegraph to Clipstone."

"I will, I will at once."

"It was noble!" Then was added, "She gave herself for the Bishop, for me." Then the eyes closed, and unconsciousness seemed to prevail. Some one came and put Clement aside, saying—

"Go now, Sir; you shall hear!"

Clement, who thought it might be death, would have stayed at hand; but he was turned away, and could only murmur an inarticulate blessing and prayer, as he meant to fulfil the earnest desire that was thought to have been conned over and over again by Bernard, as these half sentences recurred again and again in semi-consciousness. His telegram despatched, Clement returned to his sister, to hear from the two masters all they had to tell. Captain Miller, of the *Afra*, had slight hurts, which had been looked to before he should take the train for London; and Blaine had waited to tell his story before pursuing his voyage to Bristol, both, indeed, to hear the report of the patient, and likewise to collect the news of the few who had been landed at Corncastle, to the great relief of Captain Miller; but of the first boat there were no tidings, and Blaine thought there was little probability that it had not sunk or been dashed against the crags of the savage coast.

Captain Miller's account was, that not long after leaving the Mersey, there had set in an impenetrable fog, lasting for a night and a day. There was perhaps some confusion as to charts, and the scarcely visible lights upon the Maidens. At any rate, the *Afra* had suddenly struck on a reef, and, shifting at once, had been hopelessly rent, so as to leave no hope save in the boats. Every one seemed to have behaved with the resolute fortitude and unselfishness generally shown by English and Americans in the like circumstances. The sea was not in a dangerous state, and there was a steady east wind, so that the boats were lowered without much difficulty, and most of the women disposed of in the first.

Before the second could be put off however, the water had reached the fires; there was a violent lurch, the ship had heeled completely over, washing many overboard, and of course causing a great confusion among those who had been steady before, and making the deck almost perpendicular. The captain, however, succeeded in lowering another boat, and putting into it, as he trusted, the few remaining women, the Bishop, and most of the men. This was, of course, that which had safely reached Corncastle, and of which he only now heard. The last boat was so overcrowded that he, with three of his crew, had thought it best to remain for the almost desperate chance of being picked up before they sank.

He had supposed Mr. Underwood had been washed overboard in the heeling over of the ship, and that his sister had been put into the first boat; but presently he heard a call.

"Oh, help me, please!" And he became aware that Sister Angela was hanging over her brother, who lay crushed by a heavy chest which had fallen on him, and thrown him against the gunwale, though a moan or two showed him to be still alive. The remaining sailors removed the weight, lifted him, and laid him in the best place and position they could, while his sister hung over him and supported his head. To Miller's dismayed exclamation at finding a woman still on board, she replied—

"It was no fault of yours. I hid below. Other lives—the Bishop's—were what mattered! I am glad to be here!"

He believed that Mr. Underwood had revived enough to know his sister, for he had heard her voice talking to him. Yes, and singing; but it was not for very long. The wreck was in motion, being carried by current and tide along the Channel, and if it did not sink, might be perceived now that daylight had come, and a signal of distress might be seen by some passing vessel.

Seen it was, in fact, and that there were persons to be rescued; and Blaine, who was on his way from Londonderry to Bristol, in the *Muriel Ellen*, a cattle-boat, possessed a boat in which to attempt a rescue.

All that experienced sailors could do in transferring the helpless and unconscious form to the boat first, and then to the sloop had been done; but it was no wonder that in the transit Angela, more heedful of her brother's safety than her own, had fallen between, and been lost in the waves, to the extreme grief of Tom Blaine, who had been one of her scholars, and devoted to her, as all the boys of Vale Leston were.

The cattle-boat had few facilities for comfort, and all he could do was to let Mr. Bernard Underwood lie, as softly as could be contrived, on deck, and make sail for Ewmouth, so as to land him as near home as possible. How far he had been conscious it was impossible to say, though once he had asked for Angela, but had seemed to understand from an evasion, that she was missing, and had said no more, but muttered parts of these requests, as if afraid of not being capable of them.

All this had been told or implied, while messages came down that the surgeons did not think the injuries need be mortal, provided the exhaustion and exposure had not fatal consequences. The left arm, two ribs, and the leg had been broken, and were reduced before the doctors ventured on a hopeful report with which to send home the brother and sister. One sight, Clement was allowed of a more unconscious, but much less distressed face, and one murmur, "Noble! Phyllis!" and he was promised a telegram later in the day.

The two hardly knew which to feel most; grief or thankfulness, the loss or the mercy, and yet—and yet—after the fitful, wayward, yet always devout life, with all its strains, there was a sense of wistful acceptance of such a close.

They felt it all the more deeply when, a day or two later, Bernard was able to say, at intervals, for the injury rendered speech difficult and almost dangerous, as Clement leant over him—

"Yes! I woke to see her face over me, all bright in wavy hair just as when we were children, and she said, 'Bear! Bear! we are going together!' Then somehow she tried to help me to trust for Phyllis and Lily."

Then his voice sank, but presently he added, "There was more, but it is like a dream. She was singing in her own, own voice. There was 'Lead, kindly Light!' and when it came to 'Angel faces smile' there was a cry—quite glad—'There! there on the water! Felix! Coming for us! Oh! and another One! Lord, into Thy hands.' That is all I know—a kiss here, and 'Yes! thanks! For me!' But the lifting hurt so much that I lost all sense, when she must have fallen between the wreck and the boat. You are glad for her! Mine own! mine Angel!"

"Safe home!" said Clement. "Oh, thankworthy!"

CHAPTER XXXII—ANCHORED

"Safe home, safe home in port,
  Rent cordage, shattered deck;
Torn sails, provision short,
  And only not a wreck;
But all the joy upon the shore,
To tell our voyage the perils o'er!"

Safe home! It might be said in another sense for Bernard, for he was naturally so strong and healthy that the effects of exposure and exhaustion were not long in passing off, the injury to the chest proved to be only temporary; and having cased him like a statue in plaster of Paris, the surgeons decided, to the joy of his family, that the more serious injuries would be better recovered from in the fresh air of Vale Leston, than in the fishy, muddy atmosphere of Ewmouth.

So he was transported thither, and installed in Felix's study, among the familiar sights and sounds, and where another joy awaited him, and where he lay in happy stillness.

Phyllis had borne up bravely through the suspense, never relinquishing a strong assurance of hope; but when that hope was actually crowned by the first telegram, the reaction set in, and she had broken down so entirely that her mother durst not let her move at first, and indeed accompanied her and her little girl as far as the junction, being herself on the way to Larne.

And Geraldine's heart was at peace when she saw Phyllis sitting by the bed, her hand in his, content to see and not to speak. Another visitor appeared the following day, namely, the Bishop of Albertstown, who had remained at Larne till he could see his fellow passengers in safe hands. Then he had crossed to Bristol, and before his hurried visit to his sisters he could not but come to see his beloved old pupil, Clement, and share with him those reminiscences of her, who, as he had only now learnt, had given her young superabundant life for him, a man growing into age, whose work might be nearly done.

He only saw Bernard in silence, but heard from Clement the account of those last moments, which showed how entirely Angela had been conscious of what she was doing, and how willingly she had devoted herself to save those whom she loved and valued.

While yet they talked, there was a fresh arrival. Sir Ferdinand Travis Underwood, who could not forbear the running down to hear perfectly all that was to be heard, and to make arrangements that might relieve Bernard's mind, if he were indeed on the way of recovery.

In fact, almost the first thought after that of the wife and child had been the security of the drenched, stained, and soiled pocket-book; nor would the patient be satisfied till he had been allowed himself to hand it over to the head of his firm, with, "There, Fernan, safe, though smashed with me. Tell Brown."

"Never mind Brown or anything else but getting well, Bernard. I have taken our passage for next week. I shall get things arranged so that you need not think of being wanted again out there. We will find a berth for you in the office in town, as soon as you are about again."

Bernard's eye lightened. "I hope—"

But Ferdinand would not let him either thank or hope, scarcely even allow any words from Phyllis, who could not be grateful enough for the relief. To Alda, who had received her old companion, since Marilda seemed unable to let her husband out of her sight; it was explained that she was going too, happen what would. Oh, yes, it was true she was a shocking bad sailor, but she was not going to have Fernan's ships running upon rocks or getting on fire, or anything of that sort, without her. She wanted to see about Ludmilla Schmetterling, who was reported to have found a lover while studying at a class in the States, and she also meant to settle her own especial niece Emilia, whose husband was to take Bernard's place in Ceylon and who had become heartily tired of London's second-rate gaieties.

Those thus concerned met at the memorial service in the morning before the Bishop quitted them, where many parishioners gathered who had been spellbound in Angela's freakish days of early girlhood, and who were greatly touched when the committal to the deep was inserted from the Forms of Prayer to be used at Sea.

It brought a deep sense of awe and thankfulness to those who had feared and wondered through the stormy uncertain life, and now could exult in what was almost a martyrdom, and had brought their beloved one to the great pure grave, as her Baptism for eternity.

Some months later, while Bernard still lay on his couch, but could speak and be glad, he rejoiced indeed, for a sore in his heart was healed, when two fair babes were brought to him,—a boy who would be as another firstborn son, and a little maiden who would bear that name which had become dear and saintly in the peculiar calendar of Vale Leston.

CHAPTER XXXIII—FAREWELL

"Nay, your pardon! Cry you, 'Forward.' Yours are youth, we hope—but I?"

—Browning.

The visit of the Bishop of Albertstown had, in fact, been deferred till he could quit his fellow-sufferers, especially Wilfred, who could not well be left to the charge of the two girls, with the Larne doctor evidently in difficulty about his case.

It was with great joy that a telegram was received with tidings that General Mohun and Mysie were on the way, and also Magdalen Prescott, who met them at Liverpool, being unable to stay away from Agatha under such circumstances. At Belfast they obtained a trained nurse, and a doctor was to follow them.

The joy of the meeting between Magdalen and Agatha was almost that of mother and daughter, and nothing could be more entirely convincing that they were one.

Indeed, Agatha was thoroughly worn out; for the main strain of attendance had fallen upon her, since the Bishop was fully occupied with some of the seriously hurt in other cottages; and though Dolores tried to be helpful, it was chiefly in outside work, and attempts at sick cookery, in which she was rather too scientific, and found the lack of appliances very inconvenient. Besides, cousin though she was, or perhaps for that very reason, Wilfred was far less amenable to her voice than Agatha's; and if she attempted authority it was sure to rouse all the resistance left in him. Agatha had been constantly on the alert, liable to be called on every half-hour, to soothe fretful distress over impossible impatience at delay, anger at want of comforts, and dolefulness over the chances of improvements, and abuse, whether just or not, of the only accessible doctor.

In fact, Magdalen, on seeing how utterly worn out she was, and how little space the cottages afforded, thought it best, now that the patient was in the hands of sister, uncle, and nurse, to carry her off at once by the return car to Larne; and Dolores thought it best to accompany them, after Mysie had hung on her as one restored from death. But Mysie was absorbed in her brother, and Dolores had a strong yearning to be with her father, so strong that she decided not to return to England, but to procure a second outfit at Belfast, and to set forth again from thence, nothing daunted, for, as she said (not carelessly), such things did not happen immediately after, in a second voyage. In fact, though thankful and impressed by the loss of the others, she had gone through the crisis of the life of her heart and affections, and she had likewise been once in imminent peril through a convulsion of nature. Thus she was inclined to look on the wreck and the Irish cliffs as an experience in the way of business, so she was resolved to see the Giant's Causeway, and to make notes upon it for her lectures.

But it was a different thing with Agatha. She had been brought face to face with death; and though the actual time had been spent in hurry and bustle, and even the subsequent tossing in the boat had been not so much waiting and thinking as attending to others more terrified and injured than herself, and there followed the incessant waiting on Wilfred; still the experiences had worked in. She rested very silently, dwelling little to Magdalen on her thoughts; but each word she said, and her very countenance, showed that she had made a great step in life and realised the spiritual world, which hitherto had been outside her life—not disbelieved, but almost matter of speculation and study.

She was not at all desirous of falling back from Dolores, whose grave steadiness and fortitude, the result of a truly brave and deep trust, had given her a sense of confidence and protection. So they wrote, and arranged for their passage, and, with Magdalen, spent the intermediate time in needful preparations at Belfast, and in an expedition to the Causeway, where they laid in a stock of notes and observations, all in a spirit that made Magdalen feel that she knew both in a manner she had never done before, and loved them with a deep value and confidence.

Wilfred meanwhile made very slow, if any, progress.

They took him to Belfast as soon as it was possible, and his mother came to him. He was gentle and quiet, with little power of movement, and scarcely any of thought; and in a consultation of doctors, the verdict was given that he must be carefully tended for months, if not for years to come; and though there might finally be full recovery, yet it would depend on the most tender and careful treatment of body and mind. London doctors, when he could be moved thither, confirmed the decision, and he began a helpless invalid life, in which a certain indifference and dulness made him a much less peevish and trying patient than would have been anticipated. Mysie was his willing, but intelligent slave; and his mother was not only thankful to have him brought back to her at any price, but really—though she would not have confessed it even to herself—was less troubled and anxious about him than she had been since he had begun to "roam in youth's uncertain wilds." Indeed, there were hopes that slow recovery might find him a much changed person in character.

He had become so uninterested in his former predilections that he heard with little emotion that Vera was to marry Petros White.

"I thought she would take up with some cad," he said. But his family were really glad that this wedding was to take place at Rocca Marina, whither the two sisters and Magdalen were invited.

Paulina would not go. She still resented the treatment of Hubert Delrio, and she was devoted to her study of nursing at the Dearport Sisterhood; but Magdalen thought it right to take Thekla, and give her the advantages of improvement in languages, and the sight of fine scenery.

And certainly Rocca Marina was a wonderful place for marriages. Vera, handsome and happy and likely to turn into a fairly good commonplace wife, had no sooner been sent off on a honeymoon tour to Greece and Egypt, and Mrs. White had begged the other two to prolong their visit, considering, perhaps, if one or the other aunt or niece could not be promoted to the vacant post of lady-in-waiting, than Hubert Delrio came to secure specimens of marble for some mosaic work on which he was engaged. He was fast becoming a man of mark, whom the Whites were delighted to receive and entertain, and who was delighted to be with the old friends who had had so great an influence on his life. And was it Magdalen alone to whom he chiefly looked up as his helper and guide? So he thought; but before the time of separation had come, he had found out that Thekla was far prettier than ever Vera had been, and with a mind and principle—no Flapsy, but a real sympathetic and poetic nature, which had grown up in these years. Young as she was, their destinies were fixed.

And Magdalen? The railroad had obtained authority to pass through the Goyle, and thus break up her home and shelter. Still she was not tempted by Adeline White's desire to make her a companion; but rather she accepted the plan on which Dolores had first started, and on which Elizabeth Merrifield and Miss Arthuret were set, of making her the head of their home at Penbeacon, partly a convalescent home, and partly a training college for young women in need of technical instruction in nursing or other possible feminine avocations. Tom May was delighted with all it might set on foot, and Clement saw in her leading the hopes that a high and pure spirit might inspire it.

FOOTNOTES

[100] It is Russian, and means Faith.

www.ingramcontent.com/pod-product-compliance
Lightning Source LLC
Chambersburg PA
CBHW060804310726
48980CB00002B/231
* 9 7 8 3 7 3 2 6 1 9 2 7 6 *